SLEEPLESS NIGHTS

IONA KANE

IONA KANE

Sleepless Nights

Copyright © 2021 by Iona Kane

Cover design: Cath Grace Designs

Editor: Victoria Villasenor

Visit my website: ionakane.com

Follow me on Instagram: @ionakanewriter

All rights reserved. No part of this book may be reproduced or used in any manner without the express permission of the author.

This is a work of fiction. All names, characters and events are either a product of the author's imagination or are used fictitiously. Any resemblance to locales, events, business establishments or actual persons - living or dead - is purely coincidental.

For Louise
To the moon. And back.

ONE

As Tyra MacLean hit the stage, the pain in her knees made her gasp. She ran back to her drums for the final chorus and wondered if the smiling red-haired woman in the front row had noticed her momentary grimace or if she'd got away with it. She needed to take more pre-show painkillers or lay off the stupid stunts like jumping over her drum kit. She wasn't in her twenties anymore, and it was getting a bit much.

Being out on the road again was definitely not where she'd thought she would find herself at forty-seven, but she loved the thrill of performing again. And playing the club tent of a major festival was an exhilarating way to end their UK tour. It had been a long few months, reminding her of her age on a nightly basis, but she was going to make the most of tonight's euphoria. She started the drum intro of the closing number, and the crowd went wild.

After the show finished she didn't wait for the rest of the band. She showered quickly and made a dash for the van waiting to take her off site.

"Ty, where are you going? Are we not heading home together?"

She swore quietly and swung around as her much younger cousin caught her by the arm. "Sorry, Mhairi, I've got plans. Can we get breakfast in the morning, and dissect the performance then?"

Mhairi was serious about her music, and her way of winding down after a gig was to talk it through in detail. Ty often enjoyed that too, but tonight she had a different kind of de-stressing activity in mind.

"But those two are just planning a massive piss up. Don't leave me here to..." She glanced over Ty's shoulder. "Oh, for fuck's sake, Tyra. When are you going to start acting your age?" She gestured behind Ty and shook her head.

Ty grinned. Mhairi must've spotted the grinning redhead loitering by the van. "Ah, Mhairi that's not fair. You're always telling me I need to find some company."

"For life, Ty, not just for a couple of hours in a hotel room. I'll see you tomorrow. Be careful." Mhairi shoved her hands in her pockets and headed back to the lights of the backstage area without a backward glance.

The fleeting guilt at disappointing her ever-patient cousin faded as she turned back to the gorgeous woman waiting for her, and she only had thoughts for the few hours of fun ahead.

Alexandra Knight blew out a long breath. Arguing the details of her impending stadium tour with her management team had grown tedious, fast. "Aren't these the technicalities I pay you to sort out?"

"Theoretically," muttered her assistant, Ryan. "But then you criticize every tiny detail, and we have to start over anyway."

Alex watched TV over Ryan's shoulder, her attention drawn by highlights of a British music festival, bringing back memories of another time. In her early teens, she'd lapped up the Britpop music scene before her mother took her to live in the US. She'd begged to be allowed to go to see her favorite bands perform live, but her mother had always refused, claiming she was too young. Alex had known it was because she thought popular music was beneath them.

"So now that you've fired the opening act, we need to find someone suitable for North America, and that gives us very little time. I wish you wouldn't make these unilateral decisions, Alex," Linda said.

Her manager's passive aggressive lecturing was hard to focus on with the TV vying for her attention. "I didn't negotiate selecting my own opening act so I could choose a band that's halfhearted and unprofessional, Linda." She turned back to the music festival coverage which now featured a very good-looking young man belting out a catchy tune, accompanied by a female bassist who bore such a resemblance to him, they had to be siblings. The guitarist appeared to have been parachuted in from the 1980s. They were good, and the crowd in the festival tent was going wild, but the musician who really drew her attention was the blond drummer with sweat pouring down her face as she roared into the mic. Alex couldn't take her eyes off her. "Who's that?" she asked, as casually as she could manage given her interest went beyond the drummer's musical prowess.

"Some British band. Who cares? Can we just make

some decisions here, please?" Linda tapped her sharp fingernail against the table.

Who the hell do you think you're talking to? Alex chose to ignore her rather than miss this performance. She moved to sit closer to the TV.

Ryan joined her. "They're called DandyLions. They've been around a couple of years. The frontman is Jamie MacLean, a self-proclaimed rock god. He formed the band with his twin sister...Marie, I think. She's less rock star, more serious musician. They roped in their cousin to play drums. And if she looks familiar, it's because she was a teen singer-songwriter in the eighties."

"In the eighties? Jesus, how old is she? She doesn't look much older than me. What's her name?" Alex peered more closely at the screen, willing the camera to focus on the drummer.

"Tyra MacLean," he said. "She was a big feminist activist and an out lesbian way before that was cool. Had her first hit at fifteen, off the rails by her early twenties. She's avoided the limelight for a long time. Those cousins must have made a convincing argument."

"And the Vince Neil lookalike?" Alex pointed at the screen, the camera now focused on the guitarist.

Ryan chuckled. "That's Mikki V. He was in Sweden's top metal band. They split, and he came to the UK to do some session work. He and MacLean go way back. I hear she's a pretty successful producer."

Alex narrowed her eyes. "You know a lot about some British band I've never even heard of."

Ryan's face reddened. "They're very original. Jamie is an amazing singer, and he's going places. The band is top notch. And they're not bad to look at either."

Alex laughed at Ryan's shy smile. "And which

MacLean is it in particular, who's caught your attention? The brash boy or his equally gorgeous sister?"

Ryan shrugged as his blush deepened. His fair complexion made it difficult to hide his embarrassment. "I wouldn't kick either of them out of bed."

Alex turned to face Linda. "I want DandyLions as my opening act on the whole North American tour."

An hour later, Linda was still arguing the case for a more conventional choice of opening band, and Alex was starting to lose her patience.

"This isn't like you, Alex. You've never taken a chance on an unknown act for your opening band."

"Perhaps that's why they've often been underwhelming. I want an act that gets people in the mood. These guys have a different fan base from me, but their music isn't so different that it'll alienate my diehard fans. They'll give me a bit of a youthful makeover, and I'll give them a way into the US market. It's a match made in heaven."

"Alex, we've spent years honing your image to perfection and keeping it that way. You want to hook up with an unheard-of act who look as though they all belong in different bands and take them on a stadium tour? It's a recipe for disaster."

"Ryan had heard of them. That's good enough for me." She turned her back on her manager, forcing herself to keep her temper in check as she poured herself a large whiskey. "Don't be dramatic, Linda. I want to know if they're interested. Make the call. For all we know they're happy being a cult success in the UK, playing cool festivals. But I want to talk to them myself. We're in London for a couple more days. Make it happen."

Linda raised her hands in defeat. "Like anyone's gonna

turn you down, sweetheart. It's your funeral. I'll set something up."

Annoyed it had taken so long to persuade Linda to do as she asked, Alex picked up her glass and headed to her room, kicking the door closed behind her. She lay back on the bed and closed her eyes wearily, thinking through the dreary few days ahead of her. Her life was one long parade of performances, media commitments, and lonely hotel rooms. She wondered how she'd got to this point without noticing. She sat back up and pulled her laptop across the bed towards her. Maybe watching some live music would make her feel less lonely. She knew what she would search for before her fingers hit the keys.

TWO

Tyra strode into the office. She slammed the door behind her, making everyone jump, and threw her jacket at the nearest chair. "I specifically said no interruptions for at least two weeks. Less than a day, and I've got you all bleating on the phone about a 'mind-blowing opportunity', and I've got to come and hear about it immediately. This better be fucking amazing."

Jamie jumped up from the couch and grabbed her in a bear hug. "It bloody is, Ty. Bloody amazing. It might be the best thing you've ever heard."

"I doubt that. I've heard some pretty amazing things in my time." She pushed him back onto the sofa and crossed to give his twin, Mhairi, her *current* favorite cousin, a kiss on the cheek and a quick hug.

Tyra turned her attention to Lachlan Phillips, their manager, sitting in his chair and grinning like the Cheshire Cat. "Spill it, Lachie. I've got a studio to run. What's got you all smirking like you've won the lottery?"

"Alexandra Knight wants us on her US tour. For real," Jamie said before Lachie could respond.

Jamie jumped up again and seized her in another bone-crushing hug. "We're gonna be famous! We're gonna be WUUUUURLD famous."

He attempted to pull her on a dance around the room, but Ty shoved him back into his seat. She looked around at them all in disbelief, trying to make sense of what she was hearing. "What the hell are you talking about? Alexandra Knight? Mainstream, stadium filling Alexandra Knight? So deep in the closet she's in fucking Narnia? Why would she want some Glaswegian slash Swedish rock band as a support act? Is she no' a bit out of our league? Or in a completely different fucking league? I hope you've already said no." She turned on Lachlan. "Tell me you've said no?"

"Of course I've not, Ty. There's no way I would make a decision like that without consulting all of you." He cleared his throat. "I do think it's the best thing that has ever happened to DandyLions yet, mind." He clasped his hands together and smiled. "Anyway, it's not a definite offer yet. She wants to see us in London tomorrow night. Her management are making all the travel arrangements."

His smile faded as Tyra paced the room, shaking her head. "Are you kidding me? Are you all telling me you think this is what we're worth? That we can't continue to do our thing—and be *ourselves*—and be successful? You think we need to jump on the bandwagon of some American superstar who's been so molded and squeezed by record companies that she probably barely remembers why she started out in the first place? Well, you can count me out." She grabbed her jacket and headed for the door, desperate to escape and get some air. Mhairi jumped up and blocked her exit.

"Come on, Ty. Let's just go to London, see what she has

to say, and take it from there? We need to do this together. Lots of bands get their big chance this way."

Ty glared at her, not trusting herself to speak, and shouldered her way past.

She was disappointed her cousins would put the chance of success above anything else, and she needed a drink.

At the first pub she found, she sat on a stool at the bar and nursed several pints, along with her disappointment. It hurt that her cousins were so enthusiastic to be associated with someone whose values were so distant from their own, but the beer helped calm her enough to decide what to do next.

Mhairi entered the bar with Jamie trailing behind her, and Ty turned away. "Piss off." Maybe the alcohol wasn't really helping. They were young and full of enthusiasm and hadn't been exposed to the cutthroat side of the music business. Mainly because she'd worked hard to keep them away from it. How could she fault their naïve enthusiasm when it was down to her shielding them from reality?

Mhairi sighed. "Oh, come on, Ty. Lachlan was approached and asked us if we want to do it. That's his job. We need to talk about this. Come on home. Jamie's brought whiskey."

Jamie waved a paper bag enticingly. Ty sighed at the obvious manipulation. Mhairi knew better than anyone how to calm her down, using a combination of common sense and the promise of alcohol.

"Fine. We'll *talk* about it." She grabbed her jacket and followed them back to the house she and Mhairi shared.

Two hours and half a bottle of whiskey later, Ty had agreed to go to the meeting in London and hear what Alexandra Knight had to say. If they were offered the job, they'd discuss it as a band and make a decision. It was only fair to the rest of them, who were already on the plane to the States in their minds. Clearly satisfied with the outcome, Jamie headed home and Mhairi went to bed.

Ty grabbed the rest of the bottle and pulled out her laptop. There were plenty of YouTube clips of Alex Knight's performances to work her way through.

Fuck, the woman was attractive. She had unusual pale green eyes that stood out against her golden-brown skin, and her glossy black hair fell over her face as she sang, staring into the camera with an intensity that could see straight to your soul. She set Ty's well-honed gaydar beeping at full speed. Rumors about her sexual orientation had cropped up time and again throughout her career, fueled by her androgynous look combined with her refusal to discuss anything about relationships in interviews.

Ty calmed her own sense of outrage about the damage queer celebrities caused by remaining in the closet, and tried to watch her performances objectively. Alex had an amazing voice. When Ty was young, she'd wished for that kind of range. She was clearly also a very capable guitarist, although her most popular songs didn't give her skill much of a chance to shine through. Alex Knight was a top-rate performer, currently riding on a worldwide wave of success. As far as opportunities went, opening for an act with her profile was a career changer, and while Ty was perfectly happy with the direction of her own career, she wasn't the only person in the band. It didn't hurt that she'd get to spend three months in the company of someone so attractive either.

THREE

A swarm of butterflies flitted in Alex's stomach. Why did she care what this British band thought of her? Surely, she had the advantage, and they would bite her hand off for the opportunity. But she couldn't shake her edginess at the thought of the imminent meeting. She'd primed her management to impress the band to the point that they'd be too overwhelmed *not* to agree to be her opening act. A quick session of Googling had told her they liked to end a gig with a pint of Guinness. She had her team arrange for the best pub in London to bring a barrel to her suite, complete with barman. Her plan was for the band to be greeted by a perfectly poured pint, which, she'd been surprised to discover, was delicious.

Everything was in place; the meeting was arranged for nine that evening to give them time to stop at their hotel and freshen up after their flight. Her internet trawling had also revealed Tyra MacLean as a teenage star of the eighties, just as Ryan had said. She'd hit the scene with some hard-hitting but catchy protest songs that had struck just the right note for a Britain in the throes of miners' strikes and Margaret

Thatcher's reign. Her first single had been a big hit, but a magazine interview in which she casually mentioned her attraction to girls had caused enough outrage to limit her mainstream success.

Alex couldn't imagine how hard it had been to come out at fifteen, and in the eighties at that. She didn't have the guts to come out at thirty-seven in a far more progressive era. She sighed. The advice of her management when she'd started her career had been a resounding no to coming out if she ever wanted to make it big. When success had arrived, the advice hadn't changed. Why spoil a good thing? Her personal unease with being dishonest about who she was had never gone away, but she'd grown used to a life of half lies and secret relationships.

But for a celebrity in the public eye few relationships ever remain truly secret and there had always been rumors about her sexuality and questions in interviews, which she firmly avoided answering. While she'd never taken the aggressive denial approach her management had advised, she couldn't claim to have been honest to the wider world, but more importantly, to her fans.

In the last few years, as more young performers were open about their sexuality, with little or no impact on their careers, she'd considered coming out. But it was so long since she'd been involved with anyone, it felt awkward to spontaneously announce her sexual orientation to the world, not to mention daunting. But she'd promised herself that if she met someone and really believed she had a chance of happiness, she would no longer hide who she was. There wasn't much time to look for love in the schedule Linda had planned for the foreseeable future, so she couldn't imagine anything changing.

She flicked through the remainder of her Tyra

MacLean research project. News stories told a tale of a young person propelled to fame at an early age, with what appeared to be little family or professional support. The added complications of her sexual orientation and a tendency to self-medicate had led to a predictable decline into substance abuse and depression. The sudden death of her mother shortly after the release of her fourth album appeared to have been the final straw. Her subsequent tour was cancelled at short notice, and Tyra MacLean disappeared from the public eye.

Alex felt for the young woman Tyra had once been. The benefits of touring with a major star might not be as attractive to her as Alex had hoped. She couldn't find any details about where she went when she disappeared, but when DandyLions' popularity increased Jamie had been interviewed by a popular music blogger. He talked about the tragic death of the twins' mother and said that Tyra had returned—he didn't say where from—and moved into her uncle's house to help raise him and his sister. That explained the close relationship, and perhaps why Tyra had chosen to give up her anonymity to help her cousins start their careers.

She glanced at her watch. It was nearly time. She had instructed Ryan to greet the visitors and make them comfortable before she made her entrance. On the stroke of nine her phone buzzed with a message from Ryan. *They're in the elevator. Give us five and come on in.*

She paced the room for a few more minutes, wondering what her guests were thinking. Were they nervous? Excited? When she could hear the buzz of conversation in the room next door, she finally swung open the door and strode in.

The twins, Mhairi and Jamie, and their manager,

Lachlan, were sitting on the two couches carefully arranged in front of the chair Alex intended to occupy. They looked up as she entered, their faces displaying a range of expressions from terror to embarrassment. Alex wanted to charm rather than intimidate them. She smiled widely as she crossed to greet them, and they all stood to introduce themselves. Lachlan shook her hand warmly.

"It's good to meet you, Alex. I think you were aware our guitarist, Mikki, isn't able to make this meeting? He was already on his way to Stockholm when we got the call."

Alex raised an eyebrow and looked around. "I was, but you appear to be another member short?"

Lachlan cleared his throat, and his gaze shifted to the twins.

Jamie spoke up. "We're sorry, Alex, our cousin Tyra has been...delayed...unavoidably."

"Really? Is she caught in traffic?"

Jamie squirmed under her gaze. "Uh, we're not sure."

Mhairi stepped forward, drawing Alex's attention from her stuttering brother.

"Hi, I'm Mhairi." She extended her hand.

Vah-ree. Alex noted the pronunciation. If they were going to work together, Alex should at least know how to pronounce her name properly. She and her brother were physically very alike. The same dark brown hair. Mhairi kept hers in a sleek bob, whereas Jamie's hung over his collar and eyes. Their eyes were the same too, a bright blue. Mhairi's expressed sincerity and openness, without the mischievousness of her brother. They were both tall, Mhairi topping Alex's five feet seven by a couple of inches.

"I'm sorry, Alex. She isn't picking up her phone, and she promised to meet us in the foyer in plenty of time. This isn't like her, but I'm sure she'll join us when she can."

Alex nodded. "I suggest we make a start—"

"Sorry I'm late." Linda burst through the door.

Alex took a deep breath. She'd made it clear to Linda that she didn't need her at the meeting. This was merely about reassuring herself that there would be no personality clashes, and that she could bear to spend three months on the road with these individuals. Linda had argued she couldn't manage Alex's affairs properly without having a say about who she worked with. "Linda, come on in." She sighed before introducing the twins and Lachlan.

"And where's the rest of the band?" Linda looked around. "I thought the aim of this meeting was to get to know each other?"

Alex waved her hand. "We've covered that already, thanks, Linda. Let's move on." She turned back to her visitors. "I heard the band's favorite beer was Guinness, so I've arranged a little welcome drink, if you're interested?"

Jamie's face lit up as, on cue, the barman came in from a side room with six pints of freshly poured Guinness on a tray. He set them down on a side table and retreated to his room. Alex handed out drinks to everyone, except Linda who shook her head and poured a glass of water before sitting off to the side. *Miserable bitch.* She sat down and returned her full attention to the band members. "Perhaps you could tell me a bit about yourselves and the background of DandyLions? And then I can tell you about my tour."

Lachlan gestured to Mhairi to begin.

"Jamie and I come from a very musical family. Our grandparents were a big part of the Scottish folk music scene back in the day. Our dad was in a band before we were born, and our cousin, Tyra, has worked in the music industry her whole life, and she was an influential part of our upbringing."

Alex nodded encouragingly for her to continue.

"We started performing at an early age, and by the time we were in our teens, we were playing in bands and writing our own songs, that sort of thing. We started a band, but our drummer kept messing us about and the guitarist couldn't play the songs we wrote. So, Jamie asked Ty if she would join us for rehearsals, just to get the songs right to begin with. At the time, Mikki was doing some session work on an album she was producing and was staying at her house. He came along too. We all started jamming together and really enjoyed it." She stopped to sip her Guinness and smacked her lips appreciatively. "That's a good pint."

Alex smiled. She liked Mhairi. There was something trustworthy and quietly confident about her, unusual in someone so young.

"So we, well, Jamie, asked them both if they'd do the gigs we already had booked. Mikki had no plans, so he agreed straight away. Ty really wasn't keen, but we convinced her. The gigs went well, and it just seemed natural to record some songs together. The rest is history, I guess."

"But that doesn't sound like a very sustainable strategy. What are your long-term plans?" Linda asked.

Mhairi smiled at her pleasantly. "We have no long-term plans," she said directly to Alex. "We thought we might make another album, but if we came on tour with you, that would change things—"

"I don't understand why you think it would be a good idea to tour with a band on the brink of breaking up, Alex," Linda said, clearly not bothered about voicing her concerns in front of the band.

"We like to think of it more as evolving, and as I said, we don't have any plans at the moment." Mhairi smiled.

Alex resisted the urge to snap at Linda and pinned her with a glare instead. "My criteria for an opening act are…" She held up three fingers. "One, they are an entertaining warm up. Two, their music and image complement mine. And three, they're professional and completely reliable. I've never had the same band twice, so what the band does after the tour makes no difference to me." She turned away from Linda and smiled at the twins. "I don't know how much you know about my work but to give you some background, I recently finished a six-month leg of my world tour, covering the Southern Hemisphere and Europe."

"I saw you at the Hydro in April," Jamie said as if he might burst.

Alex suspected he'd been under strict instructions to keep quiet and let Lachlan and Mhairi do all the talking. "Is that right?" She smiled. "You could have come and introduced yourself. I love meeting new musicians."

"No security team in their right mind would let Jamie slip through." Mhairi laughed and gave her a twin a playful shove. "Sometimes he has trouble getting into our own gigs."

Jamie shot his sister a horrified look, and Alex felt sorry for him. "Is it tough having your twin put you down at every opportunity?" She chuckled. "I grew up an only child and always wanted a sibling, but I can see they have their downside."

Jamie rolled his eyes dramatically. "She never lets up, Alex. I'm a saint to put up with it."

They all laughed, apart from Linda, who took out her laptop and started typing loudly. Pleased the atmosphere had relaxed a little, Alex continued. "So now I'm heading out on the North America leg, an extensive tour of the US and a number of cities in Canada. Forty-two dates in just under three months. Big arena venues with a sprinkling of my favorite, smaller theaters. It will be hard work. Does that sound like something you'd like to be involved in?"

They were interrupted by a hammering on the door. Ryan jumped up and swung it open. Tyra MacLean was standing in the doorway, smirking, accompanied by one of Alex's security staff. Ryan gave him a brief nod, and he turned and left, leaving Tyra to wander in, bouncing off a wall as she approached.

"You've all started without me."

Her voice was slightly slurred as she headed for the unclaimed pint on the table. Alex stood to intercept her. Tyra was much shorter than she'd expected, but her chunky biker boots gave her an extra couple of inches. Her breath smelled strongly of whiskey, and her sparkling eyes, an even more vivid blue than her cousins', were slightly unfocused. She wore skinny black jeans and a fitted white silk shirt with the sleeves rolled back over her tattooed forearms. Her smirk grew bigger as she stopped unsteadily, inches from Alex and stuck out her hand.

"Tyra MacLean. What an honor to meet the legendary Alexandra Knight."

Alex ignored the hint of sarcasm and returned the firm handshake. She introduced Ryan and Linda, who both received a vague nod. Tyra didn't seem to be in a rush to move out of her personal space. Alex's first thought was to throw them all out and start the search again. She couldn't stand unreliability. But she reminded herself how good the band was live *and* that most rock musicians didn't live the monastic lifestyle she had chosen and decided to give her a chance.

"It appears to be you who has a head start on us, Ms. MacLean." She reached for the glass and handed it over.

"Thank you. Cheers." She raised her glass, took a

healthy gulp, and threw herself over the back of the couch between her wide-eyed cousins, somehow managing not to spill a drop.

"Alex, are you really going to continue this meeting?" Linda stared at Tyra, her face twisted in obvious disgust.

Alex ignored her, took a sip of her pint, and licked her lips as she sat, aware of Tyra's eyes on her. "So, we were just discussing the mutual benefits of DandyLions opening for me on my North America tour. I think there's a lot we can do for each other. You'll get exposure in the US, a tricky market for British acts, and a chance to tour the US and Canada—"

"An' what will you get out of it? What added value could we possibly offer you?"

Jamie's expression looked to be wavering between intimidation and fury. "Ty, maybe if you shut up and let her finish, we'll find out. If you don't want to be a part of this meeting, why don't you leave it to us, and we'll update you later?"

Tyra snorted. "It's not that long since I was teaching you to wipe your own arse, so if you don't mind, I'll stay."

"Alex, this is why you need to have a professional opening act," said Linda from the corner of the room. "Performers who know how to behave in any situation."

Alex cleared her throat. This was her meeting and her decision. She didn't know why, but Tyra clearly needed some convincing, and that was fine. It made a change for people not to fawn all over her on their first meeting. "What will I get out of it? For one, I'm a big fan." It wasn't a lie as such. She didn't say *how long* she'd been following them. "It's been a long time since I had an opening act that I'd pay money to go and see. You're talented musicians, and you all bring something very different to your sound. I like that. I write my own songs and have almost complete say over their arrangement, so I find your collaborative approach interesting. And perhaps most importantly, I'm approaching forty. I need to stay connected to a younger audience. You can help me with that." She smiled encouragingly at Jamie and Mhairi.

Tyra downed the rest of the glass in a single swallow and jumped up. "Where do I get a refill around here then?"

Attempting to negotiate the table, she tripped and dropped her glass. It hit the edge of the table and shattered across the floor.

Alex stood, not sure if she should intervene. She was unhappy with the sense of chaos this woman had brought to the meeting.

"Fuck." Tyra bent down to pick up the glass. "I've got this. It's all good."

She swore again and stood up, staring at the blood dripping from her hand.

She's a walking disaster. Everyone else appeared frozen in horror, so Alex grabbed a cloth from the drinks area and moved quickly to Tyra's side. "Let me see."

Tyra held her hand out wordlessly, as Alex wrapped it gently in the cloth.

"Come with me. We need to wash the glass out."

Tyra staggered along as she steered her toward the bathroom. "Sit down." She gestured to the side of the bath and held Tyra's hand over the sink. She lifted her chin and looked into her unfocused gaze. "Are you okay? You don't feel faint or anything?" She didn't need to be dealing with a head injury as well.

Tyra blinked and shook her head slowly. "I'm sorry. I didn't mean for this to happen."

"Of course you didn't." Though Alex wasn't sure what

Tyra *did* mean to happen when she turned up wasted to such an important meeting. "I imagine it's quite painful. You'll need some stitches in it, I'm guessing." Satisfied the wound was clean, Alex wrapped Tyra's hand tightly in a clean towel and gently guided her back to the main room, hoping one of her family would now take control of the situation.

Mhairi rushed over as they reentered, kicking her brother, who sat with his head in his hands. "I'm so sorry, Alex. I'll take her to A&E."

Tyra raised her head. "I'm fine." She pulled away toward the door, holding the hand tight to her chest. "I've had enough of this shite. I'm going to the pub."

Just what she needed, Tyra proving Linda right again. Alex clenched her jaw and fought to keep an even tone. "Ty, this was an amazing opportunity for your band. I was offering you a chance of exposure you could only dream of. I don't think I can work with someone who can't turn up sober to such an important meeting."

Tyra swung around so suddenly that Alex took a step back.

"You can shove your dream job up your arse. Go and bestow your favors on some other poor bastards. An' don't call me Ty, that's reserved for friends and family. I don't recall you being either."

Ryan opened the door for her, and she stumbled into the corridor without looking back.

As the door closed everyone spoke at once. Linda was on the phone calling their security team to eject Tyra from the building, and Mhairi was telling her that was unnecessary when Ty was leaving anyway. Lachlan was trying to apologize, and Jamie was swearing.

Alex raised her voice. "Listen, guys, I know she doesn't

speak for you all, but I need a band I can rely upon, and it's imperative the whole band really wants this. I run a tight ship, and I can't afford to let one addict mess it up. Maybe you need to go away and discuss where you see yourselves going as a band, and I'll find myself a reliable, if less interesting, opening act. Unless you want to find a different drummer?"

"She's not an addict." Mhairi's voice was thick with emotion. "She hasn't touched drugs for over twenty years. And I've not seen her that drunk for ages. She only overdoes it if she's worried about something. And we've had other drummers. No one is nearly as good."

Alex added loyalty to Mhairi's list of qualities. It was a real shame she wasn't going to be working with this particular member of the band. "So, she can't cope with the idea of being in the public eye again, or she really wanted to put me off hiring you. Either way, her plan succeeded. I'm sorry. I truly was looking forward to working with you all." In her attempt to remain calm she was coming across as cold, she knew. She walked toward her room, wanting to get away and leave Ryan to get them through the door.

"Please, Alex. This isn't like her. We'll talk to her. She's an experienced musician. She'd be reliable. We all would." Jamie's voice was desperate, his eyes brimming with tears.

Alex squeezed his shoulder as she passed. "I'm sorry it hasn't worked out, and I wish you all the best for the future. You're both very talented. I'm sure the world will be seeing a lot more of you."

Jamie stood at the door for a couple more seconds before Lachlan and Mhairi took his arms and guided him into the corridor. Alex could hear their apologies until Ryan closed the door. She leaned back against the wall and let out a long sigh. Ryan opened his mouth to speak but Alex shook her head, and he began to quietly tidy the glasses away.

"Perhaps next time you'll listen to my advice about the quality of the acts you consider working with."

Linda had been quiet for longer than expected, but it was inevitable she'd want to crow about being right all along. Alex took her firmly by the elbow and guided her out the door without a word. Ryan, perhaps sensing she needed space, followed silently. She marched back to her room and threw herself onto her bed.

Her temper had always been a problem when she was young. When she first started in the business, she'd earned a reputation as a brat who flipped when things didn't go her way. She hated the lack of control she felt when she lost her temper, so had worked hard at finding strategies to control it. Now, when she did show anger, it was of a cold, restrained variety, and she stayed in control.

Alone and reflecting on Tyra MacLean's behavior, she felt more hurt than angry. What had she done to attract such undisguised contempt? Alex stripped off her clothes and took a quick shower. She wrapped herself in a thick robe and got back into bed, where she slept fitfully, her dreams inhabited by a smirking face with unfocused blue eyes.

FOUR

Ty staggered away from the hotel muttering to herself. "Who does she think she is? I was making albums when she was still in nappies. Amazing opportunity? Fuck off."

But as she trudged through the dark streets, the cold air and the pain cleared the fog in her head, and she looked down at her towel-wrapped hand. She hadn't meant to turn up pissed, but the quick couple to take the edge off her discomfort had turned into several, and she hadn't realized how drunk she was until she dropped the glass. *Fuck. Jamie and Mhairi will never forgive me.*

Alex Knight's management had booked them into a hotel not far from the one Alex used when she was in London, so it was a short walk. Ty let herself into her room and opened the connecting door to Mhairi's. It was in darkness, but she felt she had to explain her behavior or at least try to apologize. She threw herself into a chair and looked down at her hand, wrapped in the blood-soaked towel. It hurt like hell, but she couldn't find the energy to get up and deal with it. She pressed her head back against the wall. The whiskey and darkness quickly got the better of her, and she woke to the sound of the door opening. Footsteps approached in the darkness, followed by a rattle and a muttered curse.

"Would you no' be better with the lights on?" Ty winced as the room was immediately flooded with light, and Mhairi glared at her.

"Fuck, Tyra, you nearly scared me to death. What are you playing at?"

Mhairi rarely raised her voice, and almost never swore, and Ty recoiled. She hung her head and rubbed her forehead with the hand that wasn't caked in blood. "I don't blame you for being mad at me. I'm a total fuck-up."

"I was so worried. Lachie and I have been looking for you. Why did you turn your phone off?"

"I'm sorry, Mhairi, I didn't think anyone would want to be around me. I felt so stupid, I just wanted to run away. But as I walked, I sobered up a bit and realized what a fucking idiot I am."

"Yes, you are." Mhairi hauled her up by the arm and dragged her to the bathroom. "Jamie's raging. He says he's gonna kill you in the morning."

As Mhairi washed and dressed the wound, muttering about how it should have had stitches, Ty's thoughts went back to how efficiently and gently Alex had dealt with her hand earlier. She'd acted like such a loser. What the hell had she been thinking? That was it though, wasn't it? She *hadn't* been thinking. She sagged against the bathroom wall. "Fucking hell, Mhairi, I was so rude to her, and she was nothing but polite."

Mhairi placed a pack of painkillers in her bandaged hand and a large glass of water in the other. "You need to get some sleep, Ty. We can work out how to clear up your mess in the morning."

Ty nodded and slowly headed for her room, her shoulders slumped.

"Things won't seem so bad tomorrow." Mhairi didn't sound convincing as Ty started to close the door between their rooms.

"Thanks, Mhairi, you're too good to me. See you in the morning."

Tyra's eyes flew open to the sound of hammering at the door.

"Ty, you fucker. Let me in."

She hauled herself to the door and swung it open, squinting at Jamie. "Get in here, you idiot. How many hotels do you want me to get thrown out of in twenty-four hours?" She led him into her room and threw herself down on the bed.

Mhairi appeared at the connecting door and frowned. "Jay, this is a hotel. The other residents aren't interested in your tantrum," she said and set the coffee machine on.

"And when have you ever been up at..." Ty squinted at her phone. "Before eight in the morning? Is this to show me how angry you are, Jamie? Tell someone who gives a shit." She knew that was harsh. She did care, and she was horrified she'd potentially blown his big chance. But she knew how to manage Jamie's outbursts. If something didn't go his way, he was prone to shouting and swearing, but the best way to shut him down was to join in. He didn't like being shouted at, especially by her, and would soon back off. She wasn't feeling up to an extended argument; the yelling was hurting her head, so she was relieved to see Jamie drop to the end of the bed with his head in his hands.

"Oh, Ty, you proper fucked it up. This was our one big chance. My big chance. I know the rest of you don't want it like I do, but I thought we were going to give this tour a go. And you just made us all look like idiots." He looked up at her. "I don't understand."

Ty sat back on the bed wearily. She felt slightly better than she had in the early hours but not much. "I told you, Jamie. I said I didn't want to go on tour with her."

"But you said you'd listen to what she had to say," Mhairi observed from the doorway.

Jamie nodded. "Yeah, but instead you turned up pissed and insulted her."

"It was too difficult. The closer the meeting got the more I thought about how she represents everything I've spent my life fighting against."

"Well, that's dramatic. What, like success and keeping your private life to yourself?" He shook his head.

Ty ran her fingers through her hair and tried to gather her thoughts. It was all so complicated, what she'd been through when she was young, alone and with no support. She had worked hard to ensure the twins would never go through anything like it, so why did she expect them to understand? "You know how important it is to have role models in life. What sort of message does she send out to young people when the whole world knows she's a dyke, but she just keeps denying it? It's the twenty-first century, for fuck's sake."

"So basically, you're angry because she's not a big, out lesbian like you? If anyone lives their life differently from you, they're always wrong, aren't they? If someone wants to make it big in the music business, you know better. Well, I'm sick of it, Tyra. I've had enough of having my life micromanaged by you. DandyLions are over." He marched out of the room, leaving the door wide open.

Mhairi got up and closed the door. She handed Ty a steaming mug of coffee before settling next to her on the bed. Jamie's words echoed in her aching head, which she rested on Mhairi's shoulder.

Mhairi squeezed her arm. "It was going to happen eventually, y'know. You've helped him this far, but your heart's never been fully in it. Maybe it's time to call it a day."

Ty sipped her coffee. "He's so young. That tour would have been an amazing experience for him. Probably wouldn't have harmed Mikki's prospects of forming a new band back home either."

"And I've always wanted to see America." Mhairi's smile was gentle.

"Oh, Mhairi, I've buggered it up. I could've just sucked it up for a few months and played my drums. But I got up on my high horse to make a point and didn't think about the effect that would have on anyone else." She didn't want to talk about how terrified she was at the scale of exposure the tour would entail. She had always kept some things from the twins, not wanting them to know how bad things could get.

"I'm not sure you really made a point, other than that you can't be trusted with breakable objects."

Ty rubbed her temple. "Do you think there's any chance I can fix it? Or was she totally pissed off with me?" She rubbed her head harder, remembering how badly she'd behaved. "I was so fucking rude."

"She looked more disappointed than angry...but still pretty angry. And that numpty of a manager was really rubbing it in. But I don't suppose you could make it any worse if you went back and got on bended knee and apologized." Mhairi looked her up and down as she stood. "You'll need to get cleaned up. Do you have any spare clothes?"

Ty quickly dismissed the inappropriate vision of getting on her knees for Alex and peered over the end of the bed to see the carnage from the night before. She'd dropped her Levis on the floor when she collapsed into bed, along with her favorite shirt, now streaked with blood. One of her boots was sticking out from her jeans. The other was nowhere to be seen. She collapsed back onto the bed. "It's not looking hopeful."

Mhairi rummaged through Ty's bag and found a clean T-shirt emblazoned with a long-defunct band logo, and some toiletries, which she threw in Ty's direction.

"Right, get yourself in that shower. I'll sort out these clothes."

Ty dragged herself to the bathroom, shrugging off her underwear as she went.

"I'll just pick those up as well, shall I?" Mhairi shook her head.

By the time Tyra emerged, awkwardly trying to towel dry her hair with one hand, Mhairi had done an admirable job of salvaging her clothes. She'd shaken out her Levis, folded them, and put them on the bed. There were a couple of bloodstains, but they were easy to miss. She'd even found both boots.

"Thanks, Mhairi, I'm sorry I'm such a pain." Ty was truly sorry, not for the first time, for the trouble she often caused her cousin. She had tried to put caring for the twins before anything in her life, but by the time Mhairi had been nine or ten, Ty had started to question which of them was the responsible adult. She displayed common sense and insight beyond her years, and she was a natural carer. With Jamie for a brother though, she had been guaranteed a more adventurous childhood than she might have chosen alone.

Ty pulled on the T-shirt and attempted to dry her hair into its usual style with one hand. Mhairi rolled her eyes and took charge. When she'd done her best, Ty turned and wrapped herself in her arms, needing the comfort as the reality of her predicament filtered through her aching head. "She's not gonna want to speak to me, is she? I'll never get past her security."

"You definitely won't if you don't get down there and try, will you?"

Mhairi hugged her tight. She retrieved the first aid kit and applied a new dressing to the cut. Ty risked a quick look at the wound, which was deep but looked clean. After downing some painkillers and pulling on her trusty leather jacket, Ty was as ready as she'd ever be to try and put things right. "What time is it?" She looked at her watch. "I'll be there before ten. Is that a bit early?"

Mhairi laughed and pushed her toward the door. "I don't think you should worry about looking too keen, Ty. She's flying back to the US this evening after her TV interview. She'll be up."

She took the stairs down to the foyer slowly, her head aching as she tried to think up a strategy to make things right. She wished she could curl up in bed and not think about it, but she was committed now. What could she possibly say that would earn her Alex Knight's forgiveness?

FIVE

A five-minute walk that she wished was longer took Ty back to Alex's upmarket hotel. She paused in a doorway across from the entrance to plan her next move. If she went direct to the suite, she would certainly be intercepted by one of Alex's team before she could get anywhere near her. If she called from the lobby, they'd be unlikely to give her a chance to speak to Alex and explain why she needed to see her in person.

As she mused on the best approach, a group exited the hotel. An imposing man with an unmistakable military vibe blocked her view of the people behind, but as they crossed the road, she recognized the bulky form of Ryan Weaver, Alex's assistant, at the back. Maybe she could go through him. He'd definitely seemed more friendly than Alex's vile manager. Perhaps if she explained why she needed to speak with Alex again, he'd be sympathetic. They turned in her direction, and she steeled herself to intercept Ryan. As the large guy passed the doorway, she stepped out quickly, and straight into the path of Alex Knight. Her sunglasses and baseball cap did nothing to hide the look of shock on her face. Before Ty could speak, she was slammed against the door behind her, the air driven out of her lungs. She sagged against the hand holding the front of her jacket.

"Let her go, Mike. She's harmless."

When Alex's goon released her, Ty doubled over trying to catch her breath.

"What are you doing here, Tyra?" Ryan helped her to stand upright. "It's not a good idea to jump out on Alex. The security guys don't like it."

Alex had already turned away, and Mike followed close behind her. Ty gasped as she straightened. "I'm sorry, I didn't even know Alex was with you. I just wanted a quick word."

Alex looked back. "What word?"

Ty held her hands out in apology. "The word sorry. But I also wanted to explain. It'll only take a few minutes of your time."

Alex turned and continued to walk away.

"Please, Alex?"

Alex didn't slow down or turn around. "Five minutes. And you can buy coffee."

Yes. Ty kept pace with Ryan until they turned left into a narrow street. Halfway along was the entrance to a small coffee shop. Mike turned in, scanned the room, and held the door for Alex to follow. She headed to a booth in the corner, so Ty followed. Ryan and Mike took the next booth along, which gave them some privacy.

Alex pulled off her cap and placed it on the table with her sunglasses. "So?"

"Okay." Now wasn't a time to beat about the bush, and she forced her protesting brain into action. "Thanks for agreeing to hear me out. I behaved appallingly last night, and I just wanted a chance to say sorry for that."

"And?"

Ty felt herself sweating under the pressure. Or maybe it was just the hangover. "I think you're right about DandyLions being a good match for your tour, and those kids are great musicians. It would be a shame if the reason it didn't happen was down to some cynical old loser who has too many opinions for her own and others' good." Her words tumbled out, but she wasn't sure how much time she had, and she couldn't bear the thought that she might not get the chance to explain. She inhaled and looked for a reaction, but none was forthcoming. "So, I'm asking you to please reconsider the band for your support act, either with me or with a replacement drummer. I know some great session drummers who would jump at the chance. I'd make sure they were the best." She sat back with a sigh that sounded to her own ears more like a groan. The seat was surprisingly soft, and she tried to sink deeper into its surface to avoid Alex's piercing stare. She was relieved when the waiter came and took their coffee orders.

Ty wasn't easily intimidated but she was on the back foot, and Alex clearly wasn't concerned about putting her at ease. She tried not to squirm.

"Why? Why should I trust you? Why should I put my own hard-earned reputation on the line to give you a chance?"

Ty leaned forward. She rested her elbows on the shiny table and rubbed her forehead with the fingers of her bandaged hand. "You won't be putting anything on the line. There's no risk. Well, there's the obvious risk in going on tour with an obscure support act. The US might hate us." She shrugged. "But other than that, no risks. I'll be fully committed and if nothing else, I have a lot of experience of being on the road. And like I said, if you don't trust me, I'll find you a replacement."

The waiter returned with their coffees, and Alex looked down to add sugar to the coffee that had been placed in front of her. Ty took the opportunity to take a quick sip, wishing she'd ordered an Irish coffee instead.

Alex stirred slowly as she rested her gaze back on Ty. "I think we both know that a big part of DandyLions' success is your input, surprising as that may be."

Ty heard the spoon hit the saucer, but she didn't dare break eye contact.

"So, tell me, why was the thought of touring with me so repugnant? And why the change of heart?"

Tyra leaned back in her seat and rubbed her face as she tried desperately to get her thoughts in order. She didn't need to share everything, just enough to make this right. "I'll try to explain, but you'll need to hear the full story." A curt nod gave her permission to proceed, and she sighed. "I thought touring with you was a bad idea for several reasons. When I was young, the pressure on me to break into the American market was massive. I didn't care, but my record company insisted. Tour after disappointing tour; it was one of the things that broke me. I didn't want to revisit that nightmare, and I didn't want it for Jamie and Mhairi." She took a deep breath. Revisiting those days was something she didn't enjoy. "I realize now that's not my decision to make. They're adults and should make their own choices. What they need from me is support and advice, not throwing a strop because it's not what I want."

Alex shook her head slowly. Was she taking on anything Ty was saying or was she made of stone? Ty couldn't manage much more soul-bearing to make this right.

"But there's more to it than that. You weren't just opposed to a tour of the US. It felt personal."

Shit. Ty lowered her eyes. "I was getting to that bit." Further confessions were definitely on the cards. Alex wasn't going to give in until she understood. She forced herself to resume eye contact. "As a teenager, I was very open about my sexuality. It came so early in my career no one was expecting it, so no one tried to stop me. And once I was out, there was no going back in. It had a massive impact on my career, on the way I was treated by the press and the public. People held demonstrations at my gigs to stop children buying tickets. Can you imagine how that feels? When all you want to do is to entertain people and tell your story?" Ty shifted in her chair. She'd never discussed this with anyone, not even Mhairi. The emotions bubbled at the surface, threatening nausea, but she had to press on. "But do you know the very worst thing about it, Alex? The loneliness. There was no one else out in the UK. Yes, we had Holly Johnson, and Boy George, and one of the soaps had a gay character, but there was no one like me. Big names like k.d lang and Melissa Etheridge didn't come out till much later. I was a freak. But my consolation was that for every young guitar playing queer girl who came after me, however long after, I helped make it just that little bit easier." She let out a long sigh, and met Alex's steady gaze, but she was still giving nothing away. "So, I've always had...contempt for today's closeted celebrities who live in this very different world, still far from perfect but so much more accepting, where so many of us can be ourselves and not be judged for it."

Alex opened her mouth, but Ty raised her hand. "Wait, let me finish. So, I look at these actors, and singers, and sports stars and listen to them deny, or at best refuse to confirm, who they are, and it pisses me off. But it's very easy, sitting in front of the TV, to judge someone's decisions without knowing anything about them or their life. And when I met you, I wanted to dislike you, but you came over as a warm, genuine person rather than someone who's deliberately living a lie to protect their career at the cost of being a visible role model to people who really need one." She looked away again. "And I came over as a dick." She took a deep breath. "It's none of my business what you choose to share or not share about your life, and I would really like the opportunity to work with you and to get to know you better." She sat back, emotionally exhausted, and rested her aching head against the chair. Whether or not she really believed what she said, she wasn't going to let the twins down.

Alex sipped her coffee in silence. After what felt like at least an hour, she put the cup down. "I want some reassurances about your conduct."

Ty nodded slowly, trying to hide her relief. "Understandable under the circumstances. I won't promise I'll never have a drink, but there'll be no embarrassing behavior. Jamie and I do tend to have occasional rows, but we'll keep them private."

Alex shook her head. "I don't like arguments. I thrive in a calm, organized working environment. I can't have you messing with that."

"I'll bear that in mind. My commitment will be to give you the best support act you could have. I'll look after the others, make sure Jamie doesn't get distracted, and help in any other way you need me to."

Alex's expression was still stern. "You're in. But don't expect any more chances. I'm not beyond finding a new act mid-tour."

Ty sighed and reached across the table to squeeze Alex's hand. She felt herself relax, and she grinned. "Thank you. You won't regret it. In fact, in three months' time, you'll be congratulating yourself on such amazing judgement." She saw the irritation cross Alex's face. *Shut up, idiot.*

"Don't let me down, MacLean." Alex rose to leave, looking at her watch.

Ty noticed the use of her surname and didn't want Alex to go without them being on more friendly terms. "How about that Guinness?"

"What?" Alex raised her eyebrow.

"You went to such an effort to make us feel at home last night, and I royally fucked it up. How about I start to make things up to you by buying you a pint of the best Guinness outside of Ireland?"

Alex tapped her watch. "It's not even noon. I don't think this is the best way to reassure me about your drinking habits."

"Ah, yeah, I can see how that might look." She didn't suppress her grin and hoped her charm would work its magic. "I promise you lunchtime drinking is not my normal routine, but I've just been invited to tour the US with one of its biggest stars. That doesn't happen every day, so I'd like to celebrate."

Alex's face softened a fraction. "In that case, let's go. If we're going to do this, we need to start afresh. You're buying."

She nodded to Mike, replaced her baseball cap and shades, and strode out. Ty hesitated a moment before she jumped up, not used to being told what to do. She approached the waiter to pay, but Ryan beat her to it.

"I've got this. I'm heading back to the hotel now, but you better get after her. She doesn't like to be kept waiting."

Tyra nodded her thanks and hurried out. She resisted the urge to break into a jog to keep up with Alex's pace as she steered them down another side street.

"The car is arriving for my interview at two. One quick drink, then I'll need to get back."

Ty nodded. "It's only a fifteen-minute walk. I'll call you an Uber if we run short of time."

Alex laughed. "I have a car. So, I thought the Guinness I sourced for our meeting was the best London had to offer?"

"Maybe in a TripAdvisor kind of way. This is the best pint from a tried-every-bar-in-the-city perspective. You can compare. Although hopefully the company will be more pleasant," she said, still feeling sheepish about her behavior in spite of having talked her way into a second chance.

Alex stopped and looked at her. "Look, MacLean, I meant what I said. Fresh start. Let's put yesterday behind us and make this thing work."

Ty raised her hands in apology. "Absolutely. And in that spirit, maybe you could call me Ty?"

"Maybe. But I kinda like MacLean."

Alex set a blistering walking pace with her long stride, and Mike followed closely behind. Ty was half glad the conversation had paused as she attempted to lead the way without stopping to throw up.

Alex sat at a secluded corner table, waiting for Ty to return from the bar. What the hell was she doing here? Today had really not turned out as expected. She had planned a short break from her hotel room before her final UK interview and now here she was, drinking in a bar with Tyra

MacLean, of all people. Linda wouldn't be happy at her U-turn, but she would stand by her decision. Anyone who had the guts to apologize after last night's behavior must be serious about wanting it. And Alex had admired Ty's honesty, and her sincerity about why celebrities being out and proud was so important to her. Alex hadn't tried to deny anything, and Ty hadn't pushed it any further. She pulled herself out of her thoughts as Ty approached, empty-handed.

"It takes a while to pour." She grinned. "Mike said he'll bring them in a minute." She looked around at the almost empty room. "They don't do food, so it doesn't attract the lunchtime office crowd."

Alex realized she was still wearing her shades. She pulled them off and dropped them on the table.

"Is it much of a problem being recognized over here?" Tyra asked.

"Not too bad. Much less than at home, especially in New York because people are more certain it's me. Here, it's more likely to be a suspicious look or a nudge to a companion. I've had the occasional request for a selfie, but I try to be polite."

"When you really want to knock the phone out of their hand and stamp on it?" Ty laughed.

Alex frowned. How did people always remember that story? One moment when she'd lost control and it had haunted her for years. "It only happened once. And he was a journalist. He should've known better."

Ty roared with laughter. "I never knew that. Fantastic."

Alex clenched her teeth. "Don't pretend you've never considered it."

"Oh, absolutely." Ty slapped the table. "Every overly nosey reporter who thinks your entire life is their business, and some of the really rude fans too. Good for you."

Alex forced herself to relax. Ty was laughing with, not at, her. She found she was smiling back. "How about you? Do you get recognized?"

"A fair bit. Mostly by old-school fans, and the media love raking up old stories about me, but I don't really get noticed for DandyLions. One of Jamie's best traits is that he attracts all the attention. Walking around town is already getting more difficult for him. Obviously, he loves every minute and is looking forward to the day he'll have to be driven everywhere and have his shopping done for him." Ty rolled her eyes.

"He'll learn." Alex smiled again. "You're very close to them, aren't you? Mhairi told me you helped raise them?"

Mike approached with their pints, and she thanked him and turned her attention back to Ty.

Ty nodded slowly. "Yeah, for a few years. I moved in with my uncle, Jim, when he was really struggling and couldn't afford to give up his job. I was doing nothing worthwhile with my life and I didn't have anywhere to live, so it worked out fine."

"I think you're underplaying your part. Looking after new-born twins full-time is a big ask." Alex was surprised she would play down such a selfless action and couldn't help comparing it to her own experience of parenting.

But Ty shrugged. "I loved it. They're the closest I'm ever going to come to having my own kids. When Jim met Kirsty a few years after his wife died, they got together pretty quick. She'd been bringing up her son, Ewen, alone, and she seemed happy to take on the twins as well. Jim thought he was doing me a favor by releasing me to get on with my life, but I was gutted. So I moved nearby, got a job at a recording studio in town and spent as much time as I could with them. Sorry, that's a lot of family detail." She glanced down at her as yet untouched pint and looked back up quickly.

Alex smiled. Ty made her smile more than she was used to. "I asked because I'm interested." She tipped her head towards the drink. "Are you having second thoughts about that? You must be feeling last night's adventures."

"You know what they say. Kill or cure." Tyra straightened her shoulders and picked up her glass. "Slàinte mhath."

Alex touched glasses and took a long drink. She had worked up a thirst on their walk across town, but she wondered again how she came to be drinking in a pub a few hours before a live interview on national television. She licked the foam from her top lip and saw Ty watching her closely, an indecipherable expression on her face. She wondered what Ty thought of her. She had learned long ago not to be too concerned about others' opinions, but Ty's approval mattered for some reason. She checked her watch, duty taking over as always.

"I am going to have to leave soon but I've enjoyed our chat. It was good to get to know you better."

Ty was still watching her intently. "I was hoping to learn a bit about you too." Her tone was almost shy.

Alex sighed. "I would love to sit here all afternoon chatting with you..." She meant it. She wanted to get to know this fascinating woman better. "But I've got forty-five minutes before my car picks me up for a live TV interview on the BBC. And if there's one thing you need to know about me, it's that I don't like to be rushed. Or to be kept waiting. Or for plans to change at short notice. Ha, that's three things about me." She smiled again while inside she was berating herself for sounding so uptight. But Ty's smile was warm. She forced herself to look away and caught Mike's eye. He pulled out his phone as they finished their drinks.

When it was time to leave, she slipped out onto the street with minimum fuss, Mike staying close as they were in a busy part of town. Ty tagged along behind and stuck her head in the door before Mike could close it. "Thanks, Alex. I'll see you in a couple of months."

Alex waved her in. "Don't be silly. Ted will drop you at your hotel, but I'll need to get out first. I'm pushed for time."

Ty relaxed into the seat opposite as they pulled out into the traffic. "So, you fly out tonight?"

"Yeah, back home for a few days then out to LA for some album promotional stuff. I'll hopefully catch up with my mom and my daughter while I'm out there. Then it's back home to prepare for the tour."

She didn't miss Ty's eyes widening at the mention of her daughter. Why had she mentioned Dottie? She avoided talking about her to people she knew well, let alone to those she'd only met twenty-four hours ago. Tyra made her want to open up and talk. That was interesting, and a little scary.

"Hey, the tour starts beginning of September. Why don't you come out a few weeks early to get set up?" What was she saying? She had no idea. She just knew she wanted to spend more time in Ty's company. She cleared her throat. "All of you, I mean. If that suits you."

Ty nodded slowly and bit her lip. "That would be great, but we haven't sorted out our plans for the summer. Mikki'll want to spend it in Sweden if he's going to be away for three months. Things are serious with his girlfriend, and he's worried he'll mess it up by staying away too long." She looked out of the window as they pulled into the hotel forecourt. "If I can take the time off from my studio over the summer, maybe I could come over for a couple of weeks? I've got friends in Brooklyn I really need to spend some time with, and the change of scenery would be good to help me finish a couple of songs I've been asked to write. I can't speak for Jamie and Mhairi, but I'll see what they'd like to do."

"That would be useful," Alex said. *Useful?* "We could get together and talk through some of the finer details of the tour." She was clutching at straws now to make the idea seem normal.

"That's a plan then." Tyra grinned as the car pulled up.

Mike held the door and as Alex climbed out of the car. Tyra scooted out after her. "Good luck with the interview. I'll be watching."

Alex tried not to let her expression reflect the pleasure she felt at the thought of Ty watching her. She managed a small nod. "Let me know what you think. I'll have Ryan send you my number."

"And thanks," said Ty, "for everything." They hugged briefly and Ty got back into the car. As it pulled away into the traffic, Alex stood watching for a moment. She suspected Tyra MacLean could bring disruption into her orderly life. But why didn't that worry her as much as it should? As she made her way into the hotel, she reminded herself she was the boss. If anything happened on tour that she didn't like, she had the power to make it go away.

SIX

It was early August when Tyra made her way to New York. She wasn't an enthusiastic flyer, so as the plane took off, she rested her head back with her eyes closed and thought about what was ahead. She was pleased the twins had both decided not to come along. They were facing a few months further away from home than they had ever been and had decided to spend the summer with friends and family.

Ty had been working on a challenging project in her studio for the last few weeks. The long hours had been worth it to see the job finished, but she was ready for some rest and relaxation now. Her plan was to stay with her friends for a couple of weeks and explore Brooklyn. She'd sent Alex an email with the dates she would be in town, leaving it to her to propose a meet up around her own commitments. Alex hadn't come back with a suggested date yet, but she hoped they would get to spend some time together. Alex had been warmer and more caring than she'd expected. Restrained, yes, and wary of anyone who might bring disorder to her life. But underneath that, she seemed keen to make a real connection with Ty and her bandmates.

As well as an undeniably strong desire to spend more time in her company, Ty thought it would be good to get to understand Alex better. Ty had gleaned that Alex insisted on total control over every aspect of her tour and wanted to be prepared to limit conflict. They'd had enough of that already. Ty was accustomed to calling the shots in her outfit, but she was keen to work within Alex's boundaries...as long as they were reasonable.

In the past, if she'd found herself in the company of a woman as gorgeous as Alex, whether openly gay or not, she would've been unable to stop herself from running the full charm offensive to mark up another conquest. But she'd already nearly blown it with Alex. She wouldn't risk the tour by trying anything. She found Alex intimidating enough that it would be a relief *not* to try and break down her defenses. Professional and friendly would work just fine.

Unable now to take her mind off Alex, Ty got out her iPad and pulled up the documentary of Alex's last tour she'd downloaded before she left. Important research, she told herself, as she settled in for the long flight.

Alex was working her way through the live DandyLions performances she had found on YouTube. She ignored the voice in her head asking why she needed to be so familiar with their music, because she was fascinated by Tyra MacLean in action. She never seemed to run out of energy. Alex had tried playing the drums. It was hard work, and to play at Ty's pace for an entire show, as well as doing a fair share of the vocals, was impressive. Alex had begun to feel her energy levels slowing down as she got closer to forty, and Ty had nearly a decade on her. Whatever Ty's secret was, she wanted in on it.

She forced herself to focus on the other members of the band. Mikki V was an excellent guitarist and showman who clearly loved playing live, but it was Jamie MacLean who dominated the stage. He was brash and showy but had great presence in a Brandon Flowers kind of way. There was something magnetic about him. Or maybe it was just that he was ridiculously beautiful. He played guitar on some songs, but it seemed the instrument was more of a prop for him. He didn't give the impression he spent much time honing his skills. His sister, on the other hand, handled her bass as though she'd played it all her life. She also played the keyboards, double bass, and on one number, a cello.

Alex watched them until she felt she understood them better as performers, but she found herself increasingly scrolling through the video clips to the parts that featured Tyra. Her set pieces included playing at the front of the stage with a variety of drums: tympani, bass drum, cajon, bodhran, or anything she could utilize as a makeshift percussion instrument. And she ended every set by teetering precariously on her drum stool, revving up the audience, whose chant of "Do it, do it, do it" rose to a crescendo until she finally jumped over the drum kit to land at the front of the stage.

As her opening act, the band would have to deliver a much shorter version of their show, so those antics were unlikely to make the cut. Alex pushed away the stab of disappointment that she wouldn't get to enjoy the full experience.

Ty's visit was imminent, and Alex wanted to spend as much time as she could with her but didn't want to crowd Ty when she was visiting her friends. She resolved to leave it a few days before sending a casual dinner invite. She sighed and shook her head. Keeping it casual with Tyra MacLean would be a challenge. She didn't know what it was exactly that drew her to Ty, but it was powerful. She'd need to keep a grip on her desires because above everything else, her career came first.

SEVEN

Ty's first few days in New York were fun, if uneventful. She borrowed a bike and toured the neighborhood, eating oysters and a variety of food truck offerings, trying overpriced craft beers, and wandering around vintage shops. She loved it here and visited regularly, although she was always slightly overwhelmed by the scale of the city, compared to her own compact town. When she'd first toured the US as a teenager it hadn't been fun. She was dragged around the country with no chance to explore or experience the culture. But it had made her all the more determined to travel and explore when she was older. And of all the cities she had got to know over the years, New York was her favorite.

Usually she enjoyed her own company, but she found herself wondering if Alex was busy, or if she'd been to this particular bakery or that bar. On the third morning, she cracked. *Hey, hey, guess who's in the Big Apple? Let me know when you've got some spare time, it would be great to get together.*

Two minutes later her phone rang, and she scrambled to answer it.

"Hey there, good to hear from you. How's your vacation going?"

Ty smiled at Alex's familiar husky voice. "Good so far, thanks. I've been doing some sightseeing and hanging out with my friends, Barbara and Celeste, in the evenings. They've got young kids, so it's been pretty tame. How's your summer going?"

"Busy. Plenty to do to prepare for the tour. But you need to get out and make the most of your visit. I know a great place for dinner with a view of the skyline that'll blow you away."

Ty smiled. "Sounds good. Are you free tomorrow or the night after? I don't have any firm plans for the rest of the week."

"How about tonight? Send me your address, and I'll pick you up at eight."

Ty raised her eyebrows. What sort of social life did Alex lead to be available with less than twelve hours' notice? *Ten out of ten for assertiveness, mind.*

"If that's not enough notice, we could do tomorrow?"

She must have left too long a pause because there was a touch of uncertainty in Alex's voice. "No, tonight is perfect. I'll text you the address. Look forward to seeing you." Ty hung up and did her best to hide her grin as she joined her friends for breakfast.

As Alex entered her suite of offices, Ryan looked up from his screen.

"Well, you've got a bounce in your step since yesterday.

Any Scottish drummers in town we need to know about?" He grinned.

Alex scowled at him. "Shut up, Ryan. My interest in Tyra MacLean is purely to ensure her band performs well on tour and help raise my profile among a younger demographic."

Ryan grinned widely. "If you say so, Alex." He tapped his laptop screen. "Your profile is definitely getting some attention among the middle-aged lesbian demographic."

"What are you talking about?" She looked over his shoulder.

"Tyra has a big cult following. Women who are loyal fans from her first time around, as well as a younger generation who admire her fight for LGBT+ rights. You've got a whole new market suddenly interested in your work since the announcement of the opening act for your tour. If Linda had known it would get you this kind of attention, she'd have worked even harder to get DandyLions out of the picture."

Alex smiled. "I'm taking Tyra to dinner tonight. I promised Long Island with a skyline view. Can you get a reservation at that place I love in Long Island City?"

"Tonight? You want that organized for tonight? People book those tables six months in advance."

"There's no point being assistant to one of the country's top musical performers if you can't book a table with a few hours' notice. You'll cope." She lifted his cell phone from his desk and dropped it into his lap.

Ryan shook his head and started looking up phone numbers, muttering to himself. He'd been her personal assistant for more than eight years and in that time, they'd become as close as family. Ryan had never felt he fitted in his small-town upbringing and as a teenager, he'd written her email after email, begging to be allowed to intern for her during summer vacation. When she'd been let down by an agency PA one summer, she decided to take him up on his proposal, but with a basic salary rather than an internship. The six-week placement had turned into a permanent post, and she'd never looked back. He looked younger than twenty-six, and his sandy curls and innocent face often came in useful for calling in favors. Alex's own family were always far away, geographically, and in her mother's case, often emotionally too, and Ryan's reliable affection and support had made him dear to her. Sure, Ryan was a paid employee, but Alex trusted him completely, and she allowed him to see the vulnerable side of her that she shared with no one else. She couldn't imagine life without him. And his razor-sharp organizational skills didn't hurt to have around either.

Alex wandered into her personal office space, an open plan corner with a standing desk, a yoga mat, and a comfortable couch. She grabbed her laptop from the desk and curled up on the couch to flick through her to-do list. She had a rehearsal booked this afternoon to work on her vocals and another first thing in the morning with her touring band. Perhaps Ty might want to watch the rehearsal, since the possibility of a late night with her was disappearing fast as Alex continued to check her list of commitments.

She had lyrics to learn, to perfect the songs from her recent album and to refresh her memory about a couple of classics she hadn't performed live for a while, but she couldn't concentrate. She looked out of the full-length window at the city below and wondered what Tyra might be up to.

EIGHT

Ty sat on a wall playing a borrowed guitar. She'd stumbled upon some musicians in the park and couldn't resist joining in for a few tunes. Before DandyLions, she hadn't performed officially for years, but she'd play occasionally at events as long as she wasn't on the billing. This was the music she enjoyed: spontaneous, uncomplicated, and unobserved by anyone other than her fellow musicians.

She certainly wouldn't miss the exposure when the tour was over and DandyLions disbanded. She brought in enough money as a record producer to keep her studio going. After her own experiences, she'd set the studio up to produce records cheaply for young musicians. As the advent of the internet made it easier for new musicians to get exposure, her priority had turned to giving work experience to local young people, especially those who had left school without formal qualifications. Her reputation as a producer, despite her refusal to promote herself in any way, kept a steady stream of work coming in. It was never going to make her rich, but it made her happy, and that was more important to her than money would ever be.

Her thoughts, as they often did now, drifted back to Alex. She was wary of how attractive she found her. A quick fling would be unprofessional and potentially awkward, and she had no intention of starting something serious with anyone, no matter how gorgeous. And she doubted Alex would consider getting involved with someone as visibly out as she was. On one level, she appeared so in control, repressed even. But there was a hint of sadness about her, loneliness. *That's the cost of putting your career above everything else.*

As she played with the group in the park, a larger crowd had started to gather. She spotted a couple of young guys on the periphery watching her intently. When one of them took out his phone and started filming, it was time to leave. She finished the song, applauded the other musicians, and handed the guitar back to its young owner. She thanked him and made him promise to keep practicing. Looking at her watch, she decided to take a long walk back to the East River ferry, leaving her time to prepare for her evening out. She took off with a bounce in her step, humming quietly to herself as she went.

On the way back her phone rang, and she smiled when she saw Alex's name as she picked up. "Hey there, sorry I forgot to send the address. I'll do it now."

"You weren't kidding when you said the media like to dig up the dirt on you." Alex sounded drily amused.

Her stomach dropped. "You're kidding me. What now?"

"My channels are full of images of you busking in a park. It's been suggested I'm not paying my opening act enough."

"Bugger. That's so annoying. I was just jamming with a few musicians, and these bloody kids started recording it.

I'm sorry if I've made things difficult. I thought I was staying low profile."

"Don't apologize, stuff happens. I'm just heading home to get cleaned up. You still good for eight?"

"Absolutely. I'll send the address through now. See you in a couple of hours." She sent the address and headed back to Barbara's.

Ty let herself into the apartment quietly, to avoid disturbing a nap or mealtime, but her friends were sitting on the floor, watching little Kai crawl around while his big brother, Sonny, pushed a trolley of bricks around the room.

"Hey, Sonny." She poked her head into the room. "What you got there?"

"Brummm brummmm!" He laughed as he drove the trolley directly at Ty's shins. She dodged expertly, and he ran into the doorframe, spilling bricks everywhere. She knelt down to help him reload, and Celeste's tired face appeared around the edge of the sofa.

"Hey there, we've got a lasagna in the oven for when the boys are in bed. You joining us?"

"Lasagna sounds tempting, but Alex invited me for a meal." She tried to keep her voice casual.

Barb's face appeared alongside Celeste's, and they both smiled widely. "She wants to discuss the tour." Ty rolled her eyes. "I told you that when I arrived."

"And when was this arranged?" Barb asked. "You never mentioned it at breakfast when we were telling you how much we love her music and want to meet her..."

"I only contacted her today, but it happens she's free tonight so we're going to eat in Long Island City somewhere."

"It happens she's free, eh?" Barb laughed and looked at Celeste knowingly. "How very convenient."

"Ah, shut up, will you? It's just work. What would Alex Knight want with me? She could have any woman in New York—as long as they're happy to keep it a secret. I think we all know I wouldn't meet that requirement."

She got up from the floor. "Anyway, I'm off to get ready. There'd best be hot water." She made a swift exit, but their laughter followed.

An hour later, she was ready to go. She'd brought some of her more presentable clothes in the hope she would get to wear them out with Alex. She wore her least faded black jeans, a figure-hugging short sleeved shirt, her smartest leather jacket, and she'd opted for some polished cowboy boots instead of her usual heavy biker ones. She couldn't bear facing more ridicule from her friends, so she flopped back on the bed to wait, trying to think up some engaging conversation topics. Ten minutes later, her phone buzzed.

I'm early. Outside whenever you're ready.
No problem, I'll be out in two mins.

Ty pushed herself off the bed, gave her appearance one last check in the full-length mirror, and tried not to rush out of the apartment. She shouted through the door to her hosts. "Hey, guys, she's outside so I'll be off now. Not sure what time I'll be in, but I'll keep it quiet. See you later."

The girls yelled their good-byes. "Just let us know if you're not coming back tonight. We'll only worry," Barb shouted.

She shut the door on their laughter and took the lift down to the lobby to avoid any chance of sweat patches on her shirt. She nodded to the concierge as he buzzed her out, then she trotted down the steps to a waiting limousine. The driver hopped out and opened the rear door for her. She thanked him and slid into the plush interior, smiling at Alex. "Hey, we're riding in style tonight then?"

Alex's laugh was gently mocking. "What were you expecting? A cab?"

"Mm, I hadn't really thought about it." If she'd imagined anything it was a regular car and driver.

Alex leaned over and embraced her in a warm hug. "It's good to see you, Tyra. Feels like an age since London."

In reality it was less than a month, but it felt longer to Ty too. "Yeah, it's great to be here." The hug ended disappointingly quickly but Alex took her hand and inspected her palm, rubbing the fresh scar gently with her thumb.

"Good to see this has healed. Please try to take better care of yourself?"

"Promise." Ty nodded and relaxed into the leather seat. "I've hardly had a drink since I saw you. I've been getting fit for the tour." She tensed the arm resting against Alex so she could feel the muscles flex.

Alex withdrew her hand. "Glad to hear it. Playing the drums needs a whole extra level of fitness compared to a lazy guitarist."

Ty shrugged. "I've done both. There's a lot of stage to run up and down, so maybe it's a different fitness, but it still takes it out of you."

The car pulled up. As soon as the door opened, Alex slid out and Ty followed. She looked up at the large glass fronted restaurant. Alex took her shoulders and turned her around to see the view across the East River.

Ty took in the vista of midtown Manhattan in all its glory and smiled. "You were right. That's a fantastic view."

Alex kept her hand on her shoulder and guided her toward the restaurant, thanking the driver as they went. They were ushered to a quiet corner of the restaurant with an uninterrupted view.

Ty sat down. "How long have you had this reservation? There must be a long waiting list for a table like this?"

Alex smiled. "There have to be some benefits to being a celebrity, surely? Lord knows there are enough drawbacks."

"Wow. I can get into a few exclusive clubs without queuing, but that's about it." She grinned. "And my local chip shop always gives me free mushy peas." Ty mentally cursed the stupid comment. It was unlikely to impress Alex.

"Sounds amazing. Maybe when I next come to the UK you can pull in a favor and reacquaint me with mushy peas? It's been years."

Ty laughed as they picked up their menus. Her stomach rumbled loudly, and she clutched her hand to it, hoping it hadn't been loud enough for Alex to hear. She didn't react if she had heard. Ty ordered the lobster while Alex opted for a salad. They chatted comfortably about Tyra's previous visits to the US until the main course arrived, and Ty suddenly worried about being able to eat it elegantly.

The conversation paused as they ate, and Ty gave her full focus to extricating the meat as deftly as she could. Occasionally, she felt Alex's eyes on her and when she looked up, Alex smiled slightly before returning her attention to her own plate. When the food was finished, she asked Alex about her move to the US as a teenager.

"My mom was a software engineer in the biotech industry. She did her doctorate at Cambridge where she met my dad, married him, and had me. Then she got this amazing job offer while Dad was halfway through a research project he'd spent years getting funding for. I don't think it was the whole reason they split, but it was definitely the final straw. I was heartbroken to leave my dad, and the culture here was so different. I'd just got into music, and there was nothing like Britpop over here. Everyone was into

Nirvana, and I thought grunge was lame. I didn't fit in well at first." She smiled wryly and cleared her throat. "The upside was I started taking my own music much more seriously. I guilted my mom into paying for all the guitar lessons I could get. And then I came to New York to study music. I was drawn to this city, so I only applied for colleges here. My mom didn't hide her disappointment at my choice of subject. She comes from a long line of scientists and academics." Alex paused to pour them both a glass of water, which Ty accepted gratefully. The food had made her thirsty, and she was trying to take it easy on the wine.

Alex sipped before she continued. "But coming here was like moving home. I felt as though I fit in a way I never did in California. We had seasons, for one, and people are more real."

Ty sat back in her chair. "Plenty of kids travel to the big city to be musicians. How did you get your big break?"

Alex shrugged. "It almost didn't happen. By the time I finished college I'd pretty much given up my dream of making a career out of performing. I had a young baby—" She held up a hand to stall Ty's question. "That's another story, but there were suddenly some inspiring acts around, Alanis Morissette and Sheryl Crow. So I started recording some of the songs I'd written and sent them away to record companies." She smiled sadly. "I didn't get anywhere. Then I had the chance to play at a benefit gig a friend had organized. I couldn't afford to do much unpaid work, even with my mom begrudgingly making sure I didn't starve. But it was a good cause and a chance to perform with some old friends."

She picked up a forkful of salad and chewed slowly. Ty leaned forward, eager to hear the rest of the story.

"After the show, this weird, intense guy came up to me

and said he wanted us to make a record together. I was a little skeptical, but I took his card and promised to call him. When I got home, I showed Billy, my boyfriend. He couldn't believe I hadn't heard of Nick Alonso, the well-known producer and composer. It seemed too good an opportunity to turn down. I built up the nerve to call him, and the rest is history."

Ty was aware of Alex's early career collaboration with Nick Alonso. The rumors were that he'd been a controlling influence, manipulating the young Alex Knight into *his* vision of a star. Popular belief was that she had eventually tired of his dominating rule and fought to free herself. Ty considered asking about their relationship but decided not to interrupt Alex's recollection.

"How about you?" Alex was looking at her expectantly, and she wasn't sure if she'd missed something.

"Sorry, what? How my career started?" She hoped her distraction hadn't looked like boredom with Alex's story, but Alex was nodding encouragingly. "Oh, I started out busking and playing in folk clubs. A radio DJ saw me and became a fan. I managed to scrape together enough money to get a single recorded, and he played it over and over. In the end, the labels were queuing up to get me to sign a contract. I didn't choose very wisely, but after my unexpected coming out interview, we were stuck with each other. It wasn't a happy relationship..." She ground to a stop, not sure how much more Alex would want to know.

Alex must have assumed she wanted a change of subject and waved her fork. "Is there anything else you want to know about me?"

"What happened with your child?" The question came out before she could think, and Alex's smile vanished. *Shit.*

"I'm sorry, that was insensitive of me. You don't need to answer that."

"No, it's cool. It just makes me sad to think about it." Alex took a deep breath. "My boyfriend was also a musician. We met at college and thought we were in love. When I found out I was pregnant, we decided to make a go of it. We had a little girl and called her Dorothy. Dottie. I found out I had far stronger maternal instincts than I'd ever known." Her smile was bittersweet, and she looked down at the napkin she was twisting in her hands. "It was fine until I started to get work and was out most nights. Billy took on the childcare and pretty much gave up on his own music. At that point, we both became aware that music had been our common ground. Without it, we were friends with a baby." She threw her napkin on the table and looked away. "Bringing up a child is hard work, and when you find you're not doing it with the right person it's painful. To cut a long story short, he met someone far better suited to parenting, and I gave them my blessing. My little girl went to live on the other side of the country with people who had time for her. Apparently, my maternal instincts, strong as they were, couldn't compete with my desire to perform." She cleared her throat and returned her gaze to Ty. "Tell me about your parents?"

The conversation changed direction with such a jolt Ty blinked. The last thing she wanted to talk about was her hopeless upbringing, but after Alex had shared something so intimate and unexpected, she couldn't very well refuse. "I never met my dad. I don't think my mum knew him that well. She spent a summer busking around Ireland with some friends. When she got home, she discovered she was pregnant. She was twenty and clueless. My granny helped bring me up."

"Do you know anything about him?"

"Well, his name's on my birth certificate, but I've always wondered if she really knew who he was. I didn't have any other information, so I've never tried to trace him. There are a fair few Patrick Murphys in Ireland. I assume he's short and blond 'cause I don't look like anyone else in my family."

The waiter approached discreetly to ask if they need anything else. Alex looked at her watch. "No thank you, just the check please." She turned back to Ty as she pulled out her phone. "I've got rehearsal at nine in the morning. I was going to ask if you wanted to come along." She didn't look up, seemingly focused on messaging her driver.

Ty grinned. She wasn't going to turn down the opportunity to spend more time with Alex, even at the cost of an early start. "Why not? Sounds fun. Text me the address, and I'll work out how to get there."

Alex looked up from her screen and smiled. "I'll pick you up at half past eight if you'll definitely be ready. I don't like to be late."

"Yeah, you mentioned that once or twice."

Alex insisted on dropping her back to Barb's house, and she waved her off with reassurances she'd be ready bright and early. Thankfully, Barb and Celeste had gone to bed. There was too much going on in her head to face a debrief of that magnitude. She couldn't remember a time when she'd enjoyed someone's company like she had tonight. Alex was charming and interesting, not to mention being the most attractive woman she'd ever met. As she eventually drifted off to sleep, she wondered how she was going to keep her hands off Alex for three long months in close proximity.

NINE

Alex drove up to the Brooklyn apartment block in her two-seater BMW, her favorite car for driving around town. It was nippy in traffic, and the darkened windows afforded her some anonymity. She was pleased to see Tyra waiting outside.

As Alex pulled up, Ty stuck her head in the window. "No driver today?"

"I like to drive when I can. Jump in." She noticed Ty's hand gripping the edge of the seat as they pulled away into traffic and smiled. "You're not used to city driving?"

"I try not to drive at all if I can help it. Doing my bit for the environment, you know? And Glasgow's a small enough city that there's nowhere you can't get by bike."

The studio was a converted warehouse, and Alex led the way to a large rehearsal room, set up exactly as the stage would be on tour. She looked around in approval as she strode into the space, commanding immediate attention. She pointed Ty in the direction of Ryan, so he could find her somewhere to sit and observe, out of the general fray.

Alex went around her musicians and crew, getting the

socializing out of the way before they got down to business. She was fond of each and every one of them and was pleased to be working with them once more. But despite their close working relationships, Alex hadn't seen any of them since the last leg of her tour. Keeping her work and social lives separate was important to her, not that she had much of a social life. But whatever kind of recluse she'd become in private, around her work associates she made sure to be charming and sociable, and she knew she had their total respect.

When the catching-up was done, Alex got to work. They did a sound check and went through the first half of the set. Alex was aware of Ty sitting on a stool at the back of the room, writing in a small notebook and occasionally looking up at the stage. Ryan sat nearby and occasionally Ty would lean across to speak to him.

Toward the end of the rehearsal, Alex saw Ryan nodding enthusiastically at whatever Ty was saying. Irked that Ty wasn't really paying attention and intrigued to find out how much she knew about Alex's own material, she grabbed the mic. "Hey, MacLean, we like to decide the encore songs on the night. What do you think today's should be?"

Ty looked down at her notebook and back to the stage, and grinned. "You need a couple of classics. 'Water in your Eye' is the obvious one, and maybe 'Bounce.' And finish on an old favorite that fans aren't expecting to hear. 'Road Trip to Nowhere' would get my vote." She looked at Alex directly and locked gazes. "Also, you should start with 'Reality Is Overrated.' 'Providence' is a big fan favorite, but I think they need something to warm them up first."

Who the hell does she think she is? Alex's initial defensiveness eased when she saw the playful challenge in

Ty's gaze as their eyes stayed locked. *I did ask.* It showed she'd paid attention. She smiled widely. "Then 'Water,' it is. Let's go."

Ty joined in enthusiastically with the chorus. As they finished the last song, Alex handed her guitar to a tech and jumped off the stage to join Ty. "How did we sound? Any other suggestions?" She was always a little hyper after performing. Even rehearsing filled her with an energy she found it difficult to replicate in other parts of her life. She wiped her face with a towel, then looked up to see Ty watching her intently. She raised an eyebrow and Ty blinked.

"I...I took some notes, and we can run through them later if you want? I don't want to step on your toes, though."

"Now is good. Come and have a chat with Nigel, my production manager." She called him over and left them talking while she went to get some water.

When she turned back, Ty had jumped onto the stage to demonstrate something. She caught Alex's eye to check it was okay to handle her guitars and then played through a few bars, before stopping to talk with Nigel. She looked up a couple of times as if aware of Alex watching her. She wasn't certain how she felt about Ty's input. She was used to being surrounded by people who were wary of making suggestions. She knew she didn't encourage a collaborative approach to her work, sure as she was that no one understood her music like she did. But Ty's suggestions were insightful and creative, and she knew they made sense. Her annoyance was also tempered by how incredibly attractive she found Tyra with a guitar in her hands.

When they were happy with the adjustments, Alex used her mic to thank the musicians and crew. "Same again tomorrow please, everyone." Patting shoulders and giving thanks, she made her way back to Tyra. "Let's get out of here."

Ty followed behind, and they headed back to the car.

Alex glanced at her as she gunned the engine and shot back out into the busy street. "You really do know your music, don't you? You played my songs like they were your own." And it was the sexiest thing she'd ever seen. She took a deep breath. She needed to rein it in. "Thanks for your advice. Nigel was impressed."

Ty took her eyes off the road and winked, but it looked like a struggle. "It *is* what I've been doing for a living for the past twenty years, so no problem. You sounded great. This tour's going to be amazing."

Alex could feel her watching her now and could sense an unspoken question. She glanced over. "What is it?"

"I've been thinking about your encore choices. What if you started it each night with a different cover song? Something relevant to the city we're in."

Alex raised her eyebrows but returned her eyes to the road. "I don't do covers."

"I know, but that'll make it all the more novel. Admittedly it would be easier in some cities than others, but we could find something for everywhere. I've thought of something perfect for your opening night. The crowd would go wild."

Alex wasn't certain she wanted Ty trying to influence her performance. Even the people she paid wouldn't have the nerve to suggest something so off the wall, and Tyra was a musician in her opening band. Sure, she was a producer in her other life, but in this one, she wouldn't be calling the shots. She didn't reply as she accelerated away from a junction at a speed that pushed Ty back into her leather seat.

"Just think about it." Ty's voice was tense, whether from the car ride or her reaction she wasn't sure.

She looked over and forced herself to smile. "All right, I will. Now, I'm starving. Would you like to eat at my apartment? I can show you around." She immediately regretted the offer. Her apartment was her sanctuary. What the hell was she doing opening it up so easily?

Ty frowned and then nodded, looking as surprised as Alex felt. "I'd love to see your place."

When she reached the parking garage and pulled inside her private compound, Alex saw Ty taking in her selection of vehicles parked in a row. "Are they all yours?"

"Uh, yeah. I guess I'm not much of an eco-warrior like you."

Ty shrugged. "You work hard. You should spend your money on whatever makes you happy."

Alex wasn't sure they did make her happy. She enjoyed driving, for sure, but it was just another thing she did alone, to pass the time when she wasn't working.

As the door to her private elevator opened, Ty chuckled. "You have your own lift?"

On the ride up to her penthouse, serious second thoughts flitted through Alex's mind. Ty had already expressed contempt for the trappings of fame. As they exited into the lobby, she stopped so suddenly that Ty almost crashed into her. "No teasing about my apartment, okay? I know it's excessive but it's my home, and it keeps me sane. I don't share it with many people."

"In that case, I expect the full tour." Ty smiled broadly and motioned ahead. "Lead on."

Ty's open smile helped Alex relax as she swung the door open into her lounge. Ty walked straight to the full-length windows looking out across the decking area to the cityscape. The building was one of the tallest in her neighborhood, and Alex had selected it for the open views. On one side, she had the East River and Brooklyn, and on the other, midtown Manhattan laid out beyond her beloved roof garden. Ty appeared to approve of the views and turned to survey the interior of the room. She seemed to study the wall of framed discs and photographs with other performers and celebrities closely. Then she moved across the room to where Alex stood by her favorite piece of furniture, an enormous leather couch. Old and battered, she knew it stood out from the rest of her modern furnishings, but she loved to relax on it. She had a sudden vision of lying there with Tyra in her arms, watching the sunrise. She rubbed her eyes, trying to rid her mind of the image and concentrate.

"Great settee. Where's this tour, then? I've not seen anything impressive so far."

Her cheeky grin made Alex want to kiss her. Christ, if this was how she felt after a few hours with Ty, controlling herself over the next three months was going to prove very difficult indeed.

She guided Ty into her into her kitchen, the room that had least influenced her decision to buy the apartment. But large apartments come with impressive kitchens, so she'd had Ryan fill it with gadgets—ones she didn't even know the functions of and would never use.

Ty sat on a stool at the central island and ran her hand along the hanging utensils, setting them softly jangling before she rested her elbows on the counter. "Where do you eat your meals?"

Alex shrugged. "I mostly grab something and sit out on the deck or the couch."

"No big dinner parties entertaining your people?"

She tucked her hair behind her ear. "Not really. I eat out if I've got company. I told you, this is my oasis. I don't share it often."

Ty smiled. "I'm honored then. Show me the rest."

Alex led her through another door. "This is the guest room." The huge space had a full-length window with another panoramic view.

"You'd pay a fortune for a hotel room with a view like this." Ty kicked off her boots and launched herself onto the enormous bed, before rolling onto her back and lacing her hands behind her head.

Alex turned for the door. Ty lying on her bed was more than she could cope with at this moment, and her total sense of being at ease in Alex's space was both disturbing and satisfying, yet another thing she couldn't analyze just yet. "Don't get comfortable, the tour isn't over," she called over her shoulder.

Ty caught up as Alex reached her bedroom. She hesitated with her hand on the door. Aside from her cleaning staff it had been a very long time since anyone had entered her inner sanctum. It was strange enough to have someone in the apartment at all, but it felt unusually comfortable to have Ty there. She was aware of Ty behind her, waiting, but not too close, as if sensing she needed space. She opened the door and stepped back to allow Ty access.

She knew her bedroom was stunning. She'd had it decorated in calming greys and blues, and it was on a corner of the building with two walls of floor-to-ceiling privacy glass. She slid back the doors that opened onto the deck and stepped out.

Ty followed. "It's gorgeous." She looked back into the

room. "But I haven't seen any guitars. I can't imagine you being happy somewhere without music."

Thankfully, Ty hadn't flopped down on Alex's bed too. "Ah, good point. One more very important room." Alex led her back inside to her music studio. Located in the center of the apartment, it was windowless and well soundproofed. She'd managed to squeeze in a digital grand piano, a row of guitars, and a whole wall of sound equipment.

"Nice." Ty looked around appreciatively.

"I love the light and the views from the rest of the apartment, but this is for when I need to focus and get to work. Sometimes no distractions are good." Though she was finding it pretty distracting being in such a tiny space with someone she was struggling to keep her hands off. She headed back out to the lounge. "What do you think?"

Ty followed her, a genuine smile lighting her face. "Okay, I'm impressed. You have a wonderful home, and I totally understand why you need it. I don't think you're flashy or whatever the other things were that you worried about. You've worked hard to get all of this."

Alex relaxed. "Thank you. How about we order some food in, and you can check out the deck?" She didn't know why the approval of Tyra MacLean was suddenly so important to her, but she decided to just enjoy the warm feeling it instilled.

They sat on the deck after lunch. Alex watched Ty as she went inside to get them another drink, conscious she was watching her ass a bit too closely. She thought about the last woman she'd felt anything for. Joanne was a high-profile journalist who'd been out for her entire career. She had something special with Joanne, but eventually hiding their relationship had devalued it, and Alex had begun to resent the intimation that she lacked courage. Journalism was a very different culture from the music industry, and Joanne didn't understand the pressure that Alex was under. The breakup had been angry and messy, an indication of how deeply their feelings had run.

Mutually convenient relationships with other closeted celebrities had been easier but never satisfying. The pleasure of physical intimacy was always outweighed by the inconvenience and the constant worry about being found out. So, for the last few years she'd avoided relationships and dating. She'd convinced herself she didn't miss it and had always found it easy to immerse herself in her work.

But now, with Ty, all she wanted was to spend more time with her. And she couldn't take her eyes off her body. The combination of muscle and soft curves was mesmerizing. She was constantly finding reasons to touch her. Tyra appeared to be enjoying herself just fine, and anyone with her reputation would know how to handle unwanted attention.

What she should be worrying about was how she was going to manage her attraction for the next three months. She had an unbreakable rule that she remain unattached while working. She didn't like distractions, preferring to concentrate wholly on her music and her fans, and it had never been a problem to end any liaisons before a tour or a spell in the studio. But this particular distraction was coming on the road with her, which would require a change of strategy.

She looked up to see Ty wandering back, two cold beers in her hand, and her eyes firmly on Alex, a slight smile playing on her lips. It was probably best not to know what was going on in her head.

"I was thinking." She took the beer from Ty and waited for her to sit. "You're crammed into your friends' tiny apartment with two small children, and I'm here with all this space to myself. Why don't you use my guest suite for the rest of your stay? You'd be very welcome." Alex bit her lip. What was she saying?

Ty's eyes widened briefly before her cocky grin kicked in. "I'd need to have a wee think about it. I'm used to a fairly high level of service at my current hotel. Would you be able to arrange a four a.m. wakeup call? The more piercing the scream the better, please."

"I'm sure I can arrange any sort of service you need, ma'am." She waggled her eyebrows. "This is the very best of hotels." *What the hell am I doing?* She couldn't remember ever flirting with anyone, not with any genuine meaning behind it, and now she couldn't help herself. Maybe Ty would decline the offer. With her fear of publicity and the paparazzi she probably wouldn't cope with the scrutiny she'd come under *living* with Alex. God, why had she made the offer?

Ty's eyes sparkled. "I really do appreciate the offer, Alex. I feel bad the girls have the kids in with them to give me a room of my own. If you're sure you wouldn't mind the imposition, I'd love to stay."

Alex thought her smile would break her jaw, even as doubts made her swallow hard. "It would be a pleasure." Pleasure didn't even begin to cover it. She couldn't resist the opportunity to spend more time with Ty, but she knew it would make keeping her at arm's length so much harder.

TEN

"There are towels and everything you should need in the closet. There are a couple of vintage tour shirts in there too, in case you need something to sleep in."

Ty grinned and held back from commenting on her bedtime clothing requirements. Things had moved quickly, and she'd faced a barrage of questions from her friends when she arrived in Alex's limousine to pick up her belongings. Barb and Celeste had teased her mercilessly, but she knew they were also relieved to have their small home to themselves once more. Her parting gift of VIP tickets to the opening night of the tour had sweetened them up too.

Now she stood looking at the view from the guest room, in too-close proximity to Alex, trying not to flirt and wondering where they were headed. "So, of all the places you've been in the world is New York your favorite?"

Alex tilted her head as if considering the question. "I wouldn't say that. I think it's a great city, and it's possible to live here relatively peacefully and do what I do for a living, but sometimes it's so loud and busy. I'd like to have somewhere I could go where I couldn't hear or see another single person if I wanted to. I get to stay in some amazing locations, but I've never found that one place I would want to go back to time and time again."

Ty smiled as she pictured her own favorite place. "I know exactly what you mean. I've lived in Glasgow pretty much my whole life, and I love it. But I've also got a wee cottage in the Highlands where I can escape when I need some quiet time. I go there a lot to write."

Alex sucked in her breath. "That sounds idyllic. I'd love to visit, maybe next time I'm over in the UK?"

Ty fought to keep the surprise from her face and didn't know if she'd managed it. Everything was moving really fast, and it was making her a tad dizzy. "Ah, I don't think it's the kind of place you'd be used to staying, Alex. It's awful basic, just two rooms and a tiny kitchen. And it's miles from anywhere. Even if you got an internal flight to Inverness, it's a couple of hours' drive. That's what I like about it. You don't go there unless you really want to."

"If just thinking about it puts that dreamy look on your face, I'm guessing it would be worth the effort." Alex smiled. "How do you get there, since you don't drive?"

"Oh, I drive a car if I have to, but I prefer my motorbike. I can do the journey in about four hours. It's a beautiful ride." Ty thought she saw something flash quickly across Alex's eyes. She hadn't expected Alex to be the kind of woman who would be impressed by a motorbike.

"It sounds amazing. Has that bike got room to ride double?"

Ty felt her core temperature rising at the thought of Alex sitting behind her on her bike. "Aye, it's got a very comfortable seat. It's a bit snug, mind."

"I don't mind cozying up. I've heard it's cold in Scotland.

I might need the body heat."

Ty was accustomed to feeling in control when she chatted with women, but Alex was being unexpectedly flirtatious, and she wasn't sure how to handle it. "Cold, and more often than not, wet. A four-hour motorbike ride in the pouring rain isn't as glamorous as it might sound." She smiled to lighten her comment. "But yes, I'd love to show you my place when you've got some free time. You probably wouldn't want to stay long. There's not a lot going on."

Alex's smile faded. "People always assume I'm some kind of diva needing a constant stream of entertainment and a car to drive me everywhere. I love seclusion. As a kid I spent the summers in the wilderness with my dad. They're the happiest memories of my life."

I'd love to give you some happier memories. Ty fought to hold back yet another smirk. Alex was so very sexy, and she definitely seemed interested in Ty in a deeper way than just as a tour buddy. But she had to be professional. They had a three-month tour ahead. *And now I'm staying in her actual apartment for the week. I need some distance. And a cold shower.*

"Shall I get us a drink and we can sit out on the deck for a bit?"

Cool air sounded like a good move. "Yes, please."

Outside Ty sat looking out at the view, still amazed that beautiful roof gardens like this were possible in such an urban city, until she felt Alex's eyes on her.

"What are you thinking about?" Alex asked.

"Just that money makes a difference to everything and how much easier it can make your life." She knew she had phrased it clumsily, and the silence from Alex confirmed it. She looked over to see Alex frowning. "I'm sorry, I wasn't criticizing your lifestyle. It was more of a general reflection."

"It's not so easy. If we wanted to just spontaneously go out for a drink, my choices are limited to venues that cater to celebrities. Going for a walk and wandering into the first place that catches my eye is almost impossible."

"But all the things you can do make up for that small inconvenience, surely?" Alex's expression suggested a change of subject would be wise, but Ty couldn't seem to let it go.

Alex took a deep breath. "I know I'm very fortunate, but my life is complicated, and sometimes not all that much fun." She looked away briefly.

Shit. Ty touched her arm. "Hey, I really wasn't trying to put you down. It's just a whole world away from the life I'm used to living. But I do remember how hard it can be." She felt Alex relax.

"Sorry, it's something that bugs me. People think I'm living the dream. But it's complicated, and often lonely, and sometimes I just wish I could leave it all behind."

Ty squeezed her arm and smiled. "But on the good days, you're making the music you want, working with people you've hand-picked, and half the world loves you to bits."

Alex smiled weakly and nodded. "Yeah, I guess so."

"Maybe when the bad stuff outweighs the good, you'll know it's time to stop."

"Is that what happened to you?"

Ty heard the concern in Alex's voice, but she wasn't sure she wanted to go there. She shivered in the evening air and rubbed her bare arms. "How about we get comfortable inside before I tell you about my short-lived career?"

Alex stood up. "Of course. You go and get settled on the couch, and I'll pour us a drink. Is something stronger appropriate for this story?"

Ty stood. "Depends how you look at it. Either that or a cup of tea."

"Which would you prefer?" Alex called over her shoulder. "I've got most everything. Lagavulin?"

Ty laughed. Alex had done her homework. "Perfect. As it comes, please, no messin' it up with water or ice." She threw herself onto the settee. It was as good as it looked and so large that she could fold her legs beneath her and still not be near the edge. She relaxed back into the luxurious leather.

"How d'you like my *settee*?" Alex reappeared with two glasses. She handed one to Ty and curled up at the opposite end.

"Whatever you want to call it, it's amazing."

They sipped in appreciative silence for a few minutes, Ty weighing up the heavy crystal glass in her hand.

Alex shifted to face her. "So, you were going to tell me about why you stopped performing."

It was an innocent enough question. What was wrong with her that she still couldn't talk easily about those days all these years later? In truth, she had avoided the subject for so long, it wasn't easy to drag up from her memories.

"I don't make a habit of reflecting on my inglorious past, but I'll give it a go." She rubbed her forehead and looked into her glass. Where to start?

"There's no pressure to talk about anything you don't want to. I'm interested in your story is all." Alex moved across the settee and her warm hand came to rest on Ty's knee. "I was pretty naïve when I made it big in my early twenties. And I had my mom looking out for me big time, paying for the best management company. I can't imagine how much harder that must have been at the age you were.

But you talked about knowing when it was time to stop, and I wondered when that moment came for you."

Ty shrugged. "It's okay, I'd like to give you the full story, warts and all." She took a long sip on her drink and rested her head back against the couch. Did she really want to do this before they worked together for a prolonged period? She didn't want Alex to think badly of her. Alex's hand still rested gently on her leg, and she looked down at it as she began.

"I was on the road for six years, never saying no to anything. Sex, drugs, and rock'n'roll. You can read all the gory details on the internet. By the time I was twenty-one my health wasn't great, and I was having periods of depression, so I drank more and more to try and cope. The quality of my writing declined, and so did my record sales. My live appearances, when I actually turned up, were a disaster because I was usually off my head on something. Even most of my loyal fans had stopped coming to gigs. I was in a pretty destructive downward spiral. And then my mum's boyfriend pushed her down the stairs and broke her neck." She took a long, deep breath. "I saw her in hospital before she died. The doctors said there was evidence of previous fractures all over her body. He'd been kicking the shit out of her for years and I hadn't even noticed. That was the final straw. I didn't do anything dramatic, but I did my best to obliterate the guilt and the grief."

Alex's hand moved up to stroke her arm. "If this is too painful, please stop."

Tyra looked up, her eyes burning with unspilled tears. There was a good reason she hadn't dredged this stuff up for years. It hurt too much.

She shook her head, determined to go on. "No, you may as well know, since you'll probably read it in the tabloids once we start touring. I eventually ended up in a psychiatric unit—saved by the NHS. My mum's brother, Jim and his girlfriend, Tina tried to support me, fucked up as I was. He was ten years younger than my mum and had always been more of an older brother to me. But they were trying to start a family and they had their own lives to live." Alex's warm hand moved to cover her own, and she looked down at their entwined fingers. "When I was eventually well enough to get out of the unit, I just packed a bag and got out. The record company were glad to be shot of me, but the few fans I had left had no idea where I'd gone. I treated them badly, but I had nothing left."

"Where did you go?" Alex's voice was soft, her thumb rubbing soothingly over the back of Ty's hand.

"I worked in bars for a few weeks at a time and hitched around Europe. I was lost, with no plan and no one to turn to. I was in Italy when I got a hysterical call from Jim and pieced together something terrible had happened to Tina. I jumped on the first plane I could get back to Glasgow and I've been there pretty much ever since."

Alex watched her silently, her eyes misty with compassion. "Thank you for sharing that with me."

She got up to pour them another drink and they moved the conversation on to lighter subjects, chatting into the early hours until Alex, realizing the time, abruptly called it a night.

Ty lay for hours in her room, watching the lights across the city through her open blinds, unable to sleep. She'd found herself opening up to Alex in a way she never had with anyone else, and it felt comfortable and safe in a way that was new to her. As she finally drifted off, she recalled the sensation of Alex's hand holding hers and knew she wanted more.

ELEVEN

In the morning, Alex emerged from her room in an irritable mood to find Tyra, freshly showered and dressed only in her boxers and a borrowed T-shirt, making coffee.

"Dammit. I can't believe I stayed up so late last night. I slept through my alarm, and I hate rushing."

"Well, I can help. You go and get ready, and I'll rustle up some breakfast."

Alex turned back toward her room. "I don't have time for breakfast. Coffee is fine. I need to be out of here in thirty minutes," she snapped. *Well done. I invite someone I like into my home and then treat them to a big dose of morning me. No wonder I live alone.*

She showered and immediately felt more human. As she hurried to get ready, she reminded herself the rehearsal couldn't go ahead until she got there. She headed back out to the kitchen to find a mug of coffee waiting. As she sat down Ty placed a plate piled with French toast on the counter in front of her. "That's all I could manage from the contents of your enormous, but surprisingly empty refrigerator. Get it down you. Were you never taught breakfast is the most important meal of the day?"

Alex checked the time and smiled sheepishly at Ty. "Thank you. This looks amazing. I'm sorry I was rude earlier, I'm not a morning person."

She couldn't stop her gaze running appreciatively down Ty's toned legs as she stood there in her boxers and T-shirt. She looked up to find Ty grinning.

"I did notice that. Loving the T-shirt, by the way. Do you keep a stock for women who stay over?" She modeled the slightly too snug Alexandra Knight 2012 tour shirt.

Alex laughed. "If I did, I'd have plenty of stock left." She checked her watch again. "Do you want to come to the rehearsal? You'll need to be ready to leave in ten minutes." She took the opportunity to look Ty up and down. "You appear to be slightly underdressed."

"I'll be ready." Ty's phone buzzed on the worktop, and she grabbed it guiltily. She looked up. "Sorry, the girls are being really inappropriate." She rolled her eyes as the phone buzzed again.

"Let's leave them guessing." Alex winked.

Ty's eyes widened, then she frowned. "They're discreet and would never speak to the press, but if you make a habit of being seen in public with the big old lesbian, those rumors you spend so much time denying will be back on a whole new scale. I might have a wee bit of a reputation." She looked concerned.

Alex laughed, forcing away the uncomfortable truth. "I know. I read the celebrity news columns. You may not be the big star of DandyLions, but the band has certainly raised your profile again." She wasn't about to admit that it worried her, but she'd made the choice, and now she'd have to manage the outcome.

She finished her food and jumped up. "Thank you for breakfast, that was delicious." She checked Ty out for a final time. "Get your pants on, MacLean. If I'm late for rehearsal, people will think I've been kidnapped by aliens."

Ten minutes later Dave arrived to pick them up.

"Not driving today?" Ty looked relieved as they got in.

Alex laughed. "Much as I love terrifying you with my driving, I've got a meeting with Linda straight after the rehearsal so Dave will bring you back and pick me up later."

She rested her head back on the seat. She hadn't slept well, waking throughout the night, unable to stop herself wondering if Ty was asleep in her room just down the hall. She mentally shook herself. This was why she didn't mix relationships with work. She needed to focus.

Later in the day, on her way home after a too-long planning meeting with Linda, Alex had time to think about how much she liked having Ty at rehearsal, and how so many of her ideas were solid. She was clearly a great producer, and even if it chafed a little to loosen her grip on things, Alex appreciated knowledge and talent enough to step back a little. It didn't hurt that Ty was easy on the eyes, either.

As she entered her apartment, she could hear the faint sound of a piano, so she headed for her rehearsal room. The door was ajar, and she could see Ty sitting at her digital piano, playing a slow melody. She watched for a few minutes as Ty stopped occasionally to scribble in a notebook. Eventually she looked up and noticed Alex watching from the doorway. She smiled and patted the stool next to her before turning back to the piano.

Alex sat. "I don't want to disturb you."

"You're not, just let me get this written down and you can tell me about your meeting with super-bitch." She turned back to her writing.

Alex pushed back a wave of annoyance. "She's just doing her job, Tyra. She doesn't even dislike you personally. She thinks DandyLions are a bad choice for me as my opening act, and my career is her job. She may be wrong, but her intentions are good."

Ty looked up from her notebook, a look of distaste obvious. "Her intentions are self-serving. I don't like her, and I don't think she's a good influence on your public persona." She immediately looked as though she regretted her outburst.

Anger swept through her at the sweeping statement, and she struggled to control it. "Thank you for your input." Her eyes held Ty's. "But you know very little about my career or my business, so I'm not sure you're qualified to have an opinion." It sounded harsh, but it was true.

Ty got up swiftly and headed for the door. "Sorry, it's not for me to judge who you choose to manage your life. I'll keep my mouth shut."

Alex watched her leave and heard the door to the guest room close quietly. She let out a long sigh. Half the reason she had reacted so angrily was because Ty was right. Linda was good at keeping her career moving but she wasn't sure she was a healthy influence. Still, how could Ty come to that verdict so soon? And what gave her the right?

She sighed again and went to make some tea. As she sipped it, she knew she needed to apologize. Just because she didn't like what she'd said didn't mean she didn't have a right to say it. She knocked quietly but there was no reply. She opened the door quietly to see Ty asleep on the bed, a notebook resting on her chest. She watched her lying peacefully, looking younger in her sleep. It took all her self-control not to curl up on the bed next to her. It wasn't only a physical attraction; she felt a connection to Ty that she wanted to explore further. Did Ty feel the same way about her? She was certainly doing her fair share of flirting, but she had admitted to Alex she had a reputation. Was she just acting the way she would with any attractive woman?

Ty's eyes flickered open and met her gaze. *Apologize before you even think about a deeper conversation.* But the words wouldn't come, and she just stared at her over her tea mug.

Ty rubbed her face. "Hey, y'know watching people sleep is weird, right?" Her voice was rough with sleep.

Alex couldn't help but smile as she came to sit on the edge of the bed. Ty sat up, pushing her notebook aside.

Alex turned to face her, thinking quickly about the best way to phrase what she wanted to say. "I'm sorry about earlier. You *are* entitled to an opinion. To let you into a secret, I don't deal with criticism well."

Ty's smile was warm. "Who knew? It's okay, it really isn't my business. It's just that I think you're a wonderful person and the way the public see you, through Linda's publicity machine, sometimes doesn't do you justice. But I'll keep my mouth shut from now on, and when I see her, I'll do my best to be polite."

"I've had some doubts myself about Linda's values, but she is who she is, and she's brought me this far. But thank you for saying something." She sighed and looked down at her hands, not sure if she could say what she wanted to while looking into Ty's crystal blue eyes. "And I'm very happy you'll be staying with me for the rest of your visit...but I feel we need to talk about what's going on here. Between us." She looked back at Ty momentarily but found her hands a better object for her gaze while she waited for Ty to respond. Her knuckles were white, but she couldn't bring herself to relax her grip.

Ty drew in a long breath. "Well, I'm having a fantastic time with you, and you seem to be enjoying yourself too. It seems like you need a friend." She reached out and squeezed Alex's clasped hands, giving Alex no choice but to look up into her eyes. There was puzzlement there as if she wasn't sure what Alex was asking.

Alex could feel her own eyes burning. *Why is this so hard?* "I can't remember enjoying anyone's company like I do with you." She blinked and faltered again. "But...as you've said, you've got a reputation for, well..." She pushed her hair out of her eyes. "I'm not very good at this."

Realization dawned in Ty's eyes as she leaned closer. "Alex, I spend every moment in your company fantasizing about what it would be like to kiss you." She cleared her throat but held Alex's gaze. "But you don't seem like the casual fling type, and I'm not the relationship type. I'd hate to ruin our new friendship by making unwelcome advances and then have everything go catastrophically wrong."

Alex smiled but felt she needed to give more clarity. "I've avoided intimacy for years because I hate unpredictability. And disappointment. But with you I want..." Ty's lips were too close. She pulled back and took a juddering breath. The strength of her attraction to Ty frightened her. She moved to the window and rested her head against the glass, trying to calm herself. "I'm sorry." She didn't turn around. She felt Ty's presence behind her. *No, stay away. I need the distance.* But Ty pulled her around gently but insistently.

"Hey, it's okay." She breathed deeply as she took both of

Alex's hands in her own. "Alex, I would never want you to do anything you feel uncomfortable with."

Alex looked up into her blue eyes. "Please don't think I'm not comfortable with you." She squeezed Ty's hands tightly. "But I have to be in control. I'm not used to feeling like this. Please try to understand?" How could she expect Ty to make sense of her behavior when she didn't understand it herself?

Ty loosened her grip and her thumbs rubbed soothingly over Alex's knuckles. Alex looked up into blue eyes full of empathy.

"I'll go and make dinner."

Alex watched her leave and dropped down onto the bed, letting the tension go. She had come so close to kissing Ty, and Ty had said she wanted to kiss her too. But Ty was right, they wanted different things. Not that she was clear herself about what she wanted from this. She'd always prided herself in having the strength to be single-minded in achieving her goals. But now those goals seemed less clear. Aside from her career there wasn't much going on in her life. Did she want a relationship and all the complications that came with it? And did that matter when Ty had just made it very clear she didn't? She ran her fingers through her hair and groaned. How had things gotten so confusing? She needed to try harder to keep her distance.

TWELVE

The sky was a fiery red as Alex ran alongside the East River, following her favorite early morning running route. She was pushing herself harder than usual, knowing Ty was somewhere behind. Her long legs and lighter frame gave her an advantage and she could easily leave Tyra in her dust, but Ty had stamina and Alex often found herself struggling to maintain her lead. Their runs were usually only a few miles, but she guessed over a longer distance Ty would be in with a chance of beating her.

They had spent the week in a comfortable routine of early morning runs, rehearsals, working out, and eating in. Ty was a talented cook and could rustle up something tasty from almost any ingredients. She had asked Alex how she shopped for groceries and Alex, not entirely sure of the answer, had called Ryan.

Within hours the refrigerator and cupboards were mysteriously stocked with a variety of foods. Ty muttered about choosing ingredients herself but had used what was available, and Alex was enjoying the novelty of home-cooked food. Outside of rehearsals it was just the two of them and she was loving every minute.

They hadn't talked further about their growing attraction and in an effort to avoid physical contact they had mutually stepped away from any situations that threatened to escalate. On a couple of occasions, it had been Ty who had left the room, or looked away from a gaze that lingered too long. Alex was grateful for her fortitude because she found it increasingly difficult to keep her resolve as they got to know each other better and shared more about their lives. She was developing an attraction for Ty she had never felt for anyone else before, and as someone who had spent her life avoiding unpredictability, she was more than a little afraid.

This morning, they'd gone out before dawn to run around lower Manhattan without a security escort, stopping to sit on the shoreline and watch the sun come up over Brooklyn. Or rather, Ty watched the sun come up and Alex watched Ty, arms wrapped loosely around her bare legs and chin on her knees, her tattooed shoulders on show in her tank top.

Alex couldn't remember ever finding anyone this irresistible, and as she got to know Ty and understood her strength and kindness, that attraction just continued to grow. *Maybe I do just need to sleep with her and get her out of my system.* But this was more than just a physical attraction. She looked around to reassure herself they had the place to themselves and slid down the hillside to sit closer to Ty.

She loved Ty's arms, whether in a T-shirt or fully bared. She could watch them all day: the mixture of tanned and inked skin and the muscle that moved underneath. She wondered what the rest of Ty looked like bare, and a shudder ran through her body.

Ty tipped her head to the side. "You okay?" She grinned but quickly looked back to the sunrise.

Alex, suddenly self-conscious that her thoughts were so transparent, removed her shades from where they had been resting on top of her cap and donned them quickly. "Race you home!" She jumped up and took off at a sprint, laughing at the swearing she could hear behind her but eager to make the most of her advantage.

Now, as she ran through streets that were getting steadily busier with early morning New Yorkers beginning to go about their business, she felt guiltily relieved Ty hadn't caught up and there was no chance of them being seen together.

As Ty made brunch she peered into the over-stocked refrigerator in bemusement. This was an alien world in so many ways. Alex had reiterated several times that Ty didn't need to cook, they could have meals delivered or hire caterers. But she loved to cook, and Alex appeared to enjoy the intimacy of eating together. They had gone out occasionally, to private functions or exclusive restaurants with hidden rooms or booths where celebrities could eat unobserved by regular folk. Despite this they had been photographed together often enough to garner some media attention and there was much conjecture about why the drummer of the support act would be socializing with Alexandra Knight a month before their impending tour.

Ty's colorful history was usually dragged into the story somehow. Back in the day she had become accustomed to the lies and the assumptions that were printed solely to increase sales, but she'd always found it emotionally wearing, no matter how hard she tried to ignore it. She was uncomfortable that while she was so out and proud herself, she had to worry about the assumptions people were making about Alex and her, and how Alex would feel about that. She wasn't blind, and knew that whenever they went out, Alex was careful to keep her distance. She couldn't help but feel hurt by it, as if who she was wasn't quite good enough.

Alex didn't follow the media directly, but Ty knew Ryan sent her a summary each day, highlighting the positive or negative angles of particular stories.

After eating, as they lounged at opposite ends of the leather couch and Alex flicked open her laptop, Ty thought it was as good a time as any to talk about it.

"Are you okay with all this speculation, Al?"

"We're ignoring it." Alex's tone was flat. "Once we go on the road and act normally, people will see nothing is going on between us and the stories will stop. Then, hopefully, the interest will be in our music."

Ty had found the week a confusing mix of emotions. Her connection with Alex had taken her by surprise. She was used to finding women desirable, but she usually moved in and moved on, before anything deeper developed. Spending so much time with Alex and being unable to act on their attraction was driving her mad, even if she had no earthly idea where she wanted it to lead. The thought of another few months of close proximity made her wonder if she would make it through. Her frustration finally spilled over into words. "Doesn't it ever bother you? Having to hide who you are?"

Alex put her laptop aside and looked at Ty in surprise.

"Of course it does, but I need to work like this for now. I have to be able to focus all my energy on the tour."

"It seems to me you spend a lot of your energy pretending to be something you're not." She stood up and paced the room, too agitated to sit. "And do you want me to behave normally? Normal on tour for me usually involves female company." She didn't want to hurt Alex, but that was the truth.

Alex looked awkward. "Linda did mention that. She thought I should encourage you to behave in your usual way to disprove these rumors. I'm not suggesting you feel obliged to take any of your fans to bed, but I don't feel in a position to object if you wanted to."

Ty jumped up off the couch. "For fuck's sake Alex, are you asking me to sleep around to help with your publicity?"

She felt the tears stinging her eyes and didn't want to lose it in front of Alex. She turned away and headed to her room. She threw herself onto the bed and let the tears flow, her anger a mix of disgust with Alex's seemingly indifferent approach, and annoyance with herself at her outburst. Whatever it was between them, they'd agreed not to act on it. Alex was right, she wasn't in a position to ask Ty not to sleep with whoever the hell she wanted. So why did the thought of it feel so wrong?

Alex's motivation was so difficult to understand. But she didn't need to understand it, did she? She just had to accept it and get the next three months out of the way. It wasn't as if they were doing anything that they needed to hide anyway. She pulled herself together and went to find Alex. Unfortunately, she emerged to find Alex in a conference call with Linda, Ryan, and her tour manager, Nigel. She grabbed a Coke from the fridge and headed out onto the deck, closing the door behind her. She stretched out on a lounger and tried to relax. A few minutes later she heard the door open and felt a shadow cross her face.

"Do you want to talk?" Alex sounded miserable. Ty sat up, pulling off her shades and gesturing to the seat next to her.

Alex sat quickly. "I'm so sorry, Tyra. I can't think of anything I want to avoid more than hurting you, but I need to calm my thoughts before we go on tour. I know you think I over-prepare, but usually before a tour I would be sitting at the piano every night, rehearsing my songs over and over. Instead, I want to hang out with you and talk all night about anything and everything. I need to get back into my usual routine."

Ty knew she needed to be honest about her feelings. "I know I have a tendency to act on impulse. If I like someone, I want to be with them there and then, and I don't care who knows it. I need to respect that you don't feel that way, but I think what we have between us is special and I don't know what to do about that."

Alex put her arms around her, and she leaned into the embrace, just wanting Alex's touch to calm her. But she was suddenly so aware of her warmth, her scent, and the softness of her body. She pulled back to look into Alex's eyes and found them cloudy with the same desire she was feeling. Ty's gaze dropped to her slightly parted lips, and she was lost. Alex leaned in and those lips were on hers. *Shit, this is a bad idea.* She tried to hold back but Alex was just too desirable, and logic was replaced with lust.

She moaned as she felt Alex's hand slide under her shirt and onto her breast. When it reached a nipple, she gasped into their kiss.

Alex pulled away. "We need to take this indoors." She

jumped up and pulled Ty with her towards her bedroom, both discarding clothing as they went.

Once indoors Alex pushed her onto the luxurious bed. The feeling of falling into a cloud was quickly overtaken by the sensation of Alex straddling her naked, the heat from her center feeling like it would burn a hole through her. She ran her eyes up Alex's body. Naked, she was every bit as beautiful as Tyra had imagined and more. She lifted her hands, not content with just looking, and felt Alex tense under her touch. She reached the curves of her breasts and shuddered. She couldn't think about whether or not Alex might regret it all later. She couldn't think at all, only enjoy the feelings that were overwhelming her. Nothing had ever felt so good, so surely it had to be right.

She let out a moan of disappointment as Alex's firm grip on her wrists stopped her exploring further. Her hands were pinned back on the bed behind her head and she resisted, wanting to touch Alex once more. Then Alex leaned in to kiss her and the sensation was so intense she could only surrender to it, closing her eyes. Alex's weight lifted off her momentarily, to be replaced by a warm knee eased between her legs, pushing them apart. Ty complied willingly, opening herself for Alex.

"Where do you want me, Ty?" Alex's breath tickled her ear.

She whimpered. "Inside." Her voice sounded alien it was so thick with need.

Alex sighed against her neck and her fingers moved down her body, skating around the sensitive skin at the top of her thigh. She bucked her hips towards the touch and Alex laughed quietly before she plunged inside. She moved deeply but kept the pace slow, despite the drive of Ty's hips. Ty heard herself cry out in a way she didn't remember ever doing before. Nothing about this felt like anything she had done before. Alex increased the pace and she rocked back against her, desperate for more. Just as she thought she couldn't take the sensation any longer, Alex's thumb brushed her clit and that was all it took to send her over the edge. She groaned and pushed her arms against the hand still lightly restraining her. She grabbed Alex's shoulders tightly as she came, so hard she thought it might kill her.

Afterwards Alex kissed her and held her close, spooning up behind her. She felt the sensation of warm lips on her neck and rolled over slightly so she could face her.

"Are you okay?"

Alex smiled. "Yes, I'm better than okay. That was..."

"It was fucking amazing," growled Ty. "But now I just want you even more." She pushed Alex back on the bed. If this was a one-time thing, she was going to make the most of it.

It was early evening and Alex ran her fingers along Ty's spine and watched with fascination as the fine hairs on her lower back stood up. She felt surprisingly good about having finally acted on her feelings. The sex had been everything she had fantasized about, and so much more. She knew it would need to end here, when Ty left for the airport, but for the next twenty-four hours she was going to savor every moment. She followed her fingers with a line of kisses down each vertebra, her fingers now giving some attention to the strong muscles which rippled as Ty rolled onto her side and looked at her.

"That is magical but if you keep it up, we're gonna lose

all track of time and we're supposed to be picking up Celeste and Barbara at eight."

"I was wondering about that. Would you prefer maybe to meet with them alone? I don't want to intrude on your last evening." Alex had thought about it before they spent the afternoon making love and now it didn't seem like a very good idea at all, but she felt she had to ask.

Ty turned to face her. "I am not prepared to deal with the disappointment if you don't turn up. You're definitely the main attraction of this night out. They hardly get a child free evening out together and they're so excited." She ran a hand across Alex's cheek. "Please don't pull out."

Her slightest touch lights up my whole body. Alex smiled and kissed her. "Of course not. It would be wonderful to be together on your last evening here. I'm going to miss you even more these next two weeks."

"Me too, but I'll be back with the gang soon. That reminds me, thank you for all the arrangements your people have made for us. Not many support acts get all their expenses paid. I bet Linda's havin' kittens." She smirked.

Alex shrugged. "She's not overly happy about it. But she's finally given up arguing." She very reluctantly pushed herself up from the bed and looked down at Ty. She paused as she considered how to phrase what she wanted to say tactfully. "You know she's going to be around plenty while we're on tour and I'd really appreciate it if you could try not to stress her out?" *Oh, not that tactful.*

Ty's eyes ran up Alex's body slowly, eliciting a similar response to her touch. She grinned. "If you always ask favors while standing naked in front of me, I'll agree to anything. Of course I'll behave. In fact, I'll do my best to stay out of her way completely. Now get in the shower before I change my mind about standing up my best friends."

Alex tried to relax under the warm stream of water. Every fiber of her being was buzzing. She didn't seem to be able to sate her desire for Ty. The more they'd made love, the more she wanted it. Nothing had ever made her feel so alive. But where was this going? Ty didn't do relationships, particularly secret ones, and Alex wasn't about to come out. It had felt so amazing, but would it only lead to misery?

THIRTEEN

Tyra eyed Celeste and Barb suspiciously. The car had picked them up first and they were unexpectedly giggly as she got in and sat opposite them. Barb had confided they were both a little nervous about meeting Alex. "Have you two been drinking?"

Barb grinned and waved a mostly empty bottle of champagne. "The driver said it was for us."

Celeste's attempt to hug Alex as she got in turned into more of a grope as Ty shook her head in despair. Could they not just act normally? She recalled the first time she'd met Alex and decided to cut them some slack. Alex took it in good spirit and settled herself between them, leaving Ty sitting opposite, glaring at her two friends. "I'm sorry, they don't get out much."

Alex draped her arms around the shoulders of her beaming new friends. "Well, let's give them an evening to remember. Be a darling and open another bottle."

Ty rolled her eyes and opened the small refrigerator, pulling out another bottle and expertly popping the cork.

She pulled another couple of glasses from the rack and poured a full glass for everyone.

Alex cleared her throat. "Girls, I stole away your houseguest and I'd just like to say thank you for letting her come stay. We've had a wonderful time preparing for our tour and getting to know each other."

"You're welcome." Barb laughed loudly. "She was no' much use anyway. She kept going out when we needed a babysitter."

"And drinking all the milk and not replacing it." Celeste giggled.

"Sounds like I stepped in just in time then." Alex laughed. "I'd like to raise a toast to welcome visitors. I think we're all happy knowing Ty isn't going away for long."

"To visitors!" they all repeated, and Celeste downed her glass in one. Ty topped it up but muttered, "If you want to remember this VIP night out you've been looking forward to, it may be an idea to ease off on the bubbles there."

"Ooh, Tyra MacLean giving advice about drinking in moderation! Who'da thought we'd ever see this day!" Barb howled with laughter.

"Oh, piss off, Barb. I'll never hear the end of it if you two get blootered and ruin your evening. One more glass and I'm putting it away. If you're still conscious on the way home, you can finish it then."

"You sound more Scottish around Barb." Alex's voice was low as she watched Ty interact with her old friend.

The intensity of her gaze made Ty shiver. *You can't look at me like that in public. It's not fair.*

Their unexpected afternoon of pleasure hadn't taken the edge off her desire for Alex, and she didn't know how she felt about it. She knew where she was with attraction that quickly escalated to sex, easily sated, and leaving her free to move on. This was different, and likely more painful to leave behind. But she couldn't bring herself to regret what happened, it had been too good. She knew it would end when she walked out the door tomorrow and that was how it should be. She forced herself to focus back on Celeste chatting about Sonny and Kai, spurred on by Alex's interested questions. Her phone was out now, showing off their best photos to Alex.

"They're so cute. You must be very proud of them. I'd love to meet them one day."

"Oh yes, that would be amazing. They love your music." Barb was silenced by another eye roll from Ty.

Alex had hijacked Ty's video call to Barb earlier in the week to ask where they would like to eat. Recovering from her initial starstruck-ness when Alex's instantly recognizable face appeared, Barbara had mentioned an Italian restaurant she'd heard great things about. Alex declared it was her favorite place to eat in the area and promised to pull out all stops to get a table. The gesture had clearly won over Ty's sometimes prickly best friend.

They pulled up directly outside the restaurant Barb had mentioned. "Get ready to move." Ty grabbed Celeste's hand. The moment Dave opened the curbside door, Alex swept out in her usual manner, heading straight inside with minimal delay. Ty hauled Barb and Celeste out of their seats and guided both of them quickly into the restaurant behind Alex. It was funny how she'd slipped back into this life. Who knew how quickly you could get out of a car and into a restaurant when you wanted to avoid attention? Fortunately, there were no paps in sight, so at least Alex being spotted with Ty and a lesbian couple wasn't going to be an issue tonight.

They were shown to a typical discreet table, tucked away

out of sight of other diners, but with a view of the bustling street outside. A couple of slices of heavenly pizza sobered the girls up and the meal was taken up with them asking Alex questions about her life, what it was like being recognized continuously, who was the most famous person she had ever met—the President— and how she did her shopping. Ty laughed when Alex gave a vague answer to this, knowing she had never even thought about it until recently.

Alex happily talked about her upcoming tour, the cities they would visit, which were her favorite venues, and which she would rather avoid. She reassured the girls they would have 'access all areas' passes at the New York gig, so would be able to see how the show came together. They were delighted, and that made Ty happy.

Barb wiped tomato sauce from her mouth with a napkin. "I used to think it was pretty cool to be friends with Tyra MacLean, '80s icon and queer rights activist, but to be honest, that all feels a bit B-list now. No offence, like."

"Absolutely none taken." Ty smiled across at Alex, who was laughing along with her friends.

They chatted for hours, ordering jugs of beer until belatedly realizing the rest of the restaurant was empty. The owner assured them it was no trouble, but Alex called Dave and they got ready to leave, with Alex stopping for photos with the owner and her daughter in front of their neon sign before they got in the car.

The journey back was quieter. Celeste, permanently sleep deprived, and not used to big nights out, dozed on Barb's shoulder. Barb insisted they head back via Alex's apartment and drop Barb and Celeste off afterwards.

They pulled into the parking garage. "Keep in touch and let us know how your tour preparations are going. We absolutely cannot wait to see your opening night." Barb hugged Ty tight, while a drowsy Celeste nodded her agreement as they got out of the car.

"Thank you for giving my friends an evening to remember." Ty leaned back against the wall of the elevator, feeling full of pizza and alcohol but happy, as long as she didn't think too far into the future.

Alex moved in, running kisses down her neck. "I had a fun night too. Although I didn't enjoy having to keep my hands off you." Her voice was low as she started to undo Ty's shirt.

Ty sniggered. "Some of your comments didn't leave much to the imagination." Alex's brow furrowed and she pulled back. *Shit.* "Hey, I told you they can be trusted." Ty pulled Alex back towards her, just as the elevator reached their destination.

"I know that. I'm just concerned that if rumors start now, they'll follow us through the tour, and we'll be scrutinized constantly." Alex's voice was serious as she led the way into the apartment.

Ty pulled herself together, stung at the reminder that she was nothing more than a dangerous secret to be kept hidden at all costs. "But you're a massive celebrity. What can anyone say that can possibly hurt you? I just don't understand why you would deny who you are for an easy life, when you could be a role model. What are you afraid of?"

Alex swung around. "I'm not afraid of anything, Tyra." There was a touch of ice to her tone. "We've had this conversation before. My whole business is built around my brand, my image. I need to manage things carefully." Her expression softened as she looked at Ty. "What's happened between us has been wonderful. But I really need it to stay between us. Please."

Ty shrugged again. "I won't tell anyone." *God forbid your precious image is tainted.* She was aware of how little time they had together and didn't want to spend it arguing about something they felt so differently about.

Alex moved closer. "Thank you, Ty. I do trust you." She smiled and her eyes narrowed. "Now, where were we?"

Alex jumped at the harsh sound of a familiar ringtone. Ty was wrapped around her, and she tried to extricate herself without disturbing her. Unsuccessfully, and if the scowl on Ty's sleepy face was anything to go by, she too recognized the ringtone. "Sorry, honey, I'll get rid of her." She fumbled with the phone and answered curtly. "Not today, Linda, I'll call you tomorrow. Of course it can wait. I said not now." She hung up, only for the ringtone to blast out thirty seconds later. She swore, resisted the urge to throw the phone at the wall, and switched it to silent instead.

Ty had moved to face the window, lying halfway down the bed. Alex felt the distance between them as real life intruded. She moved down to curl up behind Ty, kissed her gently on the cheek, and pulled the sheet up over them both.

When she awoke several hours later, they hadn't moved. Moving as quietly as she could she crept out to make coffee. She checked the time and was pleased they still had a few hours before Ty had to leave for the airport.

She had barely made coffee over the past week. Had she taken Ty for granted? She was so used to people doing things for her, had she expected Ty to simply take care of things? She pulled up a stool while the coffee brewed. The week had been wonderful. Alex had gotten to understand Ty's creative nature, her tendency to crack a joke when things got too intense, and they'd both shared so much about their pasts. But now they needed to put it all aside and get back to work. She wondered if there was any chance for them to pick things up when they were done working together. Their lifestyles made that unlikely she knew, but still, it felt good to think they wouldn't lose this newfound connection completely. She snagged a couple of pastries and headed back into the bedroom, but Ty was nowhere to be seen. Looking outside she saw her sitting out on the deck, strumming on a guitar.

She approached with the coffee and Ty smiled shyly up at her, continuing to play.

"Sing for me?" Alex sat down opposite and sipped her coffee. "Something from back in the day. I love your old songs."

Ty nodded and tuned the guitar some more and started to play 'Vita', one of her most well-known songs from her very first album. Alex joined in on the chorus.

When she finished Alex asked, "Will you play 'Sleepless Nights'? It's my favorite."

Ty scowled. "I'd rather not. I haven't played it for years. Nineteen-year-olds shouldn't write love songs. What did I know about anything?"

They'd never spoken about Ty's love life, and Alex wondered if the song brought back bad memories. "It's beautiful, Tyra. The innocence is part of the attraction. I don't think you need to have experienced true love to understand longing. And your ability to capture that in your lyrics is perfect." She stood and leaned down to take Ty's face in both hands and kissed her tenderly. "Please play it for me."

"That's cheatin'. You know I'll do anything if you kiss me." Ty sighed thoughtfully. "I don't even know if I can remember all the words." She strummed a few chords, humming to herself. "Okay, here goes."

She launched into the song and Alex sat transfixed, wondering how successful Ty might have been if things had been different for her all those years ago. It was a timely reminder about how important it was to stay on track, to keep control and not mess things up.

When the song was finished Alex took the guitar gently out of Ty's hands and pulled her to her feet. She cleared her throat. "Come back to bed?"

Their last few hours together were energetic and passionate. When Ty finally escaped into the shower, Alex immediately missed her presence and padded after her. Ty was under the shower, with her hands on the wall and her eyes closed, singing quietly as she let the water sluice down her body. Alex slipped in behind her. "You okay?" She kept her voice low and felt Ty shudder as she took the soap and started to lather her body.

"Oh yes." Ty groaned. "I can't believe the things you do to me. I don't think I'll have any problems sleeping through the flight home."

Alex couldn't concentrate on the job at hand and gripped Ty's short hair, pulling her head back to descend on her exposed neck.

"Alex, Dave is arriving in forty-five minutes." Ty's gasp was half pleading, half regretful. With one last lingering kiss, Alex got out of the shower and left Ty to finish up, not trusting herself to behave.

When Ty was ready to leave, Alex felt the awkwardness

between them as they stood by the elevator. Ty dropped her bags and wrapped Alex in a hug, which she tried to return warmly.

"Thanks for everything, Alex. I've had a wonderful week."

"No, thank *you*, it's been...fun." She smiled weakly as Ty stepped back and shouldered her bags when the doors opened.

Did she mean fun? She didn't want Ty to think that's all it was, but how else to describe it? They had made a connection, but this was where it ended, at least for now. They needed to put it aside before they started working closely in a few weeks.

Ty stepped in and turned as the doors began to close. "See you around, Alex." Her grin was as cheeky as ever, but it didn't quite reach her eyes. Alex stood and watched the closed doors for a few minutes, then sighed and turned back to her empty apartment.

FOURTEEN

Back home Ty tried to focus on the preparations for their tour in a few short weeks. Unlike Alex, who had a member of staff for everything, her band only had Lachlan, so there was a lot to plan and organize, including deciding what they would wear for their performances, and ensuring their kit was ready to be shipped over to the US.

Alex's management was arranging most of the details and all of the expenses, and Ty knew that was a privileged position for the band to be in, so she didn't want them to mess anything up. If they had been offered this tour on the condition that they paid their own expenses she wasn't sure how they would have managed. Although Jamie would have convinced her to try.

Mikki had finally dragged himself away from his fiancée in Stockholm and had helped with the equipment. Ty felt more empathy for his predicament now and felt guilty about all the in-or-out demands she had made on him around committing to the tour. His fiancée Siri had a demanding job but managed to plan a two-week break in October, when she would join them for part of the tour.

She spent hours poring over the tour itinerary and familiarizing herself with the cities and venues. It was going to be an intense three months with over forty dates across North America, and a week of free time every few weeks. Tyra was pleased to see that Alex was trying to minimize her carbon footprint so there were few flights, and most of the traveling would be done overnight by bus. Ty hadn't yet seen the tour buses but had been told they were state of the art. Hybrids with solar panels, they relied as little on traditional fuel as possible. There were three buses for performers and crew and another three for equipment. Pretty different from when she'd been on the road herself a million years ago.

It was going to be an epic trip, she reassured her bandmates, who were developing nerves about the scale of the tour. When even Jamie was starting to worry about what they had signed up to, Ty knew she needed to keep her own anxiety in check. Her cousins were so young, with only a couple of years' experience of performing live, and they were about to be catapulted onto an international stage. They had a right to be scared. But they needed to know she was steady. She did her best to banish the flashbacks that kept her awake at night, of her lowest moments in front of an audience, when she'd been too wasted to remember the words, or too filled with terror to get on the stage. Those times were so long ago, and yet so clear in her memory it could have been yesterday. But she owed it to Jamie and Mhairi, and to Mikki, who'd put his own plans on hold to do this with them, to keep it together. More than that, to be a strong, supportive influence. She told herself if she could get through this and make their tour a success, she would never put herself under this kind of pressure again. The rest of the band could do whatever they wanted, but she was going back to her quiet life.

She thought often about Alex and her life in the spotlight. They spoke and sent texts regularly, but Ty could feel Alex was keeping their relationship on a more business-like level. She understood why, they had been honest with each other about what they were prepared to give. So why did the distance hurt so much? She was so frustrated by her competing feelings. She didn't want celebrity, or a relationship, and she disapproved of people who refused to be open about who they were. So, what could she possibly want from Alex? And yet she knew she wanted something more than she had.

She had tried to keep out of Mhairi's way since she got home, but ever-sensitive to Tyra's moods, Mhairi had inquired a number of times about how she had got on with Alex, and even asked whether anything had happened that she needed to know about. Ty had tried to respond casually, reassuring her she had just had a pleasant break, and learned how Alex worked. But she wasn't used to holding things back and she knew she wasn't fooling her cousin. Finally, Mhairi cornered her in the kitchen one evening.

"Look Ty, I'm not trying to pry or to push you into telling me anything you don't want to but you're acting awful strange. I just wanted to say I'm here whenever you want to talk, okay?"

Ty gave her the most convincing smile she could muster. "Hey, Mhairi, we share everything, don't we? If I had anything to tell you I would. I'm just a bit jet-lagged and nervous about what's ahead."

She turned away so Mhairi couldn't see the guilt she knew she couldn't hide. She hated that the promise she had made to Alex was forcing her to lie to the person she was closest to in her life. This was what happened when you kept secrets. You forced others to keep them too.

Ty had plenty to keep her busy with her studio. She had prioritized touring with the band over the needs of her business for too long and had been looking forward to returning her full attention to the work she loved. Now she was having to find ways to fit in work before she went and was redirecting business to other studios. She hated to do that but there was a limit to how long people could wait, no matter how much they valued her as a producer.

"I feel like I'm stretching myself too thin, Kenny." She was sitting in her favorite pub with her sound engineer, Kenny MacBride. They'd worked together since she started the studio. He was one of her oldest friends, their relationship dating back to when she was a young performer. Only a couple of years older, he'd been an apprentice sound technician on her first tour, and they'd bonded over their geeky perfectionism. When Tyra started the studio, she'd sought him out and together they'd built the business. Ty had often wished Kenny would want to step up and take a bigger role, but he'd always been happy doing the thing he did so well. She couldn't fault him for that.

Now she watched him over her pint. "D'you think I'm neglecting the studio?"

He shook his head of shaggy gray hair. "You're going to be part of a massive tour that will probably launch the career of at least one of your cousins. You'll have a brilliant time, and all this will be here when you get back. And raising your profile will just bring more work in. You'll be turnin' people away once you get back. Stop beating yourself up."

"It's the massive aspect that's worrying me, Kenny." She

rubbed her face wearily. "You remember how I was before? This is so much bigger than that. What if I can't deal with it?"

"You can't possibly still be holding onto the idea you were responsible for what happened to you back then, Tyra? You were a child, and you were exploited horribly. Fed drugs to keep you compliant and forced to do what the label wanted, to make them as much money as possible. People would go to prison these days for how you were treated." He picked up his pint and took a long swallow. "What's happening now is a million miles from that. You're choosing to do this. Whether that's for your cousins' benefit, or because, despite your anxiety and previous trauma, you bloody love performing."

"I don't—"

He shook his head again. "You live through music, Ty, and the best way you express that is by performing the beautiful songs you write. Try to remember that and enjoy what you've got ahead."

Ty wasn't convinced he was right. Yes, when she was on stage it felt amazing. But sooner or later the show ended, and you had to face the intrusion and the lies that were told just to make a story. That was the stuff she didn't know if she had the strength to deal with.

FIFTEEN

Ty found it impossible to sleep on the flight to New York. A combination of increasing anxiety about the tour and the anticipation of seeing Alex again meant she was exhausted and irritable when they landed, with a headache that was threatening to crush her skull. Jamie, on the other hand, was hyper, and even Mhairi was unusually bubbly in her excitement to be in the US. As they passed security, Ty strode ahead impatiently and shrugged off her leather in the too-warm baggage claim area, leaving the twins waiting for Mikki to catch up after retrieving his beloved guitar. When she caught sight of the wall of photographers in the arrivals hall a moment of anxiety hit, and she stopped dead. *I can do this.* Everyone was relying on her and she just needed to get a grip and play the game.

She took a breath, pulled off her shades and smiled. Holding back for the others to catch up, she slid her arm around Mhairi's waist. Mhairi snagged Mikki's free hand and raised their joined hands in greeting. Jamie threw a peace sign and they posed for photos, all smiling widely.

She'd make it through this, and then go back to the life she'd made for herself. It was just three months.

Alex stopped at a photo of DandyLions on her social media feed. Ty, looking tired but grinning, all in black with her jacket slung over her shoulder. Jamie to her left, wearing what looked like a feather boa and no shirt, and Mhairi managing, as always, to look effortlessly cool and bohemian. Mikki was smiling widely and holding tightly to his guitar case. She smiled at the image. *Well, at least they look happy to be here.*

Privately, she was slightly nervous about her opening act being able to ramp it up for audiences of fifteen thousand plus. When Tyra had been at her peak, venues were far smaller. The only one of them who'd ever come close to gigs this large was Mikki, whose previous band, Masters of the North, had played a couple of smaller stadium tours before their dissolution. But as she looked at Tyra, smiling confidently, she felt reassured.

She needed an excuse to see Ty. Luckily Lachlan, who had been in New York for a few days already, was in the office and announced he was heading off to catch up with the new arrivals.

"Do you think they'd mind if I pop in to say hi?" Alex did her best to sound casual.

Lachlan's head shot up in surprise. "Of course not. They'll be thrilled to see you."

When they arrived at the hotel Mhairi opened the door to the suite and hugged Lachlan before noticing Alex standing next to him. Alex was taken aback to receive an equally warm embrace before she was swept into the large suite of rooms. Even Dan, her security escort got a hug. As soon as Jamie saw her, he dragged her to the window. "Alex, look at that view. You can see all of America!"

She laughed and pointed out some of the most iconic landmarks. *Where the hell is Ty? I didn't come here to play tour guide.*

Mhairi took pity on her and steered her away. "Sorry, he's been like that since we landed. Tyra had a bad head, and he was driving her crazy, so I sent her to bed with some painkillers. She didn't want to be left too long so why don't you go and give her a shout?" She directed Alex towards a door and turned away to entertain her hyperactive brother.

Alex slipped inside the dark room and could see a figure on the bed, facing away from the door. She sat down on the edge of the bed and leaned over. "Hey, sleepyhead, did the big journey take it out of you?"

Ty's eyes opened, showing momentary confusion until she realized where she was and sat up, grinning and rubbing her face. Alex leaned in for a hug and a kiss on the cheek. They both held on a little too long and Alex felt herself inhaling Ty's familiar scent. They pulled apart reluctantly and she looked closely at Ty's face. "Are you okay? You look tired, and Mhairi said you had a headache."

"I'm never a great traveler, but I'm feeling better now."

Alex was suddenly aware of how close they were and how they had left things after Ty's last visit. Ty looked equally uncomfortable as she jumped up off the bed and led Alex back out into the safety of company. "Hey, Mikki," she shouted. "Get off the phone and come and meet Alex."

Mikki dutifully appeared in the doorway a minute later, smiling nervously. Alex embraced him warmly. "It's great to meet you at last, Mikki, and I understand congratulations are in order."

Mikki looked surprised. "Uh, yeah." He smiled. "Thank you. My fiancée is going to join us next month if that's okay?"

"I look forward to meeting her. And can we get together sometime to talk about your technique on 'QT'? I love your sound on that song."

His face lit up. "Yeah, of course, and maybe you could teach me something new too?"

Alex laughed. "I doubt that. You're a far better guitarist than I'll ever be, but let's jam together and see where we go?" He nodded eagerly and she smiled at his enthusiasm. "Now, you get back to that call Tyra rudely dragged you away from."

Ty poured coffee for herself, and a second cup for Alex, adding creamer before handing it to her. Alex took it with a nod and a smile and noticed Mhairi watching with interest. Ty must also have been aware of the scrutiny because she moved away self-consciously.

Alex chatted casually until she was interrupted by her phone and turned away to take a call from Linda, whose irate tone could probably be heard somewhere in south New Jersey. She calmed her and promised to head back to the office.

She turned to Ty. "I'm sorry, I need to go. There appears to be a problem with the logistics company."

"Surely that's what you pay people to sort out for you?" Ty asked dryly. Mhairi's eyes widened at her tone and Ty looked away.

Alex rubbed her arm. "I prefer to reassure myself that problems are addressed."

She swung around to the other band members. "So, I'm assuming Ryan's shared our rehearsal schedule with you? The room is yours any other time you want it."

Jamie ambled nearer. He seemed to have calmed down a little. "Thanks, Alex. We really appreciate that. This time next week we'll be onstage at Madison Square fucking Garden! I can't believe it."

Ty winced visibly at his language, but Alex laughed. "Believe it, Jamie. And behave yourself this week. We need positive press coverage."

Jamie grinned at her. "Of course. We'll just do a wee bit of sightseeing and that. Totally innocent."

"Right, I need to go. How about we all have dinner tomorrow? I'll have Ryan make a reservation." Everyone smiled in agreement. *Think of a reason to see Ty on her own. Think, damn it.* She was nearly at the door. *Got it!*

She turned back and caught Ty's eye. "Hey MacLean, you remembered your running gear, right?"

"She doesn't go away for the weekend without her trainers. For three months she's probably got a whole suitcase full." Mhairi laughed and Jamie joined in.

Ty glared at them. "I've brought my kit. You know that's my stress reliever just like yours is playing more bloody music, and his is getting off his head in a club." She tipped her head at Jamie.

"Mine too. Running that is, not getting off my head." Alex laughed lightly. "I was planning to head out tomorrow around Central Park. If you go super early, it's pretty quiet. Would you like to join me?"

"Aye, why not. I was wondering about running routes. Some local knowledge and company would be good." Ty was playing along with the story.

"We've got a date then. I'll pick you up outside at five-thirty."

"Five-thirty in the morning? That's bloody disgusting!" Jamie was horrified.

121

"Good thing you're not invited then."

Tyra followed Alex to the door as she called out her goodbyes to everyone. She tried not to acknowledge how much she enjoyed the brief hug Ty gave her, but as she walked to the elevator, she knew she was screwed. Here she was, finding any excuse to spend time with Ty, and to what end?

She rested her head against the cool mirrored wall of the elevator as they descended. Dan, professional as ever, pretended not to hear her long sigh. They had agreed to end what had happened between them and she had no intention of trying to reignite anything that might cause problems later. The logical part of her knew that was the only way to handle the next three months, but there was a small part of her that asked why. So she could safeguard a career that just made her feel increasingly lonely and isolated?

As the elevator doors opened, she drew herself up with a renewed sense of purpose. No. She'd worked damn hard to get where she was, and negative thinking about feeling lonely wasn't going to get her anywhere. There was nothing wrong with enjoying Ty's company. If having her as a friend was the best she could do, it was better than nothing. For now, she had a tour to focus on.

SIXTEEN

The stage was dark as Ty slid onto her seat and readied her drumsticks. The crowd was noisy and there was a heavy sense of anticipation. She didn't look beyond the first few rows so the size wouldn't freak her out. She felt sick, but then she always had in those quiet moments before the lights went up or, when she'd played solo, before she ran onto the stage. She knew that the moment she started playing she'd be fine.

She had done her best to calm her cousins' nerves, but they had all been struggling with the scale of what they were about to do. Until Alex had turned up at their dressing room door. Dressed in tight jeans, cowboy boots and a green shirt the exact color of her eyes, just the sight of her was enough to settle Ty's anxiety. Her easy confidence filled the room. "Okay guys, you are gonna rock the Garden tonight. I'm really proud to have you opening my tour and I want you to remember that as you go out there."

After she wished them luck and left to prepare, Ty continued the pep talk. "You heard her. Alex Knight believes we can do this and who are we to argue? It doesn't matter if there's twenty people out there or twenty thousand. We go out and we entertain them. We know how to do that!" She slapped Jamie on the back. "Twenty thousand people are going to get to see how fucking awesome you are." Jamie had whooped with excitement as Mhairi smiled her soft smile, and Ty knew they would be okay.

Now, alone on the darkened stage, she started a slow beat, soft at first but growing in volume. The crowd went quiet and then roared as they realized their night's entertainment was beginning. A spotlight hit Ty and the crowd began to clap and scream. Mikki joined in with a guitar riff, the lights picking him out as he ran onto the stage. Next came Mhairi on bass. The crowd was ear shattering now, and as Jamie ran onstage the rafters practically rattled. He milked it as usual.

"Good evening, New York. We are DandyLions. Do you want us to play for you tonight?"

The crowd went wild, and Jamie launched into their opening number.

Ty was used to playing for over an hour, so she was surprised at how quickly the time went before they broke into their final song. Their biggest UK chart single, it had barely scratched the US market.

But it's going down all right now. She smiled in satisfaction. She had enjoyed all the live performances with DandyLions, and they'd been comfortable with the scale of their success but playing to this number of people was something else. She looked out at the rows and rows of people, as far back as she could see against the lights, and it reminded her of the exhilaration she had felt in her early days of performing. When it was new, and way before it had all gone so wrong. The buzz of knowing you had the attention of a whole room of people—whatever size that room might be—and they were having a great time, was unbeatable.

Jamie thanked the crowd, and they ran off stage to thunderous applause.

Alex was waiting on the side of the stage, clapping, and smiling widely.

"That was awesome. Told you they'd love you." She gave Ty a peck on the cheek and squeezed Mhairi's hand encouragingly. "Gotta go get into my clothes. See you later."

Ty now knew her well enough to see that, despite the weeks of rehearsals, sound checks and her crew double-checking the equipment, Alex the perfectionist was still on edge. She gave her a reassuring smile. "Good luck. We'll be watching." Alex smiled back and was gone.

Ty beat the others back to the dressing room, stripping off her leather jeans and sweat-sodden tank top on the way in, and hit the shower. She quickly dressed in a comfortable pair of cargo shorts and a baggy Alex Knight tour shirt she had succeeded in scrounging.

She was still towel drying her hair as she headed toward the stage to watch Alex's first moments of the tour. Backstage was busy, as Alex's show involved a number of set changes. Alex and her band were still in their dressing rooms so she grabbed some popcorn, a banana and her water bottle and looked for a space where she wouldn't be in the way.

There was a large steel equipment case against the wall. She hopped on top of a speaker and pulled herself up. From her vantage point she had a full view of the stage but wouldn't be in anyone's way. She chomped on her banana, hungry after even a shorter set, and waited for Alex to make her appearance.

Technicians were making final adjustments to equipment on stage, but in the rushed way that conveyed to the crowd that the show was imminent. The foot stomping started and the chant of *A-lex, A-lex, A-lex* grew louder and louder. The band members ran out to loud applause. The backing singers took their places at the mics and started a slow clap in time with the chanting.

She looked down and saw Alex standing below her feet, just out of sight of the crowd, waiting for her moment. Ty couldn't resist the temptation and Alex jumped as a piece of popcorn hit her head. She swung around to the battered Converse at her eye level, and her gaze rose to Ty's laughing face. "I couldn't let you go without a final good luck. Knock 'em dead, superstar."

She got a flash of a brilliant smile before Alex turned and ran onto the stage as the crowd went wild.

Ty watched Alex's performance in awe. She commanded the attention of the twenty thousand concertgoers like nothing Ty had ever seen. She did her best to manage her own stage nerves by imagining she was in a room, playing to a small group of people she liked and wanted to share her music with. Alex behaved as if every single person was there because she had personally invited them. It was powerful and intimate at the same time.

The show flew by and before Ty knew it, Alex was thanking her band members individually and going into the last song before the encore, the biggest hit from her most recent album.

Alex ran off stage, wiping her face with a proffered towel, then balled it up and threw it at Ty's head. Laughing, she ran off for a comfort break and returned with her two stylists in tow, giving her hair a quick revival and complaining about shiny, sweaty faces. Alex laughed them off and ran back onstage with her band, to tumultuous applause. They performed "Water in your Eye" and then Alex quieted the crowd. "Hey, everyone, we thought we'd end this night in my adopted hometown in a special way. I'd like to sing you a song I think you'll know. And I'd like to invite my amazing opening band, DandyLions, to come out and sing it with me. What do you think?"

She looked up at Ty and grinned. "I think they're a little shy so you may need to help me encourage them."

The crowd stamped their feet and cheered enthusiastically.

Jamie, clearly not shy at all, was first out onto the stage, radio mic in hand. Mhairi followed, saxophone slung around her neck, and Mikki brought up the rear with his guitar. They had showered and changed back into stage clothes. Ty suddenly suspected she was the only one not in the loop. She looked down at her T-shirt and cargo shorts and wondered what her hair must look like after its towel dry and no hair product. *What the hell, it's not like I've got any reputation to uphold.*

Jumping down from her perch, she grabbed a worn cap from the head of an unsuspecting roadie and pulled it on backwards, managing to capture most of her wayward hair. As she ran onstage Alex started to play the opening bars of the cover song Ty had suggested weeks ago. Suzi was on drums and Alex indicated with her head for Ty to join her at the piano. They played the piano part together, Alex launching into the vocals.

As she ended the first verse, she nodded at Ty. "Your turn," she mouthed.

Ty tried to look calm. She sang lead vocals on some of

DandyLions' tracks, but Jamie and Mhairi were there on backing vocals. This was just her voice and a piano in the biggest auditorium she'd ever played, and for a moment she panicked. But Alex didn't break eye contact and smiled with such confidence she couldn't help but start to sing. At least she knew all the words.

Mhairi played the sax solo impeccably. Ty didn't remember ever hearing her play it before, so this was starting to feel like a set-up. She wanted to be angry but performing with Alex felt so good she couldn't help but enjoy herself. They finished to thunderous cheering and foot stamping, and Ty and her bandmates left the stage to leave Alex to one final song.

"What the fuck was that?" She grabbed Jamie as they got offstage.

"Why are you havin' a go at me? It wasn't my idea. I barely even got to sing."

Mhairi pulled Ty's hand from Jamie's collar. "It really wasn't his idea, Ty. Alex talked us into it. She said you wanted her to play the song, so it would be fun to surprise you. And it was great, wasn't it?"

Ty had enjoyed herself immensely but had no intention of letting them off the hook so easily. She didn't like being the last to know things, and there was no way she wanted to set the precedent that it was okay on the very first night of the tour. She gave them both withering looks as they waited for Alex to leave the stage.

"That was fantastic." Alex ran off the stage towards them. Clearly still on a high from her performance, she took Ty's face in both hands and planted a sweaty kiss right on her lips. She winked imperceptibly and then turned and did the same thing to Jamie. He looked for a moment as though he might lunge for a longer embrace but he settled for a wide smile.

"Please don't ever do that to me again." Tyra tried not to sound too annoyed. "I've just been on stage in my oldest shorts and no hair product. The world does not need to see my hair in its natural state."

Alex ruffled the curly mop, now free of the cap. "You know, I like it best like that." She grinned. "You were fucking awesome. You all were. Well done, guys. And you," she faced Ty again, "just need to find us a song for the next gig and make sure everyone can play it." She laughed and walked away to congratulate her band, clapping them on the back and exchanging hugs.

"What?" Ty shouted to her. "What are you talking about?"

She turned back briefly. "Give me twenty minutes, then come to my dressing room and we'll discuss it."

Mhairi shoulder bumped Ty. "C'mon. You know you loved it, and you sounded amazing." She looked at Ty with a smile, but the worry in her eyes was clear.

"It was pretty cool. But don't make a habit of it, eh? You know how I feel about surprises." She hugged her cousins, who left to relax, and she leaned against the metal container, out of the way of the bustle, as she considered how she felt. When it became too messy, she headed to Alex's dressing room.

She knocked loudly and Alex opened the door with a toothbrush in her mouth. "I said twenty minutes." Her voice was garbled by the toothbrush, and she turned away to finish up.

"I'm not good at doing as I'm told." Ty grabbed two glasses for the ice-cold bottle of champagne on the table and popped the cork.

Alex took her glass and dropped heavily into a chair.

Ty didn't join her. "What was that all about? You know I'd have played with you if you asked me. Why put me on the spot like that?"

Alex patted the chair next to her. "I think you perform better spontaneously. And your band needed something to take their minds off the size of tonight's crowd. They were crapping themselves. Once I convinced them you wouldn't really murder them, they were happy to play along. Mhairi is very talented, isn't she?"

"She is. And thank you for giving them a distraction, but I don't enjoy surprises any more than you do. Although I'm glad you took up my suggestion, and...well, performing with you is a dream."

Alex's face lit up as she sat forward in her seat. "So that's why I thought we should do this every gig. You choose a song; we all perform it together. It'll give Jamie even more chance to shine."

Ty knew the last was added to ensure she couldn't say no. She shrugged, although she wasn't sure how she felt about being up front like that for the whole tour. At least it was just the one song, though. "Fine, with one condition. I choose the songs, I arrange them. No discussion."

Alex sat back and took a sip of her drink, watching Tyra as she swallowed slowly. Ty hoped she could agree to hand over control of this one part of her performance. Rehearsals would give them more reason to spend time together, even if she wasn't sure if that was a good idea.

Alex finally nodded. "Done."

Ty kept her expression businesslike. "Okay, I've got something in mind for Philly. We'll go for a straightforward arrangement, nothing too exciting. When we've got more time, we can get a bit more playful. We'll go through it first thing tomorrow. Now can we go and eat, please? I'm starving."

Alex laughed, and Ty followed her from the dressing room, glad to be out of the intimate space. Around other people she could almost forget what she and Alex might have had.

SEVENTEEN

Ty was lounging on the tour bus, tipped back almost horizontally on her chair while she scrolled lazily through the news on her phone. "Fucking hell. I hope you're happy, Jamie. This is what you've always wanted." The success of the first two weeks of the tour, with the encore covers proving a particular highlight, had driven sales of DandyLions' back catalogue through the roof, propelling them up the Billboard charts for the first time.

"Too right." Jamie beamed. "Famous at last! And bloody rich!"

She frowned. "You won't be so smug when you can't go to the pub without getting hassled constantly. Or when every girl you've ever slept with sells their stories to the press."

Jamie's smile didn't falter. "I'll worry about that when it happens. And I've never treated anyone badly or done anything to be ashamed of."

Mhairi snorted from her corner where she was eating cereal and reading the newspapers that appeared every day on the bus. "What about that time I was driving us to a gig in Inverness because you were hung over and sleeping in the back? Until you felt sick and vomited into a bag. Not your bag, which was right next to you, but my bag."

"Okay, there's a few things I'm not proud of but most of them are between us. You're not gonna sell me out to the papers are ya, Mhairi?" Jamie threw himself onto the floor next to her chair and looked up at her beseechingly. She rolled her eyes and threw a cornflake at his head before going back to her reading.

Jamie rolled over, bored. "Hey, cuz, what you up to today?"

Ty looked up from her screen. They'd got into a routine of gathering for breakfast each day on Alex's tour bus as there was more room for everyone to get together. If they had a gig that night, Alex would talk through rehearsal plans for the day, and if it was a free day, they would discuss what they planned to do with their downtime. They were currently parked in Boston ahead of a two-night stint at the TD Garden and Alex had yet to come out of her room.

"We need to rehearse these songs, then maybe you can have the afternoon off. After tomorrow you've got a week to do whatever you want."

"But I don't know what I want to do." His whining voice was starting to get on Ty's nerves. "Mhairi wants to stay in Boston and do boring history tours. The minute Siri's plane lands, Mikki'll be off to the nearest hotel room to shag his brains out, and you're buggering off to the middle of nowhere. There's no one to play with so I've got to head back to New York with your girlfriend." He rolled his eyes.

Ty got up and stretched, casually kicking Jamie in the elbow as she passed. "I've bloody told you, stop calling Alex my girlfriend. She'll go mental if she hears you." She retrieved her laptop and sat back down, scratching her head.

"These encore songs are a pain in the arse. I need more time to arrange them."

"Well, some of them are no' that imaginative, are they?" Jamie rubbed his elbow as he got off the floor to help himself to another pastry.

"But they're fun, and Alex loves a good guitar solo. And a romantic ballad." She thought about Alex singing the song she had chosen for the following night and smiled. Admittedly, it would be a duet with Jamie, which took some of the shine off, but still.

"All of their amazing songs and you had to choose that one? D'you not fancy having a go at something a bit less, y'know?" He mimed sticking his fingers down his throat.

Ty shrugged. "Nope. I love that song."

Alex emerged from her room, noticing Jamie's gesture. "What's making you sick, Jamie Boy?" She slapped him on the back as she passed.

"Ah, nothing, Alex." Jamie looked guilty as he stuffed the pastry into his mouth.

"Jamie doesn't like some of my song choices. He thinks Sunday's cover is too soppy."

Alex was skimming through the newspapers on the table. "Doesn't Jamie realize we don't get a vote? That this is a cover song dictatorship?"

Ty chuckled. "I think he was hoping to influence the dictator with his skills of persuasion."

Alex looked up at her. "Did it work?"

"Nope."

Alex laughed. "So, we need to do a quick run-through of tonight's song. Then sound checks are from three this afternoon. Who wants to come for lunch?"

Jamie, still eating, put his hand up. "Me, I'm starving."

Ty smiled apologetically. "I'd love to join you but Barb's in town and I've arranged to meet her for lunch. Sorry."

Alex nodded and turned away quickly. Ty watched her enter the rehearsal room and sighed. Things between them were purely professional. Alex was friendly, sure, but no more so than she was with Jaime or Mhairi, and Ty couldn't deny it still hurt. But so be it. She'd made her bed, and Alex wasn't in it. She shook herself into action.

"Right, you lot, let's get this thing done so we don't make idiots of ourselves tonight."

Alex picked at her lunch as Jamie chatted away, oblivious to her subdued mood. She would never have suggested lunch if she'd known Tyra wasn't free, and now she was having to sit through Jamie's incessant chitchat. The generous side of her had to admit his stories were always entertaining but she just wasn't in the mood today. Mhairi and Ryan were nodding enthusiastically at Jamie's tale, and she found her thoughts drifting to the regular subject.

She wanted to ask Ty to spend a few days with her at her apartment during their week off, but she didn't know if that was a good idea. Last time Ty had been there, their relationship had been on a very different footing. But she knew she missed their long chats and Ty's take on problems she herself thought were insurmountable.

In a few weeks they would be on the West Coast, and she would need to spend time with Dorothy. She had barely spoken about her daughter to Ty, but now she wanted to tell her about their problematic relationship. She knew Ty would see things in a different light and she longed for her advice on how to handle the situation.

Something else was bothering her. Since they had gone out on the road, Ty had shown no sign of looking for female company, much to Alex's relief. She didn't think she would be able to stand it, whatever she'd said in the past. But over the last week she couldn't help but notice Ty was spending more and more time with Ruth, one of Alex's backing singers. She'd noticed them chatting alone quietly on several occasions and earlier this week they'd gone off in a car together one afternoon, and no one seemed to know where they had gone.

Ruthie had been with Alex for over ten years and Alex had never heard any suggestion she might be interested in women. But then, she didn't exactly model a culture of openness on that particular subject, did she? She had no right to know what was going on in Ty's life but the hurt she felt at the thought of her being with someone else surprised her with its intensity. Perhaps she should just ask her. At least then she would know, instead of torturing herself with imagining what might be going on. But then...she'd know, and she wouldn't be able to un-know it. She looked up to see Mhairi's concerned gaze had settled on her. Jamie was still mid-yarn, but Mhairi must have noticed her preoccupation. She smiled to reassure her and made an effort to listen to Jamie for the rest of the meal. Anything to distract her thoughts from Ty.

Ty's lunch date felt like an interrogation into how things were going with Alex.

"What is it with all the questions, Barb? I told you, the tour is going great. Everyone's getting on really well and we're getting great reviews. Is there something else you want to ask me?"

Barb, naturally a plain speaker, frowned. "Celeste told me to be subtle. Is it not working?"

Ty breathed out slowly. "What do you want to know?"

"Well, when we met up over the summer you and Alex seemed pretty close. I know she has her profile to think about, and she's not out publicly, but it was pretty self-evident." She put her hand up to stall Ty's reaction. "I'm not asking you to 'fess up to anything, Ty. I'm just saying what we saw. You seemed happy together and that was good to see."

Ty shrugged, focusing on her food, a good reason to avoid eye contact. "We get on well together and we share a love of music. It was a good trip."

"Yeah. But the next time we saw you together on your first night of tour there was a very different vibe. You both seem to be going out of your way to stay at arm's length. We wondered whether something had happened."

Ty decided it was better to say nothing.

Barb finally gave up waiting. "It's a shame, that's all. You deserve to find someone who makes you happy."

Ty threw her napkin down, giving up on the idea of enjoying her meal. "Do I, Barb? I've spent the last ten years looking for quick satisfaction, nothing more. Why should I change any of that now?"

Barb rolled her eyes. "Stop being so dramatic. You've never properly got over Marianne and you like to tell yourself you're better off on your own."

Ty resisted the urge to get up and leave. She respected Barb's opinion on most things, but she wasn't sure she wanted to hear her judgement on this particular subject.

"But you know that's bullshit. You couldn't write the

songs you do if you didn't believe in love. So maybe you need to fight for it, Ty. Like you told me to all those years ago."

Ty nodded, feeling if she disagreed this could go on even longer. "I hear you, Barb. But things are complicated and I'm dealing with it in the only way I know how."

After they finished up their lunch and said goodbye, Ty wandered the streets for a while, thinking about Barb's words. They had been friends since childhood and sometimes Barbara remembered the idealistic, romantic teenager she'd been a little too vividly. Yes, of course she believed in love. But wasn't it a little too late for her now?

EIGHTEEN

Alex lay in her room staring at the ceiling in the near dark as her bus left Boston. She should be happy with how the tour was going. They had delivered two more top rate shows, and she was enjoying the covers more than she could ever have imagined. They had become a favorite with fans, and there was a storm on social media before each gig, with competition to guess what the next one would be. Ty managed to keep everyone on their toes by swaying between the obvious and the obscure.

Her PR company wanted to maximize the added interest and encouraged Alex to maintain the mystery each night. She had moved all rehearsals into her small studio on the tour bus, which was easy for the more straightforward piano or guitar-led songs, but when they needed to pull in her backing singers or horn section, the room was a little on the snug side. However, the joy of working with experienced musicians was that everyone simply made it work.

Ty sometimes selected songs that challenged Alex to learn a complicated guitar solo, or complex lyrics at short notice, but she was lapping it up and felt a sense of liberation that sometimes the performance wasn't perfectly polished, but everybody loved it. She had enjoyed singing the romantic ballad the night before with Jamie, but the irony of the lyrics wasn't lost on her.

This morning she had finally asked Ty if she would like to spend their free days together back in New York. She knew she should have asked sooner, but she'd been weighing the pros and cons as she tried to figure out the best plan. Her heart still felt as though it was being crushed when Ty explained her plans.

"I just need a few days to myself, Al. Off the grid. I'm gonna leave my phone off. Mhairi's got my itinerary and I'll check in with her every evening, but that's it. Just me and the trail for a week."

"Oh. That sounds like fun." Alex tried to keep her voice light. "What about the encore songs?"

"This week is supposed to be actual time off, right? We'll have time to work on them as we go. I can be back in New York City by the tenth and travel to Indianapolis on the bus. We can rehearse then?"

"I guess." Alex turned away to hide her dejection and Ty didn't appear to notice. To make matters worse, Ryan had asked to have a few days off, which was unheard of. Alex had agreed, only to overhear him suggesting shyly to Mhairi that he could show her around Boston.

Now she was faced with a week of her own company. Ordinarily this was exactly what she would be craving after a few weeks on the road, but she wasn't looking forward to the solitude. With no other distractions she would have plenty of time to think about her relationship, or lack of it, with Ty.

Did Tyra want anything more? She'd made it clear to

Alex she didn't do commitment, but Alex needed to know if that could change. What she knew for sure was that anyone dating Tyra would need to be open and transparent about who they were. Could she be that person?

When she couldn't stand the mental torture any longer, she sat sipping coffee on her deck, but looking out over the sprawling city made her feel more alone than ever. She wished she could talk to Clara. However, her best friend was also her daughter's stepmother, and she couldn't face talking about Dorothy as well as everything else going on in her head. She flipped her phone over in her hands. Perhaps if she stared at it long enough Tyra might call and they could talk. In the end she sent a quick text asking if they could meet as soon as Ty returned. She dropped her phone to the chair and headed back to her rehearsal room. If she couldn't fix everything in her life at least she could ensure her performances were perfect. In fact, maybe it was a good time to put pen to paper and draft some new songs. Emotions like the ones rambling around in her were good fodder for music.

Tyra checked her compass to confirm she was on the right trail. It was the last day of her trip and it had been just the workout she needed. Although the tour was physically demanding, she'd been missing the long runs and bike rides that served as her stress relief. Open spaces where she could breathe deeply and not hear anything other than birds reminded her of her cottage, and she couldn't deny the taste of homesickness.

As she walked, she mulled over the last few weeks. Performing had been less stressful than expected, and the anxiety she used to feel had eased. She knew a large part of her enjoyment was due to the close proximity to Alex. They worked well together musically, and she believed they could have a creative future together, if that was something Alex wanted.

But did Alex desire more than that? And did Ty even know what she herself wanted? She had convinced herself for years that all she needed was her close network of friends and family, and her regular casual hook-ups saw to her physical needs. But meeting Alex had turned everything on its head. In her heart she longed for more, but there were so many things in the way, she couldn't imagine how it could happen. Alex valued her as a musician, and she was confident in her own abilities as a songwriter and producer. She knew where her strengths lay. *But Alex Knight is a superstar. Why would she turn her whole life upside down for me?* Alex had been very clear back in the summer that what had happened in New York was over. So why couldn't she let it go?

Catching her foot in a root she just caught herself from sprawling face first on the trail. Injuring herself would be stupid, and she needed to concentrate.

She sighed and sat down on a nearby rock, pulling out a snack bar and some water.

She turned on her phone and checked her messages. There was one from Alex asking to catch up as soon as she returned, and another from Ruth, Alex's backup singer. Ruth had asked Tyra for help a few weeks ago when her nephew had come out to his parents as transgender. Ruth had been supporting him for a couple of years and had advised him against making any big announcements to his very conservative parents while she was away, but the situation had deteriorated and had ended in her sister and brother-in-law throwing their fifteen-year-old child out on the streets. Ruth had been torn between her commitment to her work and ensuring her nephew was safe, so Tyra had called in her community contacts to make sure Dylan had support and somewhere safe to stay until Ruth could get back. Ruth was with him now and had sent photos of them together, thanking Tyra for her help. She replied, sent a quick text to Mhairi letting her know where she was, and turned her phone off without replying to Alex's message. Work could wait, and she needed to clear her head, to stop thinking about what could have been with Alex and get on with her life.

She pushed her hair back under her cap as she stood, slung her pack back on her shoulders and took off at a punishing pace.

NINETEEN

When Tyra got back to the city it felt even more loud and crowded than she remembered. The calm she'd felt, that she only ever really experienced when she was outdoors, quickly dissipated under the oppressive shadows of the high-rise buildings. She headed straight for the studio and immersed herself in arranging the cover songs for the next few gigs.

Alex turned up at the studio late in the day. "I thought you were going to let me know when you were back?" She didn't manage to hide the hurt in her tone.

Ty felt a pang of guilt that she'd thought it would be easier to focus on work without being in close proximity to Alex. "Ah, sorry, I just got stuck in and the day ran away from me. D'you want to run through what I've been working on?"

Alex shrugged. "We might as well now I'm here."

Ty shared the songs she had chosen, and they experimented with playing them. Alex scheduled in a couple of full band rehearsals for when they were back on the road. She appeared pleased enough with the songs, but

Ty felt the awkwardness between them, and looked up a couple of times to see Alex watching her, an unfathomable look on her face. Tyra felt conflicted. Part of her was so happy to be back with Alex again, she couldn't deny she'd missed her. But she had renewed determination to keep a professional distance. Anything else would only end in her getting hurt.

As they packed up their instruments Alex called Mike for a pickup. "Do you need a lift anywhere?" She looked up at Ty, her smile hopeful.

Ty forced herself to stay strong. "Uh, no thanks, I'm gonna take a walk."

Alex's expression darkened as she nodded. "See you on the bus tomorrow then. Enjoy your evening." With the briefest of hugs, she was gone, leaving Ty to head back to her hotel room in a somber mood.

The next morning was a very early start back on the road and Ty's mood wasn't helped by Mhairi arriving relaxed and full of historical facts about the American War of Independence. They were eating breakfast together when Mhairi asked, "Have you seen Jamie?"

Ty shrugged. "He's not been around since I got back." The truth was she had been relieved not to have to deal with whatever drama was going on in Jamie's life but now she felt guilty she hadn't checked up on him. "D'you think he's okay?"

"I'd say things are more than okay for him. He can't stop grinning." Mhairi slid her phone across the table.

Ty picked it up. The screen showed numerous images of Jamie, always in the company of the same smiling, familiar-looking woman. Ty looked closer at the screen and scrolled through the article. It was all about Danielle Coburn and her new escort. Ty wasn't the biggest expert on celebrities, but she knew who Danielle was. She had seen her in the lead role in several blockbusters. She was a fully-fledged movie star. "Fuck, Alex told him to keep a low profile." She got up, her lunch abandoned as she went in search of her wayward cousin.

She found him packing his belongings back on the bus and pulled him into a quiet corner.

"I leave you alone for a week and you're out there getting your face plastered all over the papers?"

"Hey." He held his hands out in defense. "Alex told me to behave myself, not to hide away like a monk. She's fine with it. I've been out with Dani a few times, but no one else. It's not my fault we make such a gorgeous couple people can't keep their cameras to themselves!" Jamie laughed in a lame attempt to make the gorgeous part sound less conceited.

"A few times? Like more than once? Do you like her, then?"

Jamie smiled. "What do you think? She's smart, funny, and dead famous. Plus, my favorite quality of all, she's a big Jamie fan. What more could I want?"

"Well, she's clearly got no taste." Ty rolled her eyes. "Are you seeing her again?"

"She's headed back to LA for work now. I've put her on the guest list for the gig there and I'm hopin' we'll meet up."

Jamie's smile was so wide, Ty decided not to interrogate him further. He wasn't shagging around and seeing a movie star regularly would be better than a string of casual liaisons. She squeezed his shoulder and left him to unpack.

As musicians and crew assembled to join their

respective buses for the next leg of the journey, she saw Ruth hurrying over, and pulled her aside. "How was it? Did you speak to your sister?"

Ruth looked exhausted. Family crises probably weren't the best way to spend your downtime. "Yeah, but she refuses to see Dylan." She ran a hand over her face. "The good news is our youngest sister was out of town for work but she's back now. She's furious with Margie but she's trying to be diplomatic. Dylan is going to stay with her for a while, so at least I know the poor kid has some stability. I really hope Margie and George come around eventually."

Ty pulled her in for a hug. "They will, I'm sure. And you've done everything you could to help." Over Ruth's shoulder she recognized Alex's car with its blacked-out windows pulling up alongside her bus.

"Thanks to you. Your contacts made sure he had somewhere to stay and people to talk to. What sort of monsters throw their own child out on the street?" Ruth didn't seem to be in a rush to end their embrace, so Ty held her tight, hoping to reassure her, as she watched Alex slip out of the car and ascend the steps to her bus. She turned as she went, and her gaze landed on Ty. Ty smiled a greeting, but Alex looked away without returning the smile and continued her journey onto the bus. When Ruth eventually let her go, they got onto Alex's bus just as the driver was starting up the engine. As they pulled off, she joined the other musicians in the rest area, catching up with those she hadn't seen since their break. They all had their instruments ready for the rehearsal, but Alex was nowhere to be seen. Ty knocked quietly on the door to her private quarters and when Alex's head appeared, she grinned. "Hey, Alex, how's it going? Are you still good to rehearse the songs with everyone?"

Alex seemed distracted. "Yeah, but I wanted to discuss something first. Let's find somewhere quiet."

Ty followed her back past the other band members, to the rehearsal room, wondering what was going on. Alex closed the door to the room firmly and turned to Ty. Her expression was unreadable.

"I like your song choices generally, and I know I agreed you choose them, but it doesn't feel right going to Indiana and not playing a John Mellencamp number. He's one of my biggest influences."

Ty opened her mouth to object and Alex help up her hand.

"So, we're *going* to do Jack & Diane. It's a far better song to perform together than the one you've arranged. You can play that cool drum filler." She smiled confidently, but it was the fake smile she used with the press. Ty knew it well.

Ty was struggling to understand what had happened. "You committed to me having full control over the covers. You can't go back on that. Also, Jack & Diane? Seriously? You don't have any problem with those lyrics?" She slapped her hand against the wall, feeling the anger rising. "If you really wanted to do Mellencamp we could've talked about 'Small Town' or 'Cherry Bomb' but you never said a word, and now, on the day, you want to change it? Absolutely no fucking way." She was shouting but she didn't care. This was about more than a song. Alex couldn't hand over control, and apparently, she couldn't even honor a simple agreement, either. What would a woman like that do to her heart?

Alex's expression had gone very still except for where a muscle in her jaw twitched. Tyra had only seen her get really angry on a couple of occasions, but all the signs were there now.

Her voice was quiet and icily cold, in stark contrast to Ty's yelling. "How dare you tell me what I will or will not play at my own performance? I have given you and your band every opportunity imaginable. I've let you choose each song we've performed together so far. And now I have one request and you point blank refuse?"

"But it wasn't a fucking request, was it? It was a demand. And the moment anyone dares to disagree with you, you throw your toys out the pram an' say you're in charge. You simply can't handle not having control over everything and everyone around you. Fuck you and your bullshit." Ty flung the door open so hard the handle embedded itself into the wall. She marched out, ignoring the shocked gazes of the other musicians, and headed for the front of the bus. She needed to stay on her own bus from now on. Distance was the key to her sanity.

Alex put her head in her shaking hands and breathed deeply, trying to calm herself.

Why did Ty have to react so extremely to everything? How well suited could they be if they could make each other this angry?

She hadn't meant to demand the change of song. She had been hoping to have a civilized discussion about it. Once the idea of the new song had stuck in her head, she had pursued it in her usual driven way, which must have seemed to Ty like an order. No, that wasn't fair. She'd made it an order, still stung by Tyra avoiding her on her return. Seeing her with her arms around Ruthie in the parking lot had been the final straw.

She groaned into her hands. She *had* promised her full

control of the cover songs. What had gone wrong? She had returned after their break with every intention of talking to Ty about her feelings. But Ty had actively avoided her, which hurt more than it should. It was so much easier to focus on the parts of her life she could control, even if it meant taking it from someone else. *Fuck.*

She heard a cough and looked up to see Mhairi standing hesitantly in the doorway. "Are you all right, Alex?" She hesitated in the doorway.

"Leave me alone, Mhairi. Go look after your foul tempered cousin." She ran her hands through her hair. Mhairi ventured a couple more steps into the room.

"She's far too foul tempered to approach for a while. And she can't come to any harm. We're on a moving bus." As she spoke the bus slowed and came to a halt. Mhairi shrugged. "She'll just be gettin' on one of the other buses to give herself time to calm down a bit. She'll be fine."

"She'd better get her shit together because if she messes up tonight's gig, I'll replace her for the rest of the tour." Alex growled. "There are plenty of well-behaved drummers out there."

Mhairi shook her head slowly. "No, you won't. And she won't let you down. She gave you her word, and for Ty, her word is unbreakable." She paused, as if not sure whether to go on. Alex raised her eyebrows. "I was just wondering if you mind me asking what you argued about?"

Alex stood, stretching her neck and shoulders, aware of the audible crunching. Mhairi was going to find out anyway, but somehow, she couldn't bring herself to say it out loud.

Mhairi winced sympathetically. "Sit back down on that stool and I'll rub your neck. I promise I know what I'm doing."

There was something reassuring about Mhairi's calm

and common-sense approach. It might have been a natural talent or honed through a lifetime of dealing with Tyra's temper and Jamie's histrionics, but against her own expectations Alex found herself slumping back onto the piano stool and letting herself relax under Mhairi's strong hands.

"I guess she may have felt I was going back on my word to her. I wanted to change tonight's cover song and perhaps I could've raised it more sensitively. Shit, you really are good at this."

"Your shoulders are knotted as anything. It feels like you hold a lot of tension there."

Alex rotated her neck a little more freely. "I feel particularly tense at the moment. This feels amazing, thank you."

"Ty is an incredibly loyal friend, but she values trust above almost anything and if she thinks you've broken a promise over something, she can get pretty angry. But even for her, this seems an extreme reaction." She paused and then asked quietly, "Can I ask you something?"

Alex tipped her head back to look at her. "Is it about what happened over the summer?"

Mhairi nodded and pushed Alex's head back down gently.

"How much do you know?"

"I know she spent a lot of time in your company, and stayed at your apartment, but she was awful quiet when she came back, and didn't want to talk about her trip. She was focused on preparations for the tour, so I let it go. We talk a lot usually, and it felt as though she didn't want to share something. But we don't have the sort of relationship where I would keep pushing for details." Her thumbs pressed into Alex's shoulders. "But it's not like her to keep secrets."

Alex could hear the disappointment in her voice. *Crap, I made her agree not to tell anyone about us. I took away her support network.* She let out a slow breath. "We became close in that week, but we agreed to end things when Ty's visit was over. Neither of us wanted a relationship, and even if we had, we live our lives in such different ways it could never have worked." Was she trying to convince herself or Mhairi? Things didn't seem as clear-cut now as they had in the summer.

Mhairi continued the massage, quiet for a while until she continued. "Ty has had one serious relationship that I can remember. Ask her about it sometime, but the way it ended had a big impact on her." Mhairi's tone was deliberate, as though she was really thinking about what she was saying. "She's guarded her feelings ever since, preferring the company of people who are only looking for fun. It's worked for her so far, but if she's got close to you, she must trust you. And if she thinks you've betrayed her trust, she'll find that hard." She stepped around to the front of the chair and Alex felt a surge of disappointment that the massage was over.

"Why don't we get tonight over and done with and maybe she'll be ready to apologize and talk some sense?"

"Thanks, Mhairi, you've got an old head on those young shoulders. Speaking of which, I can't remember the last time mine felt this loose." Alex stood and hugged her, surprising herself.

Mhairi returned the hug warmly, then turned to go. Opening the door, she roused the others. "On your feet, you lot. We've got a new song to learn for tonight."

TWENTY

Tyra avoided everyone for the rest of the day, turning up dutifully at sound check, replying civilly to her band mates, but refusing to discuss anything more than the needs of their performance, not wanting their empathy, or their judgement. She knew it was harsh, but she just didn't have the emotional energy to deal with them *and* play a set in front of another massive crowd.

The moment their performance was over she almost ran back to their bus and was showered and in her bunk before Alex's set had barely started. She could hear the performance from the bus, whether she liked it or not, and instead of putting in earplugs she lay and listened, checking off the songs on Alex's playlist until the end of the set. The roar for Alex to return was deafening, even out in this distant parking lot. Alex came back on stage and Ty could hear her voice without making out the words. Then a deafening cheer as whichever musicians were performing the cover song returned to the stage.

She heard the intro and realized Alex had changed her song choice. 'Small Town' blasted out, with Alex and Jamie taking each verse in turn. Not the song she had planned, but not the one she had been so opposed to. Was Alex trying to show compromise? A compromise they could maybe have reached if she hadn't lost her shit and shouted in Alex's face. She shoved her earplugs in, pulled the pillow over her head and, emotionally drained, fell quickly asleep.

Her mood hadn't improved the following morning as she sat on her bed looking at their schedule. They had a long way to go on this tour and now she was facing weeks of awkwardness. If Alex even allowed her to continue the tour. It was her own fault; it was Alex's tour, and she could overrule anything she wanted.

Mhairi hadn't returned to their shared room after the show, probably too disgusted with her temper tantrum. Their performance last night had been acceptable, and they were all professional enough to be able to get away with putting on a good show, even if they themselves knew it wasn't their best. It hadn't been fun, and she couldn't even think about how badly she had missed performing alongside Alex.

She jumped at a quiet knock on the door. Mhairi's head poked around it.

"Hi, how are you doing? I thought you needed some space last night, so I stayed on the crew bus, but I do need some clothes."

Oh God, even Mhairi doesn't want to be around me. "Sorry, Mhairi, please come in. You didn't have to stay away."

"No problem, we stayed up late chatting and I didn't want to disturb you. How you feelin' today?"

"Pretty shite, to be honest. Does Alex hate me?" She pulled the duvet around her. Mhairi sighed and dropped onto the bed next to her.

"No, she doesn't hate you. She'd like the chance to talk with you. Quietly. Like normal people." She squeezed Ty's hand.

Ty pulled away. *Was Mhairi Alex's messenger now?* "Have you been talking about me?"

"Ah, Ty, for God's sake, you've not spoken to anyone for nearly twenty-four hours. People need to get on with their lives, you know? Just go and see her."

"Why do I have to go and see her? She knows where I am." She knew she was sounding petty now.

"Because you're scary when you're angry and nobody dares approach you."

The pettiness vanished and Ty again felt ashamed of the way she'd acted. It didn't matter how undermined she had felt, she'd lost control of her temper again. Something about Alex brought out the passion in her, for better or worse. She let out a long breath. "Okay, I'll throw myself on her mercy and she can decide whether to spare me."

"Oh, Ty, stop being such a bloody martyr. Don't get yourself into these situations if you don't like apologizing!" Mhairi got up and started rummaging through her clothes.

"Right. I'm on it." Ty left Mhairi in peace and hurried to the shower. The buses had been driving since the early hours but had parked up for a couple of hours for the drivers to rest and change over. She had a short window if she wanted to get on Alex's bus before they left.

No one was about as she crossed the parking lot, heading for Alex's bus with its steel blue livery.

The door opened as she approached, and Ryan stepped down with a relieved smile. "Hey, Tyra, good to see you.

Everyone's just finishing up eating and about to do a quick rehearsal for tomorrow's song. Go and join them."

She nodded and headed towards the communal area where she found Jamie, eating as always, and Mikki tuning his guitar. They both got up and hugged her while she muttered apologies about being miserable the day before.

"Alex is in the rehearsal room on her own," Jamie stage-whispered.

She rolled her eyes and headed to the door, which was slightly ajar. She could hear the strumming of a guitar and she poked her head in cautiously. "Okay if I come in?"

Alex looked through her fringe of hair. "Will you smash the place up if I say no?"

Ty bit her tongue. "Is that not a bit unfair? I slammed a door. I'm sorry, I'll pay for the damage." As she closed the door, she could see the repairs had been made, with no visible sign it had ever happened. She headed over to a comfy chair crammed in the corner and sat facing Alex, who stayed very still, hunched over her guitar.

"I really am sorry for losing it. I overreacted."

Alex let out a deep breath and her shoulders relaxed. "As did I. I'm not proud of what I said to you. I hope we can get past it."

Resisting the urge to throw herself into Alex's arms, Ty rubbed her forehead. "I'm totally committed to this tour, so whatever you need of me, I'll do it. If you want to decide which covers we perform, I'll do my best to arrange them. You're right, it's your tour and we're here only because you gave us a chance."

Alex put her guitar down and moved across the space, kneeling in front of Ty, and taking both her hands in hers, she looked up, her eyes shining.

"I really am sorry, Tyra. I played the power card and

undermined your decision. I don't even really understand why I did it. But I do know how much we missed you last night, and if they're not your song choices I don't want to do them."

Fuck, I want to kiss her so bad. Ty chased the thought out of her head and stood, pulling Alex with her. "In that case, can we just rehearse tonight's song and move on?"

Alex smiled warmly and pulled her into a brief hug before they went to join the band for rehearsal Ty was glad they'd put the argument behind them, but she didn't know how much longer she could go on pretending, to herself or to Alex, that they could just be friends.

TWENTY-ONE

Alex barely heard the soft knock at her door as she sat thumbing through a magazine on a well-earned rest day. "Hello?"

Ruth, her longest-serving backing singer stuck her head around the door. "Is this a good time?"

Alex swung her legs down off the couch and put the magazine aside. "Of course, Ruthie, come on in." She had an open-door policy with all her band members and crew. She'd noticed Ruth had been looking rundown over the past few weeks although it had never affected her performance. She'd briefly wondered if, as she'd suspected, there was something going on between Ruth and Ty and Tyra had hurt her in some way. But she'd dismissed the thought immediately. Knowing Ty as she did now, she knew she would never intentionally hurt anyone. She may prefer to keep her relationships casual, but she'd always been honest about it.

Ruth sprawled on the couch as Alex got up to pour them a glass of wine. "Is everything okay, Ruth? You've been looking kind of tired."

Ruth's face crumpled and she sobbed as she poured out her story of how her older sister had reacted badly to her child's gender identity. The nephew was now safe and living with another aunt, but Ruth was distraught that her older sister, who she had looked up to all her life had turned out to be a narrow-minded bigot who could desert her child. Alex hugged her close but didn't feel she had much insight to offer about sibling relationships. And abandoning children wasn't a subject she wished to discuss.

"Hey, we can get you straight home today. We'll find someone to cover you and there are only a couple more dates before the next break anyway. Go to your family if they need you."

Ruthie took the proffered tissue and blew her nose noisily. She moved out of Alex's embrace self-consciously. "Sorry, Alex. I didn't mean to dump all this off on you. Things are more stable now and I'll go back as soon as we get a break." She sniffed. "But Tyra said I should talk to you and let you know what's going on."

Alex felt her shoulders tense. "Tyra? What does she have to do with this?"

Ruth looked at her oddly. "Oh, Alex, she's been so good. When it all happened, I was halfway across the country and my sister was in Europe. Tyra got in touch with an organization she knew of in our hometown to make sure Dylan had somewhere to stay. They were so good to him. Without Ty's help he would've been out on the streets."

Alex wanted to ask why Ruth hadn't come to her first, but she knew why. Throughout the tour Ty had organized fundraisers and supported causes for LGBT+ charities in the places they passed through. She was such a visible role model and ambassador for her community, it was something Alex had grown to admire. She knew being in the limelight didn't come easily to Tyra, but her determination and courage were inspiring. And people loved her for who she was, the whole package. There were always the haters, but Alex had her share of them too. She dragged her attention back to Ruth, who was talking about all the other little things Tyra had done to help, to keep her functioning until she'd been able to go home and see her nephew. "And since we've been back on the road, she checks in with me every day, takes me out for walks and sits with me late at night when I just need to talk. I don't know what I'd have done without her."

Ruth left reassured that Alex would support her, whatever she needed. Alex, however, felt less sure about anything than she had in her life. She had wanted to talk to Tyra for a while but their fight a couple of weeks ago had unsettled her. The conflict had hurt so much she hadn't wanted to do anything to cause further anguish between them. And they'd settled into an amiability that seemed to be working, so why mess with it?

The tour continued to be a massive success. Jamie had begun to add costumes and gimmicks to the ever more popular cover numbers. Running on stage in a wig at one show, he made Alex laugh so hard she had to delay the start of the song. He had taken that as a challenge and brought something more ridiculous to every song. One night, he came on stage in beard, hat, and shades, handing Alex another set to complete the look. The fans at the gigs, the people scanning YouTube for the first phone camera video, the acts whose songs were being showcased, and people who had never been interested in Alexandra Knight before were following just to see what the hype was all about. Everybody loved the covers, and even Linda was forced to agree they were useful publicity.

But now they were about to start their overnight journey to Memphis, and after that was a week of free time. Alex was planning to spend it in LA. She had asked Ryan to rent an ocean-front beach house and she was planning to sit watching the ocean with a good book in hand. But what she really wanted was Ty there with her. Was that a good idea? She would never know if she didn't suggest it.

She would see both her parents while she was in LA. She had no real choice but to spend time with her mother while she was in the city where she lived. And her dad was on a rare conference trip that happily coincided with her plans. That was a lot of family plans to impose on Ty if she joined her, but she could choose to come along or not as she wished. And there was Dottie. Her last visit over the summer had ended in a fight with her daughter that had left her tearful for days. She was never quite prepared for how much Dottie's jibes hurt.

She shook her gloomy thoughts away and forced herself to go in search of Ty, and eventually found her deep in conversation with Mhairi on the band's own bus.

Alex stepped up behind them. "Sorry to interrupt. We'll be leaving shortly, and I wondered if you wanted to ride with me? I've had some food delivered and I thought maybe we could talk about the songs for the next leg?" Her attempt to sound casual was a million miles from how she was feeling inside.

Ty frowned and rubbed her forehead. "Ah Alex, thanks but I'm absolutely whacked. I was just gonna grab a sandwich or something and get to bed. Could we catch up tomorrow?"

Alex plastered on the most genuine smile she could muster. "Of course, I'm sorry, you know what I'm like. I find it hard to switch off. Tomorrow will be fine."

Shit. She said her goodbyes and climbed back onto her own bus lethargically. *It's my own fault. I've insisted on distance and now I'm feeling sorry for myself when she'd rather be elsewhere.*

She used the bus intercom to let the driver know he could leave whenever he was ready, then wearily dropped onto her couch. The journey would take around six hours so she should have time for a good night's sleep, but she felt too tense to go straight to bed. She had always enjoyed having her own tour bus, with the small rehearsal room allowing her to assemble her band, but also to send them on their way when she needed space. Suddenly it felt ridiculous to have a whole bus to herself, not to mention lonely. As she selected some music on her phone, she heard the doors open at the front of the bus. The driver said something, and an indistinct voice replied before the engine started up. It was probably one of the technicians offering to ride with Rog to keep him company on the late-night drive. They knew to leave her in peace, so she didn't mind. Joni Mitchell started to sing as she relaxed into the couch and closed her eyes.

"I thought you were looking a bit sorry for yourself, but Joni has just confirmed it."

Alex opened her eyes to see Tyra standing behind the couch, hands stuffed in her pockets, a searching look in her blue eyes.

"If you've changed your mind about the company, Rog can drop me back to the other bus, no problem. But that fake smile never works on me. Do you want to talk?"

Seeing Ty standing there made her stomach flip. "I haven't changed my mind, come and sit down." She sat up and tucked her legs under her, leaving room for Ty to sit, but she was already on her way to the kitchen.

"I'm starving, to be honest. Where's this food you mentioned?"

That gave Alex a couple of minutes to gather her thoughts about what she wanted to say. The food heating in the kitchen wasn't helping as she realized she was hungry too. Ty re-emerged with a bowl of jambalaya and a cold bottle of champagne. "Thought we might celebrate a successful tour so far?"

"Yeah, that sounds good." Champagne was the last thing she wanted. She already felt lightheaded, but whether from hunger or Ty's close proximity she wasn't sure.

Tyra tucked into the food, giving out moans of delight at the succulent prawns in the dish. She scooped some up and held the fork to Alex. "You've got to try this."

She took a mouthful gratefully. "Oh, that is delicious."

"You don't eat enough." Ty jumped up and quickly returned with a second bowl.

How does she always know what I need? They ate in silence until Alex became aware of Ty watching her intently. She raised an eyebrow.

Ty's look was concerned. "Are you okay? You look a wee bit pale."

"I'm good. Just tired and looking forward to putting my feet up for a few days." She watched Ty deftly open the bottle and pour two glasses, wondering if she should speak and risk ruining the moment. She decided to see how the conversation went. *Coward.*

"To you." Ty raised her glass. "Thank you, Alex, this is the most amazing experience for all of us. Getting the job was fantastic enough, but you've really brought us into your tour family. You didn't have to do that."

She raised her own glass. "And to DandyLions." She savored the sensation of the cold champagne in her mouth.

"I'm glad you're enjoying yourselves. You're a talented group of musicians and good company to be around. You've made my tour fun, the reviews are great, and our encores are becoming a thing of legend. It's a two-way thing." Keeping the conversation focused on their music felt safer. She shifted to stretch her tucked up feet. They were starting to feel numb, but she didn't want Ty to move away.

Observant as ever, Ty pulled some cushions onto the floor alongside the couch, and dropped onto them without spilling her drink, indicating to Alex to stretch out her legs. She leaned her head against the leather and sighed.

"I am knackered, though. This leg of your tour will be more than enough for me. I can't believe you've toured the Southern Hemisphere and Europe already this year. Where d'you get the energy?"

Alex felt a swell of emotion as she looked down at Tyra. It was time for honesty about how she was feeling. She took a breath. "For most of my career work was what I lived for. Writing, recording, and performing. It completed me. Or so I thought." She lowered her hand to Ty's face, unable to resist touching her. She ran the backs of her fingers tenderly down her cheekbone to her jaw, which tensed at her touch.

Ty reached up and stilled Alex's hand with her own, looking into her eyes. "And now?"

"You've made me realize there's more to life than work and being successful. Being with you makes me feel more alive than I ever have. I want more of that." She swung her legs off the couch and pulled Tyra up to sit next to her, not breaking eye contact. "I know we live different lives, Ty, but I want you to be a part of mine, and I'll do anything I can to make that happen."

Ty pulled her hand free and propped herself against the arm of the sofa, her arms wrapped around her knees.

"Different lives is putting it mildly. We live on different continents. I avoid media attention whenever possible, you live in the public eye." She raised her eyebrows. "And then there's the big one."

Alex ran her hands through her hair. How could she convince Ty to give them a chance? "I don't know all the answers to how we can make this work, Ty. I only know that I really want to try, that I need you to be part of my life. Can we take things slowly and work it out as we go?"

Tyra was still frowning. "I'm not being anyone's dirty little secret, Alex. I've been there and I won't make the mistake again."

Alex moved closer, unclasping Ty's hands from around her knees and holding them in her own.

"I want to be with you, Tyra. And I know that means being open about being with you. I want that too, you're too wonderful to be hidden or denied. I *will* deal with it, but I need to know you trust me enough to try in my own way and time."

Ty sighed. "I know I want more with you, but I don't know how much I've got to give. I've been on my own a long time, Alex. And I admire the way you live your life. Well, most of it. But I don't know if I can live like that."

Alex looked down at their hands, rubbing her thumbs across Ty's knuckles. "But are you willing to try?"

She looked up to see a slow smile spreading across Ty's face. "If that's what you want, it would be rude to say no."

Alex felt relief spread through her body and her own matching smile spread across her face. She shifted closer and moved in to capture Ty's lips with her own. Kissing Ty felt like the most perfect place to be as the pleasure quickly turned to a fire building inside her. She forced herself to pull back.

"We're both exhausted. Maybe we should get some sleep and talk more tomorrow?"

Ty smiled again. "I've been wanting to touch you for so long. You're not getting to sleep yet!"

She pulled Alex on top of her and kissed her again. Alex relaxed into the kiss until Ty flipped them over so that she was pinning Alex with her body. Alex fought her natural instinct to fight for control and relaxed, closing her eyes to fully savor the sensation of Ty's mouth on hers. Finally, after all those weeks of fantasizing. But the kiss and Ty's weight were suddenly gone, and she opened her eyes in frustration. Ty was sitting back, watching her, the desire in her eyes so clear Alex felt herself tighten in response.

"Take your shirt off." Ty's voice was low.

Alex scrambled to comply, pulling her T-shirt quickly over her head. She held her breath in anticipation, but Ty held back, still watching. Just as Alex thought she couldn't take the anticipation a second longer, Ty lowered her head. Alex felt her nipples harden as light kisses trailed down her collarbone. Ty moved in that direction, her fingers deftly moving to rid Alex of her bra and allow her full access. Alex thought the sensation would drive her crazy, until Ty lifted her weight once more and started to remove Alex's jeans. Taking her time with the belt and slowly lowering the jeans and underwear, she continued to kiss Alex's skin. Alex felt more than naked as Tyra sat back, still fully dressed, and gazed down at her. She squirmed. "I need you. Now."

Ty raised her eyebrow.

"Please, Ty."

Ty smiled as she lowered her head. Alex shuddered as she felt her hot breath on her sensitive skin. She ran her hands through Ty's hair, grasping handfuls of curls in case she had any ideas about moving away. But Ty seemed committed to making her feel in ways she had never felt before. As Ty's warm tongue entered her, she stopped thinking and surrendered herself.

Ty lay watching Alex sleeping in her arms. The night hadn't gone as she had imagined when she got on the bus, concerned for Alex's mood. And now here they were, back in bed. But they had talked about starting a relationship. Was that what she wanted? Being with Alex made her feel like she didn't want to be alone any longer. And if that was all that was on the line, she could imagine being able to take it slowly, building trust as they went. Alex the person was everything she could ask for.

But then there was Alex the celebrity to deal with and going slow wasn't really an option with her lifestyle. It had taken Ty years to get over the panic attacks, and being with DandyLions had allowed her to ease her way slowly back into performing and facing media attention. But being with Alex would push that to a whole other level and just the thought of it made Ty's heart start to race, and not in a good way.

And was Alex really ready to come out to the world? Ty guessed the longer you spent hiding who you were, the harder it would be. But that was something she could only support Alex with. The decision, and how she managed it, rested solely with Alex.

She must have dropped off to sleep, because she drifted into awareness to a very pleasant sensation. She stirred and reached down to run her hand through Alex's short hair as her tongue flicked her nipple.

Alex looked up, her eyes heavy-lidded. "We're just getting into Memphis. It's morning."

"I could get used to this kind of wake-up call."

Alex winked. "That can be easily arranged." She moved up and captured Tyra's mouth with her own and the conversation stopped for a while as they explored each other more leisurely than they had the night before.

Later, Alex lay behind her, kissing her shoulders. "Being with you gives me strength. I need you to believe I will make this work."

Ty rolled over and looked her in the eyes. "I do believe you. We've both got a few things we need to get our heads around but if we keep talking, we can get through it." She didn't know if that was true, but it felt more doable if they both believed it. She focused on the immediate future. "Can I see you this week? I know you'll have plans, but when you've nothing else on, I mean. A week away from you nearly killed me before. I had to walk myself to exhaustion every day just to try and get some sleep."

Alex leaned on her elbow, a little smirk on her lips. "I have nothing as important as being with you. I've been wanting to ask you to spend the week with me, but I didn't want to be disappointed. And it's good for my ego that you thought of me that much while I was pining over you in New York."

Ty felt her heart beat a little faster. "Sounds like we're both in luck then. Mhairi, Jamie, and Mikki are off to Mexico for a few days. I said I had something planned but I was lying to get out of going with them."

"Perfect." The look in Alex's eyes made her feel warm inside. "I get you all to myself. I've rented a beach house. We can plan my coming out. I need to see both my parents, and my daughter, Dottie. Will you come with me to visit?" Her smile faded.

"If you want me there, of course I will. Are you worried about how they'll react?"

"Not really. My dad will be thrilled for me, and he'll love you. My mom will be glad I've found someone to make me happy, I hope. My daughter, however, is always a difficult audience." Her face clouded for a moment before her smile returned. "I really thought I'd messed things up with you, and it made me realize what's important."

She moved closer and they kissed again.

Ty woke with a start as her phone rang. Rolling out of bed and searching through her jeans on the floor where they had been discarded, she finally located it and answered Mhairi's call.

"Where the hell are you? I've just woken up and your bed's not been slept in. Are you okay?" She sounded so worried Ty felt terrible, but she wasn't sure what to say.

"Hi, oh, God. Sorry, I should've said. I'm uh...with Alex. We stayed up late writing and well...playing some...stuff." She looked helplessly at Alex, who was laughing.

"No more lies." She got up and took the phone from Ty. "Hey there Mhairi, sorry to worry you. Your cousin spent the night in my bed, and I'm hoping it'll become a regular habit. Why don't you guys come over for breakfast in an hour? Fantastic, see you then." She hung up and tossed the phone to Ty, smiling. "That's a start. Begin as we mean to go on, don't you think?" She strolled off to the bathroom.

Ty stared after her, wondering just how serious she was. If Alex was approaching being out and proud with the same level of commitment she gave to everything else, Ty hoped she was also prepared for the public scrutiny and the inevitable backlash her coming out would generate. She shook off that thought and smiled to herself as she headed for the bathroom. An hour was far more time than they needed to shower and dress.

TWENTY-TWO

Alex felt as if a weight had been lifted from her shoulders. She could barely keep her hands off Ty in public, but they had agreed she should talk to both her parents and her daughter first. And Linda hadn't taken the news well. She was insistent that Alex did nothing hasty in the middle of their tour and had brought in their PR manager as backup.

"We can manage this after the tour, Alex. We'll plan every step and ensure we have the right positive media coverage. There's no need to rush something so huge." Kelly was always efficient, and Alex employed her because she knew the business so well. But she didn't want her and Ty to be business, it was too important.

The Memphis show was a great success, and Jamie's performance of the encore song was one of his best yet. The performance was probably helped by the high spirits the band members found themselves in.

Mhairi and Jamie didn't hide how delighted they were for Tyra. Jamie turned up at Alex's dressing room to tell her personally. "I can't tell you how long we've been waiting for Ty to meet someone who could make her as happy as she deserves. She's the kindest, most loving person in the world, Alex."

Alex patted him reassuringly on the knee. "I know, Jamie, you don't need to convince me how wonderful she is."

"But she's more sensitive than she lets on, and she's been hurt before." He looked more serious than usual. "But we both know you'll be really good for her, and you'll always treat her well."

Alex thanked him and promised she would do her best to make Ty happy.

Briefly, she wondered if she had the courage to continue what she'd started, but then she thought about how good it felt to sleep in Ty's arms, and her doubts receded.

The next morning, as they all headed their different ways, Alex spotted Mhairi looking less than her usual upbeat self in the hotel foyer. "Are you having second thoughts about tagging along on the boys' trip to Mexico?"

Mhairi looked embarrassed. "No, of course not." Then she shrugged. "I don't know, Alex, I've always wanted to go to Mexico, and I don't want to miss the opportunity, but I don't think the itinerary will be what I would have planned."

Alex gave her a hug. "If you're not enjoying yourself, just call Ryan. We'll book you a flight and you can come stay with us. There's plenty of room."

"Thank you for watching out for her," Ty said as they got into the car to head for the airport. "But will you stop inviting people to stay with us? I'm in no mood to be keeping the volume down."

Alex gulped at that mental picture, then smiled. "You haven't seen the size of the house Ryan found us. I think we'll be okay."

"I'm gonna need to go shopping," muttered Ty, donning her sunglasses as they stepped off the plane. A droplet of sweat slid down the side of her face. "It's bloody warm here."

"That can be arranged. Have you ever been to Beverly Hills?" Alex grinned.

"Stop showing off. You know I've never been to LA. I'm looking forward to exploring it with you, though."

Alex turned around to face her as they headed for customs, keeping her voice low. "Much as I would love to show you the city where I spent my teenage years, my plans include very few vertical adventures." She lowered her shades and winked.

Ty's cheeks colored but she kept a cool smile plastered on her face. "Well, if you want the paparazzi in arrivals to snap me snogging the face off you, just keep telling me about those plans."

Alex immediately turned back to the front of the line, ignoring the playful nudges from Ty behind her. She focused her attention on how irritating it was that LAX didn't have VIP suite facilities. Of all the places in the world.

Ty had only laughed at her complaint and made jokes about Alex having to slum it in first class immigration and customs queues. "You should try waiting in a queue to board with Ryanair."

But now under the scrutiny they faced in public she was sure Ty would have appreciated a more private VIP experience. They were soon through immigration, with Ryan leading the way to get them to their driver as smoothly as possibly. Alex had replaced her cap and shades and as they emerged into arrivals there were a few quiet seconds before she was recognized, and the shouts and flashes began.

As they'd mainly travelled by bus so far, she was aware Tyra hadn't had much exposure to this level of unplanned media attention, and Alex kept half an eye on her as she waved to journalists and fans, stopping for a selfie with a young girl and her family, giving Ty a chance to muster up a smile and catch up. She could see the strain on her face and wondered if her memories of the past would prove too much.

On the journey to the house Ty stared out of the window at her new surroundings, as Ryan and Alex discussed practical matters around their stay. Alex watched her chewing her bottom lip and knew she was struggling. In an attempt to draw her into the conversation she called her name twice before Ty looked up absently.

"Huh?"

"Ryan's worried about us not having our usual level of security here. I said you would protect us from unwanted visitors."

Ty raised her lip in a snarl and let out a low growl. Ryan laughed and Alex raised her eyebrow suggestively. Ty smiled back but quickly returned her attention to the streets outside.

They were soon at the house, a large white structure with blue shutters located behind a massive security fence that was well away from the house. Once they were parked Alex led Ty inside while Ryan helped the driver and security escort with their luggage.

The house was bright and spacious, with three floors, all facing the ocean, and floor to ceiling windows. The ground floor had a patio leading to the beach and the upper floors had large balconies. Ty wanted to head straight out to see the ocean, but Alex took her hand and pulled her up the open staircase. They needed some time alone.

The top floor was one massive suite. Opening the doors to the balcony, Alex gave a nod of satisfaction that it was high enough to afford them total privacy. Still towing Ty behind her, she moved outside, checked again that they weren't overlooked, and wrapped her in her arms. "Are you okay?" She lifted Ty's chin and forced her to make eye contact.

"I'll need to get used to it, won't I? Sorry, I'm not meaning to make things hard work. It just all came flooding back, the intrusiveness and the rude, insistent questions."

"Don't be so hard on yourself. It took me years to find it normal, and you've got some bad memories from the past that can't help but resurface. It will get easier with time, and I'll always be here next to you." She moved in for a kiss. What started gently soon became insistent and hungry. When they eventually parted, breathless and flushed, Alex gasped. "I've been dreaming about that all day." She held Ty's face in her hands. "I love the ocean but now I'm wishing I'd just got us a very private hotel room."

The kiss had clearly revived Ty's spirits because her cheeky grin was back. "Oh no, you're doing the whole tour guide thing. We've got a full week. There'll be plenty of time for all activities." Ty ran her hands through Alex's hair, gripping it to pull her in closer.

A cough from inside the room revealed Ryan standing in the doorway, laden down with bags.

"Sorry, Ryan, come on in. Thanks." Alex hurried over to help him, while Ty headed to the rail to look over at the ocean. She thanked him again and promised they would join him downstairs later, before she closed the door quietly, moving back out to join Ty on the deck. Alex moved closer, placing her hands on the rail on either side of Ty, savoring the contact as Ty leaned back into her. She ran her teeth gently along the side of her neck and Ty groaned. She forced herself to pull back. "Before we get carried away, how hungry are you?"

Ty turned around, put her arms around Alex's waist and pulled her in tight.

"Ravenous for you." She tipped her head. "But also, fairly peckish. Let's eat."

Alex laughed. "Do you want eat in or go out? Ryan can arrange anything, whatever cuisine takes your fancy."

"How about just a burrito or something and we can eat here?"

Alex smiled, sharing Ty's desire to get eating over with as quickly as possible. She kissed the top of her head and pulled away to go downstairs to talk to Ryan.

When she returned Ty was emerging from the shower, wrapped in an enormous fluffy towel. She beamed at Alex. "I needed that. I feel a million times better."

She discarded the towel, pulling on a pair of boxers she had left out on the bed. Alex stayed where she was, transfixed by the view, until Ty turned to look at her with raised eyebrows. "Are you just gonna stand there watching me?"

Alex moved across the room. "That wasn't what I had in mind."

Ty laughed and pulled her down for a kiss. "Go and shower and I'll give your shoulders a rub before the food arrives. All you did the whole flight was moan about them."

Alex took her shower in record time, keen to make the most of this time with Tyra, just the two of them alone. Well, nearly alone, but Ryan was an expert at being unobtrusive and would stick to his side of the house unless she needed him. The quiet break would be good for him, too.

She could barely believe that in a few short days she and Ty had gone from friends to being together, and she was about to introduce her to her family. But they still had so much to work out, including how they would make their relationship public and deal with the consequences of that. Not to mention how they managed their separate careers on different continents in the future. She dismissed her thoughts and went to find Ty. Her worries could wait till later.

Ty wanted to ask Alex a question but wasn't sure how it would be received. They'd emerged from the bedroom and were hanging out with Ryan in the living area. Alex was reading a book and Ty scribbled in her notebook, looking much busier than she really was. *Just ask her.* Finally the words came out in a rush. "Aren't you keen to catch up with your daughter?"

Alex looked up and blinked. Ty had asked few questions about Dottie since she realized Alex didn't like to talk about her troubled relationship with her child. But they were in the city where she lived. Why would seeing her not be a top priority?

"I'd love to see her, but I'm not sure how she feels about seeing me. She knows I'm in town. I'll call her tomorrow."

"You're seeing your dad tomorrow. We don't have plans for tonight. Why don't you go and see her?" Ty somehow kept the smile on her face as Alex pinned her with the most intimidating stare she'd seen in a long time.

"Leave it, Ty. I'll see her when it's convenient for everyone."

Ty shrugged. "Sounds like you're putting it off. Call her, at least. If she knows you're in LA, will she not expect you to make contact?"

Alex jumped up from the chair, grabbing her phone as she marched towards the stairs. "Fine, I'll call her. Anything to get you off my back."

Ryan looked up from his laptop. "That was brave. She's not accustomed to being told what to do."

"I know that. What's her problem with calling her daughter?"

"She's carrying a lot of guilt about not being there for her over the years. She tried her best, coming out to LA whenever she was free, taking Dottie to New York for Christmas every year. She has a great relationship with Dottie's dad, Billy, and his wife Clara, but when Dorothy got to maybe twelve, she got resentful and said she didn't want her drifting in and out of her life. Alex was distraught. They only saw each other about once a year for a while, and it was strained. Things have improved a little over the last year, but Alex is terrified of being rejected again. Go easy on her."

Before Ty could reply, they heard the door open upstairs and Alex taking the stairs two at a time.

"Right, MacLean, this was your idea. You're coming with me."

"Are you sure? Would you not prefer some alone time with Dottie?"

"Oh no, you're not ducking out now. On your advice I'm going to the house of my ex-husband and my oldest friend to have dinner with the angriest young woman I've ever met and her two overly excitable half-brothers. So you get to enjoy the whole experience too. Oh, and it turns out my daughter, who has hated every record I've ever made, is a massive DandyLions fan. She's disappointed I can't just magic Jamie from nowhere, but she'll make do with you. I've called the car. We leave in an hour." She turned and stomped back up the stairs.

Ty hadn't moved. She turned to Ryan.

"I get the feeling this might not be much fun?"

"She'll be fine when she gets there. It's a good sign Dot wants to see her at all, but sometimes she just lays into her. Take care of her, will you?"

"Always." Tyra smiled reassuringly. "It's my job now." She didn't feel so confident inside as she pushed up out of the chair to prepare for their visit. Maybe she should've kept her mouth shut. She didn't want Alex to get hurt and surely she knew the best way to handle her own daughter. And now she had roped herself into meeting Alex's child and closest friends. She'd promised to be there for Alex, but it didn't feel like the gradual approach she needed. She took the stairs slowly, preparing herself to be upbeat and positive. She'd face her own concerns when this ordeal was over.

TWENTY-THREE

On the journey, Ty teased more information out of Alex. The car had a privacy screen, so Ty made use of it and wrapped Alex in her arms, ignoring the resistance she encountered.

"So, Clara was your best friend?" she asked. "From before you and Billy?"

Alex sighed and relaxed a little. "Yes, she came up to me on my first day in my new school, and told me she would be my friend, even if everyone else thought I was weird. And she kept her word. She was the most loyal, loving friend anyone could ask for. When I went to college, she stayed out here, got a part in a long running serial, and ended up a pretty successful actor. I got pregnant when I was twenty, and when Billy and I got married Clara used to come visit. She was worried I had made a terrible mistake starting a family so young, but she and Billy got on really well." She laughed bitterly. "When I finally got my recording contract and had to come out to LA to record with Nick, Clara insisted we all stay in her new house. She had plenty of room and she was on a break from her soap opera. Her character had gone traveling or something, so she had plenty of time to help look after Dottie. I was at the studio twelve hours a day, so it seemed like the perfect arrangement. She was Dorothy's godmother and I wanted them to build a bond. But it wasn't just my daughter Clara made a connection with. After a few weeks even I, distracted as I was, could see what was happening."

She looked up at Ty, her eyes glistening.

"I confronted them, and they denied anything was going on. And it wasn't. They were both such good people, they would never have betrayed me, however strong their feelings. I finally lost it in a pretty spectacular way and told them to get on with it. I knew if I took Dottie home with me, she would spend her life being cared for by nannies and paid assistants and here she had two people in a loving relationship who were much more capable of giving her a stable, loving upbringing. I went back east on my own, even though it broke my heart."

Ty could see the tears in her eyes and couldn't imagine the loss Alex must have felt. "But you had regular time with Dorothy, and you were a part of her growing up, yeah? And you maintained a good relationship with Billy and Clara. Loads of good parents don't get to spend every day with their children."

"I know all of that, Ty. But I've never been able to get over the guilt that I let her down when she needed me most. Every time I see her it's all I can think of. It was bad enough when she was small, but when she was old enough to accuse me of exactly what I feared, it became so painful I was secretly glad whenever she cancelled a meet-up. And then the guilt just got worse." She rubbed her eyes. "Can we talk about this later? I really need to get my shit together now."

Ty stroked her hair. "I'm sorry, I was asking so I know

what we're walking into, I didn't mean to drag all the pain up. I'm just here to support you."

"Yeah, I know." Alex shook herself and straightened her shoulders. "Okay, so the main points are Billy and Clara have been together for, uh, nearly fifteen years. As well as Dot they have two sons, Nathan and Ethan." She cleared her throat. "They're a real close family but I've somehow managed to remain a part of it."

Ty squeezed her arm. "It's gonna be fine. I've got your back." When the car pulled up at the house Ty stepped out first and gave Alex a hand to get out. She was wearing a turquoise shirt that made the green of her eyes stand out. Her light brown skin was glowing, and Ty was taken aback all over again by how beautiful she was.

"Will you stop letching at me and get on with this." Alex scowled and swung the duffle bag at Ty's middle. "Make yourself useful."

"Oh, yes, ma'am, of course. Forgive me for assuming Alexandra Knight could carry her own bag." Ty didn't let up as they walked up to the house, hoping her light-hearted teasing was easing the mood.

A lanky, sandy-haired man answered the door, smiling broadly. He embraced Alex in a warm hug and turned to greet Ty.

"Ty, meet Billy Montgomery. Billy, this is Tyra MacLean. She and her band are touring with me at the moment."

Ty winced internally at being designated a work colleague. They hadn't made any announcements, but it still struck a nerve. She shoved it away and smiled.

"I know who this is." Billy laughed. "I live with one of DandyLions' biggest fans!"

He grasped Ty's proffered hand in both of his and shook

it enthusiastically.

Billy led them into the house and a large open plan living area. Two boys aged around ten and twelve, both with Billy's sandy hair, were cutting vegetables at an island in the kitchen area. When they saw Alex, they abandoned tools and ran over to hug her.

"I might make you smell like onions 'cause Mom made us cut up all the veggies," the smaller one confided.

"Less complaining, more chopping." A tall blond woman with striking cheekbones and dark brown eyes swept into the room. She threw herself at Alex, wrapping her up in a hug that lifted her off the ground. "I've missed you so much, short stuff. It's been far too long."

Ty laughed at the endearment. She was accustomed to forever being the shortest person in the room so hearing Alex being teased for her height was a novelty.

Alex regained her footing and some of her composure and smiled back. "Missed you too, Clara. You know I've been touring all year, right? So plenty of opportunities to come and see me."

Clara chuckled. "We've missed you, but not quite enough to travel to Europe." She turned and pulled Ty into a three-way embrace. "Tyra MacLean, it's very good to meet you."

Alex freed herself from Clara's arms with difficulty. "Ty, this is my oldest and dearest friend, Clara Montgomery." She waved towards the two boys. "And these two vegetable-scented angels are Nathan and Ethan."

The boys dutifully held out their hands to shake Ty's, then, seeing their opportunity, made a dash to escape further kitchen duties. Clara shook her head in mock disgust as she led them to a pair of high stools on the far side of the kitchen.

"Come talk to me while I finish this damn cooking. You can tell me about the tour."

She poured them both a very large glass of wine and topped up her own. "I'm sorry, Tyra, dinner may be delayed. Billy is the chef in this house. I offered to cook to impress Alex but to be honest, I'm not sure what I'm doing."

Alex rolled her eyes. "Actors!"

Ty stood, laughing. "I really don't think you should be judging anyone's cooking abilities." She turned to Clara. "Can I replace your recently departed assistants and get some of that chopping done?"

She turned back from washing her hands to find Clara sitting down next to Alex, glass in hand. She chuckled and focused on the job at hand, listening to the two friends chatting away.

"I'm impressed, Alex. Domesticated, a talented musician, and very pleasing to the eye. You've chosen your 'opening act' well."

Ty looked over her shoulder to see Clara grinning as she did air quotes. Alex was half smiling but looked preoccupied. There hadn't been any mention of her daughter.

Ty cleared her throat. "I hope you two are not objectifying me over there."

Alex looked over at her, an intense look in her eyes. She turned her attention back to her friend. "To be completely honest, Clara, Ty is a lot more than my opening act, and I want to talk to Dot before it gets out there." She sighed and smiled at Ty. "Which will be pretty soon because I can't keep my hands off her."

Ty blew her a kiss and saw Clara's eyes widen before she broke into a wide smile. She took Alex's hands in her own. "I'm so pleased for you. But two things about Dory.

Her initial reaction will probably be anger for confirming you've been in the closet all these years. You have to remember she's fifteen and has no idea what it was like to come out back in the day. You need to prepare yourself for that, honey. Secondly, please don't call her Dot. She's told you so many times she's Dory now. I know she'll always be your little Dottie, but you push all her buttons when you ignore what she wants to be called. Make an effort."

"Okay. Dory, like the damned fish," Alex muttered.

"And no comments like that." Clara swatted her in an exasperated manner. "Sometimes I think you're trying to get a reaction." She turned to Tyra. "Dory is a polite, intelligent young woman. But somehow, when these two get together it goes head-to-head pretty quickly."

Seeing Alex looking miserable, Ty leaned over from her cooking duties to give her a peck on the cheek. "It'll be okay."

Billy entered the kitchen and looked from Ty, busy at the stove, to his wife sitting drinking wine and shook his head. "Wow, Clara, it didn't take you long to hand over the oven mitts."

"It's fine." Ty waved a wooden spoon. "I love cooking, and the boys had done all the hard work."

Billy smiled at her warmly. "Well, thank you for ensuring we don't all starve." He mock glared at his wife and turned to Alex. "Dory's on her way down. She had her headphones on and didn't hear the door."

Alex gave a brief nod. "Of course."

They heard a loud tread on the stair and the kitchen door swung open. Ty hadn't thought much about what to expect of Alex's daughter, but what she hadn't anticipated was a smaller, slighter carbon copy of Alex. She had the same golden-brown skin and glossy black hair, although cropped very short. The icy green glare was also familiar, and she was relieved to see it soften as they made eye contact.

"Hey, Dory." Alex's voice was soft and hesitant. She stood and Dory embraced her awkwardly.

"Hi, Alex."

Alex's face fell.

"Dory!" Clara barked. "Speak to your mother properly."

Dory sighed dramatically. "Sorry. Hi *Mom*, how are you?"

Alex smiled and squeezed her daughter tight. "I'm all the better for seeing you." She turned, her arm still around Dory's shoulder. "Dory, I'd like you to meet Tyra MacLean, I think you've heard of her. Ty, meet my amazing daughter, Dory."

Dory removed herself from her mother's clutches and moved quickly across the kitchen to shake Ty's hastily wiped hand.

"Hi, I love your band. I can't wait to see you in a couple of weeks. What cover song will you be doing? Will Jamie be singing it?"

Ty grinned, laughing to herself at how the subject of conversation had moved to Jamie in record time. "Hi, Dory, it's good to meet you. The covers are kept top secret, and we don't really decide until near the time. Jamie would sing them all if we let him."

"Maybe you *should* let him. Can I meet him?"

"Of course, but you might be disappointed. He's very loud, and boring, and he's got really bad breath."

Dory looked horrified for a moment until Alex stepped in. "Ty, don't be a tease. The poor boy isn't here to defend himself. Dory, of course you can meet Jamie, and the rest of the band."

Dory looked pleased and even smiled briefly at her mother. Ty realized Billy and Clara had been holding their breath for the entire exchange, and now the mood in the room tangibly lightened. She spoke up. "Let me finish off this food. Should be about ten minutes. Where are my kitchen staff? Have they got table laying duties to carry out?"

Fifteen minutes later everyone was sitting around a large dining table, passing a salad bowl. Alex and Ty sat beside one another, facing Dory and the smaller brother, who Ty was reasonably confident was Ethan. The older one sat next to Alex, and their parents were at either end. Conversation was amicable.

"Alex, did you bring us some merch?" Both boys had expectant looks on their faces.

"Ethan, remember your manners. Eat your food and stop bothering Alex," Billy growled.

Alex winked conspiratorially and Ethan grinned.

Ty had prepared a large bowl of pasta with a fresh sauce she had cooked up, and some chorizo fried in red wine. Everyone made appreciative noises as they started to eat.

"This is amazing, not at all what I had planned with the ingredients." Clara laughed. "You've all had a lucky escape."

"Alex can't cook either. You should see her kitchen. It's straight out of the showroom." *Shit, was that too much detail?* She looked at Alex uneasily.

Dory was looking from one to the other with interest. She smiled slyly. "So what exactly is your role on this tour, Tyra? And how much time have you spent in my mother's kitchen?"

Alex took a deep breath and put her knife and fork down. "Tyra isn't just a musician on my tour, Dory, we're seeing each other. It's a recent thing but I wanted you to know first."

Ty had been wondering how Alex would broach the subject with her daughter but hadn't expected it to happen quite so early in their visit. Neither had Alex, if the tension coming off her was any indication. Ty took her hand under the table, squeezing it supportively as she looked around at the silent diners.

Clara was smiling, Billy looked surprised but pleased, and the boys were grinning, watching their sister for a reaction. Dory's face was still as she looked at her mother steadily, clearly making her mother wait for a reaction.

Dory turned her head and caught Ty's eye. "Well good luck with that, Ty. My mother has a poor track record of making people happy." She picked up her fork to continue eating.

"Dory!" Clara's shocked voice was louder than the exclamations from her father and brothers. "We've talked about the way you speak to your mom. That is not acceptable. Don't you want to congratulate her?"

Ty saw the tears in Alex's eyes and placed their joined hands together on the table in full view.

"It's okay, Clara, Alex wanted to come today and share our good news. If Dory isn't mature enough to be pleased for her mother, that's a shame, but our happiness doesn't depend on her blessing."

Dory looked up, shocked. Ty got the impression she wasn't used to being spoken to in that way. She looked around the table for someone to leap to her defense, and when that wasn't forthcoming, she threw her cutlery down and stormed out of the room, stomping up the stairs two at a time in a way that reminded Ty of Alex's behavior early in the day.

Alex looked down at her plate and picked at a piece of chorizo. Billy cleared his throat. "Boys, why don't you take your bowls into the playroom. You can watch TV while you eat. Special treat!"

The boys didn't need to be told twice. They rushed out of the room as fast as they could without spilling food. "Yeah," Nathan said as he left the room. "And you guys can stay and talk about what a bitch Dory is."

"Nathan Montgomery, you can look forward to your punishment when our visitors have left." Clara's tone was ominous. When they were gone, she turned back to Alex. "Please don't take it to heart, Alex. I'm sure she's pleased for you; she just doesn't know how to express it."

Alex looked up, tears escaping down her cheeks. "I sometimes wonder if I'll ever do anything she'll be proud of."

"She was pretty hyped about you having Ty's band on your tour. She hasn't stopped talking about it for weeks. I think she just finds it hard face-to-face, and she lashes out." Billy got up to clear the now empty bowls, squeezing Alex's shoulder on his way past.

Ty felt she had to do something to help Alex. She stood up. "D'you mind if I go and have a chat?"

Alex and Clara both looked up, surprised. Alex shrugged and Clara smiled warmly. "Of course not, but don't be surprised if she doesn't let you in. Top floor, the door on your left. You'll know it by the DandyLions poster."

Ty smiled more confidently than she felt as she left the room. "If I'm not back in half an hour, call the emergency services."

Clara pulled up a chair next to Alex and drew her into a hug. "I really have missed you. Why don't we relax on the couch and Billy will bring us some wine?"

The couch was white leather and the size of a regular living room. Alex was sure the whole family could fit on it at once. She slumped into it alongside her oldest friend. "It's so exhausting. Do you think she'll grow out of it?"

"Of course she will. We've talked about this so many times, Alex. The important thing is that she knows you're there for her, no matter how often she tries to drive you away."

Alex sighed and rested her head on Clara's shoulder. When she had first realized Clara and Billy were falling in love, she had thought her whole world was over. But it had turned out for the best. "I know it's been difficult for us at times over the years but I'm so glad it's you who's been there for her, Clara. If it had to be anyone other than me, I would always have chosen you."

Clara pulled her closer. "It's been my honor. She is a wonderful young woman, most of the time, and *so* like you, it's been a pleasure to have you in my life in some way." She stroked Alex's hair soothingly. They both started at an unexpected voice behind them.

"I'm sorry for being rude to you, Alex. Mom, I mean. I'm happy for you, and pleased you feel you can finally live your life honestly. Openly, that is." Dory stood in the doorway, head high and fists shoved in her pockets. Ty waited in the corridor behind her.

"And Mom." She turned to Clara. "I'm sorry I embarrassed you and Dad in front of our guests."

Alex tried to keep her face neutral. She had never known Dory to back down and apologize. Her usual pattern of behavior after an outburst would be to hide in her room until her parents insisted on her presence, and then to sit moodily in a corner, ignoring everyone. Alex had often cried the entire journey home after one of those visits. She wondered what mystical powers Ty possessed, and then remembered she had helped raise the twins. She couldn't imagine Mhairi had been a difficult child, but a teenage Jamie would undoubtedly have given anyone a run for their money.

"Come and sit down, sweetheart." Clara patted the couch next to her. "Apology accepted."

Alex nodded her own acceptance and smiled at Dory, not trusting herself to speak. She came to sit, but instead of where her stepmother had indicated, she squeezed herself between Clara and Alex, both of them shuffling over to give her room. Ty strolled in nonchalantly and pulled up a nearby beanbag to sit on the floor by Alex's legs. Alex looked down and raised her eyebrows. Ty smiled back and shook her head imperceptibly.

Billy appeared, juggling champagne glasses, and did a double take at the scene before him. "Did I miss something?"

"Only Dory apologizing," Clara replied.

"Can I have champagne?" Dory smiled a saintly smile.

"A small one, and don't gulp it." Billy went to fill another glass and returned, handing it to her and raising his own glass. "I'd like to raise a toast to a very special member of this family." He looked over at Alex.

She would prefer less fuss, but he had always been more inclined to make big emotional scenes, even when they had been very young. She always knew exactly where she stood with him because he told her. *Maybe that's where I went wrong.* She shook herself back into the present. Billy was still making his speech.

"I've hoped you would one day find the kind of happiness Clara and I have together, Alex. To Alex and Tyra." He raised his glass. They all repeated the gesture, and Alex and Ty clinked their glasses and smiled.

Nathan and Ethan appeared suddenly. "Why do we always get left out of celebrations?"

"Because the thought of you two fueled by alcohol is chilling," their mother replied.

"Anyway, we found this bag. Like, just abandoned by the door." They displayed Alex's duffle bag between them, eyes wide. "We were worried it might be a bomb or something."

Clara raised an eyebrow. "So you brought it in here to show us?"

"You want us to deal with a bomb on our own? We're just kids!" The boys shook their heads in fake indignation. Laughing, Ty got up and took the bag from them, handing it to Alex. Unzipping it, Alex removed a full set of her branded items for each of the boys, who started ripping off their T-shirts to try everything on. Billy looked on expectantly until a tour cap appeared. He grinned and put it on backwards as Clara was handed a T-shirt. Finally, Alex pulled out a DandyLions hoodie, with the band logo emblazoned across the back.

"We'll get Jamie to sign it for you when you see him," Ty said.

"Thank you, that's amazing." Dory beamed. She looked across at her brothers in their AK World Tour t-shirts. "But is there a chance I could get one of those too, please?"

Alex smiled and nodded, as casually as she could manage. "Of course, I'll get one sent over." Inside, her heart melted with joy.

TWENTY-FOUR

Later, in bed, Alex asked if Ty would tell her secret for Dory-taming.

Ty laughed. "What can I say, I'm a teenager whisperer. Sometimes if someone's trying to shock with their behavior, the trick is not to react. And I, as you well know, am not easily shockable." She gazed down at Alex who lay on her side, resting her head on Ty's chest. "When did she start calling you by name? It must really hurt you."

Alex wrapped her arms around Ty's middle. "When she was small, Dory called both me and Clara mom, but when she hit her teens, she claimed it was too confusing and began to call me Alex. Clara and Billy pulled her up on it all the time, but she could see how much it hurt me, and she used it to full effect. When we were alone it just felt easier to let it go."

"Y'know I'm not really into the whole therapy thing, but do you think maybe the two of you could do with some counseling? From the outside it looks like you've been a great parent, spending as much quality time with Dory as possible. But it seems she feels you deserted her. And you've got a lot of guilt going on. I guess it's the norm in society for fathers to have that kind of relationship with their children and no one bats an eyelid. Women get accused of deserting their kids, however genuine their reasons for being the part-time parent. Maybe you could talk some of that through?"

She felt Alex's deep sigh reverberate through her rib cage. "You may be right. I'd do anything for more evenings like tonight. I would need to talk her into it."

Ty took a quick breath. "Maybe you could mention it if she comes down to San Diego?"

Alex sat up. "What? When was this agreed? Ty, you know I hate it when things are arranged without my knowledge. Times that by ten when it involves my tour schedule and my kid."

She definitely could've handled that more smoothly. She put a soothing hand on Alex's shoulder. "Whoa, calm down, Al. It was just an idea. Dory mentioned tonight she'd never been on the road with you. I had a quick look at the schedule and thought if she got herself down to San Diego before the gig, she could travel back up with us over the weekend and it would give you two time to hang out. I checked with Billy but asked him to hold off on telling her until I had run it by you. Sorry, I shouldn't have sprung it on you."

She continued the shoulder rub, giving Alex time to process the idea.

Alex looked up. "Ryan would look after her during the show. We'd have all the next day to ourselves and she could see the logistics of setting up for a gig. It could be fun."

Ryan was right, Alex did like to process things herself. "Hey, Al, that's a great idea, well done!"

Alex turned to face her, frowning. "There's no need to

be sarcastic. And I'm sorry I snapped at you; it does sound like a good idea. But if I'm honest, Dot...Dory, makes me really nervous. What if she lets loose in front of my crew? That would be..."

Her mouth snapped shut and Ty could see the internal catastrophizing going on. She gently pushed Alex back down on the bed. "You mean, your employees might see you've not got one hundred per cent control over every aspect of your life? That you have a teenager to deal with?" She deepened the massage on Alex's ever-tense shoulders. "Don't worry, I'll make sure she's kept occupied. I'll get Jamie on the case."

Alex's head shot back up again, her eyes hard. "You make sure that walking heap of testosterone understands she's a child. If he did anything inappropriate, I'd kill him."

Ty drew back, frowning. "Hey, that's a wee bit offensive. I understand you feel protective, but Jamie is not the kind of guy who'd take advantage of his friend's kid. Or any kid. She's fifteen, for fuck's sake."

Alex ran her hand over her face. "I'm so sorry, Ty, that was totally out of order. I know Jamie is an honorable person. And that probably has a lot to do with his upbringing." She sighed. "I overreact sometimes when it comes to Dory."

Ty took a deep breath and let go of her anger. "And I just did the same thing for Jamie. You probably feel even more of a protective instinct because you've never had the opportunity to look out for her as much as you would have wanted to." She returned her attention to Alex's shoulders and felt them relax. "She's a great kid, I really warmed to her. And she does love you, she's just got problems expressing her feelings. Have a think about the therapy."

As Alex's breathing slowed and she drifted off Ty lay

for a while longer in the dark, wondering at how quickly she had gone from someone who didn't believe in relationships, to advising Alex on her how to deal with her child. It felt natural, but at the same time, the speed at which things were moving was disconcerting.

The next day began with a drive to meet Alex's father, Sunil for brunch. Alex took Ty's hand. "I'm sorry. I lured you to LA with talk of lounging by the ocean, but all you've done so far is met my family. I promise there aren't many members left, and we'll try and put my mom off until later in the week."

"No bother." Ty laughed, squeezing her fingers in reassurance. "Meeting your family gives me insight into you, and you're my favorite subject."

"You sweet-talker. You may not be so keen on the insight you get from meeting my mother, but Dad is lovely."

The restaurant Ryan had selected had a large terrace overlooking the ocean. They were directed to a private table with a great view. Sunil was already there and stood to greet Alex with a warm embrace.

When they separated, Alex turned. "Dad, I'd like to introduce you to Tyra MacLean."

Sunil gave Ty an equally enthusiastic hug. "It's good to meet you, Tyra. As this is the first time my daughter has ever bothered to introduce me to anyone in her life, I can only assume she's found her match."

Ty smiled, slightly taken aback by his broad Yorkshire accent. "Great to meet you too, Sunil, I've heard a lot about you. All good," she added.

Sunil was a tall man with a thick head of hair, clearly

where Alex got her lustrous locks. Ty had assumed it was Alex's mixed heritage that had given her lighter eyes and was surprised to see Sunil's eyes were the same green.

They sat and ordered food, before Sunil asked, "How is my favorite daughter?"

Ty looked up at that. Alex had never mentioned siblings. She raised an eyebrow at Alex, who laughed.

"That's Dad's idea of a joke. I'm definitely his only daughter, his only child. That's why the pressure was always on me to succeed."

Sunil's bellow of laughter drew a couple of looks from neighboring tables. "You put enough pressure on yourself, I didn't need to bother. You're truly your mother's daughter in that respect."

"Hey, Dad, no spoilers, Ty's looking forward to the full Francesca Knight show later in the week."

Sunil laughed again and then sighed in pleasure as their food was delivered to their table.

Alex definitely hadn't got her repressed emotion from this side of the family. Ty watched them interact with fascination.

Sunil managed a question as he tucked into his food with enthusiasm. "So, what news have you got for your father? I haven't seen you since February and you've been so busy with your tour, I haven't wanted to bother you."

Alex bit her lip before answering. "Nothing much. I've mostly been on the road, writing some songs, starting a relationship with Ty, and it's likely to go public soon, just the usual sort of thing." Her food was still untouched, and she twisted her napkin as she spoke.

Sunil put down his knife and stilled her hand, covering it with his own larger one. "Alex, it'll be okay. You're at the height of your popularity. Look at this tour, it sold out in days, didn't it?"

She nodded slightly.

"And your performances with Tyra's band have been some of the highlights. Any negative press will be far outweighed by the positives."

"Thanks, Dad, I know that. And I know you support me, but I wanted you to know before the shit hits the fan."

"I appreciate that. What I appreciate even more is the opportunity to meet Tyra MacLean." He turned to Ty. "I loved your music in the Eighties, but Francesca was *not* a fan. She thought you were a troublemaker, a lefty."

"She was right." Ty grinned. "Still am."

"How did I not know this?" Alex shook her head.

"You didn't manage to educate your daughter with your taste in good music? She'd never heard of me when we first met." Ty thought Alex was in need of some teasing to lighten the mood, and she seemed to have a good relationship with her father.

Sunil rubbed his chin. "Why did I not introduce my eight-year-old daughter to songs my wife wouldn't let me play in the house? Why was that now?"

After a pleasant meal with plenty of laughter, they parted company. Alex was pleased to hear that her father had managed to arrange a meet-up with his granddaughter around his busy schedule. Sunil hadn't seen Dory for three years, Alex explained to Ty in the car afterwards, which was yet another source of guilt about her daughter.

"He's a grown man. He could have organized a visit before now. Stop taking on everyone else's responsibilities."

"He lives on another continent, so it's much more difficult for him. And he's not my mother. She's spent at least a weekend every couple of months with Dory since she was a baby, whether anyone else wants it or not. She sees far more of her than I do these days."

"I can't wait to meet her," said Ty. "She sounds impressive." She looked out through the tinted window at the glimpses of sun-kissed ocean between the buildings. The variety and sprawling scale of the place was difficult to appreciate for someone who'd spent most of her life in what was a tiny town by comparison. Sometimes she wondered if Alex noticed her mouth hanging open in wonder like a tourist. "What are our plans for the rest of the day?"

"I'd love to say sitting on our balcony, reading, and watching the ocean, but Clara asked if we wanted to join them at their beach club after the boys finish school. What do you think?"

"I think that sounds fun. Let's not make any plans for tomorrow though, hey? I need some Alex time."

Alex slid across the car seat and kissed her neck. "You can have me all night long if you want to."

"Sounds good to me. For now, unless you want me parading in my underwear on the beach later, we're gonna need to go shopping."

They detoured to Beverly Hills and Alex had fun showing Ty around her favorite shops, holding up unsuitable items and making Ty laugh hysterically. When they had everything they needed, they headed back to the car. Alex was in her usual disguise, but Ty noticed a few cameras and phones pointing their way. "You okay with this?" she asked.

Alex nodded. "Yeah, but I'll be happier when I can hold your hand in public and we can turn speculation into fact. We need to talk to my mom."

When they met up with Clara and the boys, Alex was surprised and delighted to see Dory had also turned up, although she was fully clothed while everyone else was dressed to play in the surf. But after an encouraging comment from Ty, she'd run to get changed into her wetsuit.

The boys howled as Ty revealed her new shortie wetsuit. "You're gonna freeze! It's nearly winter."

She kicked sand at Ethan. "Are you kidding me? It's warmer here than it is in the middle of summer at home. You kids need to toughen up!" She took off, laughing at the boys' outrage as they chased her down the beach.

Alex stopped to appreciate the sight of Ty running in her close-fitting wetsuit.

Clara nudged her. "You can't keep your eyes off her, can you? I don't blame you, she's great for her age." She ran away after the boys, laughing at Alex's look of indignation.

Dory joined the boys in their amusement at Ty's attempts with a board, but Alex was surprised to see her spend time explaining technique. Ty was a quick learner, and her low center of gravity gave her an advantage. Alex was happy just watching them.

As she was walking up the beach Ty caught up with her. "Did y'see me? I stood up for ages!" She was grinning from ear to ear, but her lips had a blue tinge.

Alex raised her eyebrow. "Are you starting to wish you'd chosen a warmer wetsuit?"

"Oh, absolutely. I can't stop moving or I'll freeze in place but I'm not giving those two clowns the opportunity to say I told you so. None of those bloody movies show the surfers freezing to death. Who knew the water would be so *cold*?"

"Why don't we call it a day?" Alex leaned in close.

"And don't worry, I'll enjoy warming you up later." She felt Ty shiver before she ran off back down the beach to round up the young people.

As they walked back, Alex followed behind Dory and Ty, who was talking about Jamie's love of surfing. "He goes as often as he can to a place in Kintyre. It's so beautiful, but really isolated."

"Do you think I could go there one day? Maybe you and my mom could take me?" Dory looked hopefully at her.

Ty caught Alex's eye and winked. "I don't see why not. Maybe during summertime. The water's pretty cold there at the moment." She laughed and rubbed at her goosebumps. "Not that it's warm here, either."

Alex felt a strange mix of gratitude for Ty building a relationship with her daughter, and envy at the easy way they interacted. Dory went to get showered, and Ty wandered over, shaking her head and covering Alex in droplets of cold water, laughing as she jumped back.

"Did you hear that? Dory wants us to take her to the UK to walk in the footsteps of the almighty Jamie. She's gonna be so disappointed when's she meets him. Oh, and did you hear the M word?"

Alex took her face in both hands and kissed her hard.

Ty kissed her back but pulled away quickly. "Alex, we're in a public place. Are you sure you're comfortable for this to hit the news right now?"

"I couldn't help myself, you're so sweet. And this is a very exclusive club. People pay good money to keep their privacy intact."

Ty smiled, her teeth chattering slightly. "I do love kissing you, but I've spent the last hour pretending I can still feel my extremities. Can we continue that kiss at home?" She ran off toward the beach house to change.

Alex sat down on the sand, alone with nothing but the sound of the surf sliding over the pebbles. Life was changing rapidly, and she needed to remember to slow down and relax or she would freak out. Tyra was amazing, but their conversation had started her worrying. Dory had asked about them taking her to the UK, and it made her think about their future and its possibilities. They hadn't talked much about anything beyond the immediate future yet, it seemed too soon. She sighed and tucked her chin on her knees. She wasn't accustomed to thinking about relationships, and all their complications and uncertainties. What if she screwed everything up? She could lose everything she'd worked so hard for by gambling on what she had with Ty. It felt worth the risk, but what if she was wrong?

TWENTY-FIVE

Thoroughly warmed up and relaxing on the couch that evening, Ty had to gently nudge Alex to make arrangements with her mother.

"I know. I just don't want to." Alex stuck out her bottom lip but picked up her phone. "Please stay?" She waved Ty back as she started to leave the room. "But I can't put her on speaker in case you listen in and make me laugh."

Ty settled back on the couch next to her, doing her best mock serious face. Alex slapped her arm playfully and turned away as the call connected.

"Hi, Mom...Yes, I am... Just a few days... I've been spending time with Dory, and I needed to see Dad while he was in town... No, you're not last on my list. I checked your availability, and you were busy the last few days...I know, Mom, I checked with your office months ago and changed my dates to make sure you weren't away while I was here... No, I didn't get those messages, sorry."

Alex rolled her eyes, and her tone became slightly impatient.

"Okay, we're free Wednesday through Friday, do any of

those days work...Tyra MacLean, my friend, she's staying with me... No, Mom, she's my guest, and I'd like you to meet her, she's definitely coming... Thursday at eight at the usual place... Yes, I'll make sure it's a private table. Look forward to seeing you then. Love you, Mom, good-bye." She dropped the phone on her lap and leaned back on the couch, her eyes closed. "I can never get anything right with her."

Ty turned her around so she could reach her shoulders. "Wow, you're tense. She really gets to you, doesn't she?"

"Every word is laden with disappointment. She wasn't impressed you're coming to dinner with us." She turned her head to kiss Ty's fingers. "I don't want her to be mean to you."

Ty laughed. "Does anything you've learned about me so far suggest I'm easily intimidated? Let's go to bed and I'll take your mind off tomorrow." She smiled convincingly and stood, pulling Alex with her.

She was happy Alex wanted her to meet her family, and to tell them about their new relationship, but she had hoped for a few days of relaxation and a chance to discuss their hopes and dreams. And what they wanted from the relationship neither of them had expected to ever have. But so far, she had enjoyed getting to know Alex's family. She hoped her mother wouldn't be the exception. Surely, she couldn't be as intimidating as Alex was suggesting.

Halfway through the fanciest meal she'd eaten for years, Ty was starting to suspect Alex had actually underplayed her mother's forceful personality. After a formal round of greetings and introductions, Francesca had launched into a list of poor decisions she felt Alex had made recently. Alex didn't like to surround herself with sycophants and grovellers, but most people in her life treated her with a level of deference. Her mother clearly did not.

Now that the inquisition into Alex's business affairs was finally over, Francesca turned her beady glare to Ty. There was no warmth in her gray eyes. "I'll be honest, I'm unsure why Alexandra has brought you along today."

Ty swallowed her food hastily before she opened her mouth to speak, but Alex beat her to it.

"Mother, Tyra and I are seeing each other. I care very much for her, and the time has come for me to be honest about who I am." Her voice was firm but strained.

Francesca sighed and put down her fork. She rested her hand lightly on top of Alex's. "I am pleased for you, Alexandra. I did worry you would never find someone with whom to share your life." She smiled slightly. "I thought you were, like myself, too much of a perfectionist."

Alex smiled back. "Thank you, Mother, that's good to hear."

"However, I do think you need to be prepared to face a lot of media interest. Your career is stable enough to be able to withstand any negative backlash you might get from what is unlikely to be a large section of your audience. But you will need to accept that not everyone will be as happy about this as you are." Alex nodded her understanding and Francesca turned her attention back to Ty. "I remember your name vaguely from long ago. Tell me what you have been doing since then."

Ty answered as briefly and honestly as she could, without going into too much sordid detail, but Francesca had clearly done her own research. "I understand you were briefly in psychiatric care after your career ended?"

She doesn't pull any punches. She kept her face calm.

"That's right. My mother's violent death had a profound impact on my mental health." She continued her story until she reached the last couple of years, performing again with DandyLions.

"And it didn't feel uncomfortable at your age, performing with young people in their twenties?" Francesca raised her eyebrow.

She laughed. "Maybe a little, yes. I am definitely too old for this game. The sooner I can put away the drumsticks and get back to my recording studio, the better."

That seemed to be the right answer, as Francesca nodded and returned to discussing Alex's tour. She was clearly pleased when Alex explained Dory was going to join them for a few days on the road, and that she was aware of their relationship and fine with it.

Alex looked relaxed and smiled through the rest of the meal. When they said goodbye to her mother and got back into the car Alex took Ty's hand and kissed her fingers. "I can't believe how well that went. Thank you so much for teaching me a lesson in how not to rise to the bait." Her gaze was soft as she looked at Ty.

Tyra squeezed her fingers. "You're very welcome. Now, just so we're clear, there are no more family visits and I've got you all to myself for these last few days."

TWENTY-SIX

Alex felt a sense of calm as she stared out at the scenery passing by on their drive to Phoenix, despite the pain in her back that was getting gradually worse. Ty was leaning on her shoulder, snoring softly and she didn't want to wake her so she could stretch.

She had been impressed with Ty's handling of her interrogation by Francesca a few nights ago. And with her mother's approval of her decision to go public with their relationship, she felt positive and ready to face a new chapter in her life. Their time together, both with her family and the couple of days they'd spent alone, had made her sure she wanted to be with Ty, whatever the consequences, but she'd avoided talking about what might happen after the end of the tour, and Tyra hadn't brought it up either.

They had changed their original plan to travel the day before to allow them a final visit with Billy and Clara and the kids, so they had made an early morning start, with little opportunity to stretch their legs. And now she was struggling, but she only had herself to blame. *Always stick to the plan.*

They'd made arrangements for Dory to join them in San Diego in a couple of days. She'd been so excited Alex wondered why she had never invited her to watch her perform in the past, then she remembered that Dory had always claimed to hate her music. Jamie was meeting them in Phoenix, and Tyra had promised they could both give him an in-depth briefing on acceptable behavior.

Jamie and Mikki had decided to take a road trip from Mexico to Phoenix, and Mhairi had messaged Ty to say she was heading back to Phoenix after only a couple of days with the boys in Mexico. She had assured Ty she had plenty to do and would be fine alone. That explained why Ryan was so keen to travel down with the equipment earlier than he needed to.

Alex saw the two of them drinking coffee near the buses as she approached. They looked very comfortable, like a couple who had been together for some time. Alex was pleased for them. They both deserved to be happy but being Alex's assistant meant being on call 24/7 and working long hours. She couldn't imagine Ryan being able to do what he did and juggle a relationship. Add in the fact that Mhairi lived on a different continent, and she wondered how they could ever make it work. She didn't want to think about the similar problem she and Ty faced. Ryan looked up as she approached and stiffened.

"Hey, you two, did you have a good break?"

Ryan's gaze shifted between Alex and Mhairi and his cheeks colored. "Yeah, we just bumped into each other down here, so we rented a car and did some sightseeing."

Alex made a mental note to have a talk with him about living his life. She had always known he would need to move on one day, and she didn't want him to jeopardize his chance at happiness. She refused to think about what that might mean for her, but she needed an assistant who could keep up with her intense workload. She returned her focus to the conversation, as Mhairi talked animatedly about their break.

"We drove down to Tucson and saw a lot of desert. It's so beautiful." Her smile was wide. "I've always wanted to visit Arizona."

"Because she luuurves Stevie Nicks." Jamie's loud voice intruded as he strolled up to see what he was missing.

"Well, tonight she gets to show us how much." Alex headed towards her bus, putting aside all thoughts of relationships. "Let's get rehearsing."

The gig was fantastic, as all their shows were, and the cover song was perfect. She sang beside Ty, feeling like it was the most natural thing in the world, and when it was over, she was floored by how grateful she felt for the life she got to lead. And when Ty pulled back the covers on the bus and she slid in beside her, exhausted, it was even better.

Alex rubbed her back and tried to get comfortable in her cramped studio space. She had spent the day showing Ty the sights of San Diego. Ty had wanted to see the city and Alex had promised a day exploring. That had been before her back had begun to spasm in earnest. It had been getting gradually worse, but she hadn't wanted to disappoint Ty, so she had downed some painkillers and gritted her teeth. Now she wanted nothing more than to be lying down, preferably with a strong drink. But Ty was uncharacteristically agitated about their next cover song.

They had been rehearsing with Jamie on vocals, but she wasn't satisfied with the sound. "It's boring, predictable." She was pacing the rehearsal room as she tried to think of a different approach.

Alex knew she needed to tread carefully so she kept her voice soft, tentative even. Which was definitely not her usual style. "You could try the vocals?" Ty looked up sharply and she shrugged to show it was just a suggestion. "You know it well and it would certainly give it a different sound."

Jamie's face dropped at the prospect of another night consigned to backing vocals.

Ty ran her hands through her already disheveled hair. "I don't know. I guess we could try it and go back to Jamie if it doesn't work."

"Oh, yeah, just use me and discard me when it suits you." Jamie threw his hands in the air, only half joking as he stomped out to find Suzi to take over on drums.

Ty's interpretation of the song was original and funny, and they made it a typical Alex and DandyLions crowd pleaser. After another hour of rehearsing they were happy, and Alex heaved a sigh of relief and asked everyone to leave her in peace.

"Are you feeling okay?" Ty's face showed her concern as everyone filed off the bus. "Do you want me to stay?"

"No of course not, Ty. Go and spend some time with your cousins before the show. I'll see you back here later. I just need a bit of time to myself."

Ty nodded, still frowning and gave her a quick kiss before following Jamie outside.

Alex headed straight for her bedroom via the bottle of painkillers in the bathroom cabinet. Some calm and a little sleep and she'd be fine.

Ty was still worrying about Alex as she sat down at the table with her band. Something was bothering her, and she looked unusually strained. She took a long swallow of her beer before Jamie's voice filtered through her thoughts.

"Are you even listening to me, Ty? I'm proper upset here."

She blinked. "No, you're not. You're a bit put out." Alex had earlier issued Jamie with a list of do's and don'ts about his behavior in Dory's company, which he had accepted huffily.

"I know how to behave around kids, you know." His voice cracked slightly.

Ty realized he probably was quite offended. "I know that, Jamie, and so does Alex. No one is accusing you of anything, it's just that you don't always damp down your... you-ness, even around kids." She rubbed his arm. "Alex is very protective of Dory and the kid is pretty nuts about you." She shook her head. "God only knows why."

Jamie grinned, immediately forgetting his indignation. "Because I'm gorgeous and super-talented. Or maybe it's because I'm so famous."

Ty laughed, relieved to see his change of mood. "Well, her mum's a lot more famous than you and that hasn't done much to impress her. On that note, anything you can say to big up Alex to Dory would be greatly appreciated."

"Good to know I'm useful for something. Trust me, I'm a professional." He laughed and downed the rest of his beer. "Mhairi, is it your round?"

Ty sat back and let them chat. She wondered how Alex was going to move things forward, now she'd talked to her family. She'd promised she would handle things, but they hadn't discussed details. Ty wished now she'd raised it during their week off, but she had been enjoying the intimacy and peace so much she hadn't wanted to disturb it. She trusted Alex but she wondered how difficult she would find it to take the next step.

TWENTY-SEVEN

When Dory arrived from the airport Alex had just enough time to take her for food before the show. The pain in her back was making her feel more anxious than usual and she was concerned Tyra wasn't allowing herself enough time to get to the arena.

"Stop worrying." Ty laughed as Dory tucked into her dessert and Alex looked at her watch for what felt like the thousandth time. "Y'know me, a quick squirt of deodorant, a new T-shirt, and I'm good to go." She grinned at Alex, both of them knowing it wasn't quite true. The occasional bad hair day had shown Alex a more high-maintenance side of her nature.

"See, Alex, not everyone is uptight all the time, like you." Dory smirked.

"Hey, your mum's professionalism and attention to detail have made her the success she is today," said Ty. "Without her, I'd be back in Glasgow, and you wouldn't have an access-all-areas pass to the biggest gig in San Diego tonight. So watch your mouth, kid."

Dory's face dropped. "Sorry, I just meant you could be

successful and still be fun." She looked down at her plate. "I didn't mean to be rude."

"Your mum *is* fun. Do you think I'd hang out with someone who wasn't?"

"No. I'm sorry, okay?" Dory's bottom lip quivered.

"Apology accepted." Alex tried to sound upbeat. "Let's finish up here and get Ty back to the arena before the curtain goes up. You may even get to meet Jamie before they go onstage."

That was enough encouragement for Dory, and they were soon back in the car, with Dory chatting away, seemingly over the earlier incident.

They saw Ty to her dressing room. Jamie wasn't there so Alex took Dory for a quick tour backstage, allowing her to poke her head out to see the audience starting to stream into the arena. Ryan materialized and offered to take Dory to meet Jamie as the band went onstage. Alex agreed gratefully and retreated to her dressing room for some much-needed calm and stretching. Her back was still painful and another day on her feet today hadn't helped. As she did her back stretches, she thought about how different her life was since she'd met Ty. In the past, at the slightest twinge of her back she would have spent an entire day having therapy or confined to bed. Whatever was needed to ensure it didn't affect her performance. Now here she was hoping her back would hold out tonight, because she had been too busy actually living her life to worry about it. She knew she couldn't do this every night without repercussions, but it felt good to have other interests in her life to balance the work.

When she heard the crowd roar in reaction to DandyLions' appearance onstage, she slipped out to watch their first couple of numbers. She never tired of watching Tyra in action.

Dory was on the side stage, as close as she could get without being visible, Ryan close by. Alex moved up and stood by Dory, who, to her total shock, pulled her close and leaned her head on her arm.

"Thanks for arranging this, Mom, it's so cool."

Alex thought her heart would burst. "Anytime, Dory, but Ty did most of the arranging."

"Maybe. But like she said, none of us would be here without you."

The lump in her throat made it difficult for Alex to speak, so they stood in silence watching the band play. Jamie frequently turned to sing the lyrics directly to Dory, giving her, and her mother, a cheeky wink. Dory was thrilled. Alex, who couldn't see Ty properly from where they were standing, was less impressed. Towards the end of the set, she told Dory she needed to prepare for her own performance. She left a rapt Dory with Ryan, and headed back to her room, Dory's words washing away the worry about her back.

As they came off stage, Ty bypassed Dory talking animatedly to Jamie and headed straight for Alex's dressing room. She was wrapped in an embrace as soon as she entered. "Hey, careful, I'm soaking. You'll stain your shirt."

Alex kissed her roughly. "God, you turn me on when you perform."

Whatever other doubts Ty had about performing live, the effect it had on Alex was definitely a benefit. She broke free, holding her at arm's length. "I could barely see you. I thought you only had eyes for the sexy singer."

Alex shook her head and let Ty go. "You're getting me mixed up with my daughter."

Ty moved towards the shower. "Let me clean up and I'll be back out before you go on."

When Ty re-emerged, Alex had left the room. She donned some black combats and a tight T-shirt, styled her hair and was ready in record time. She could hear the chanting but judged she'd make it before Alex went onstage. As she arrived, the band were playing the intro, waiting for Alex's appearance. The crowd was going wild with anticipation. Alex's guitar tech was standing nearby with her guitar, but Alex was stretching, reaching down to her toes.

"What's wrong?" Ty dropped to her knees next to her.

"Just a cramp in my back, it's been niggling for days. I should've had someone take a look, but it seems to ease when I stretch my hamstrings."

"Why didn't you say anything?" Ty ran her hand over Alex's back until she groaned. "Here?" She massaged the area over Alex's ribs.

"We were busy having fun and I didn't want to put a damper on things." Alex's voice was rough. "Mm. Thanks, that'll have to do. They're waiting for me. Can you ask Ryan to have some more painkillers ready when I come off stage, please?" She retrieved her guitar and slung it on, giving Ty a reassuring smile and a quick kiss. "I'll be okay, honey, don't look so worried." She ran onstage to thunderous applause.

Ty, watching attentively, could see Alex wasn't moving around the stage with her usual grace. She had painkillers ready the moment Alex came to the side of the stage for a guitar change. Alex swallowed them gratefully while Ty rubbed the painful area.

"It's not too bad, Ty, honestly I'm fine." She took Ty's face in her hands. "But I love how you look after me." She smiled broadly and Ty got another quick kiss.

As the show progressed Ty was relieved to see Alex moving more normally. When it came to the encore, the crowd were chanting for Alex and DandyLions in equal measure.

Alex ran back onstage. "Hey, San Diego, would you like to hear a special song we've been practicing especially for you?" The crowd went wild. "Okay, let's welcome back to the stage my very good friends, DandyLions."

The crowd roared. Mhairi and Mikki ran on, Suzi got back behind her drums and Ty and Jamie ran on from either side of the stage, joining Alex. Ty grabbed the mic. "This is a song by, in my opinion, the best band from San Diego." The crowd managed to ramp up the noise another level as they recognized the intro.

When the song came to an end Alex joined Ty at the front of the stage. "Did you enjoy that, San Diego?" The crowd roared their approval and Alex kept going. "Do you love DandyLions?"

Again, plenty of approbation. "Do you love Tyra MacLean?" She slung her arm around Ty's neck. The crowd roared louder and Ty gave Alex a subtle look of confusion. "I'm happy to hear that because I really like her too!"

Ty's eyes widened before she was pulled into a passionate kiss. Instinct overruled shock and she kissed back until she remembered they were onstage in front of almost twenty thousand people. She stiffened and Alex pulled back, smiling.

She was vaguely aware of Dory and Ryan jumping up and down and clapping, and the whole stadium appeared to be going crazy.

As Alex's band filed back on for the final two numbers, Ty left the stage in a daze, waving on autopilot.

Dory was waiting for her, her face lit up in a smile. "Did you know she was going to do that?"

"Fuck, no." Ty rubbed her face, still dazed by Alex's grand gesture. She looked at Dory suddenly. "Did you?"

Dory blinked. "Well, no. But she was telling me she had no reason not to be open about how she feels about you now. She said she doesn't care what anyone thinks as long as the people she loves support her."

"Well, we absolutely support her, don't we? So it's all good." She ruffled Dory's hair and grinned. "I wouldn't have minded a wee heads-up though."

Alex came off stage like a whirlwind, kissing Ty briefly before turning to Ryan, smiling widely. "You'll need to fix me a call with Linda first thing tomorrow."

"Too late, she already called. She's on your schedule for nine tomorrow morning. I figured you wouldn't want to deal with her tonight."

"Perfect. Right, be ready to leave in half an hour. We need to celebrate." She threw each arm around Dory and Ty and steered them towards her dressing room.

"What about Jamie?" asked Dory. "Is he coming too?"

"Of course Jamie's coming. And Mhairi, and everyone. Let's go."

If hell was other people, Ty was securely stuck there for several hours as they celebrated. She desperately needed to discuss with Alex what had happened, but entertaining Dory was the immediate priority, so she made do with meaningful looks and the occasional whisper. It felt like far too long until they finally headed back to the parked-up buses which would leave for LA early in the morning. After Mhairi led Dory away to join Jamie on their bus, Alex pulled Ty up her steps and turned with a contented smile. "We never need to sleep apart again." Ensuring the door was secure and they were alone on the bus, she sighed. "Well, that day went differently than I was expecting." She led Ty into the bedroom.

"A bit of warning would have been good." Ty nuzzled her neck and started to undress her. "Where did that come from?"

Alex pulled back, her eyes unusually dark with emotion. "You were so concerned about my back. I realized I had never had someone look after me just because they cared. People look after me because I pay them to, or because they want to ingratiate themselves. I'm honored to be the person you care about, and you certainly don't deserve to be denied or kept secret."

Ty took her face in both hands and looked searchingly into her eyes. "Whatever journey we're on now, we're on it together. I'll be here for you whatever happens." All she could hope was that Alex wouldn't regret it in the morning.

In the deep dark of the night, Ty stirred, sensing that Alex was awake next to her. She turned and could just make out her profile in the darkness. She propped herself on her elbow, but Alex continued to stare at the ceiling.

"You okay, sweetheart? It's been an awful long day. You need to sleep." She kept her voice low.

Alex turned slightly. "Do you think that was a rash thing to do?"

Ty laughed softly. "Well, for you it was pretty spontaneous. Is my influence rubbing off?" She leaned in closer. "I know you can't help but overthink it, but you're not regretting anything, are you?" She tried to keep the worry out of her voice, but Alex must have picked up on it.

Alex's warm hand stroked her cheek. "Not at all. I'm relieved it's out in the open. And I'm happy we can be publicly together. I'm probably going to have to do some interviews in the next few days." There was a pause. "Will you come with me?"

Oh, great, TV interviews. My all-time favorite thing. She pulled Alex close and wrapped her arms tightly around her. "Of course. I'll be right by your side whenever you need me."

She lay listening to Alex's breathing even out until finally she relaxed into sleep. Was Alex really ready to deal with the fallout of her impulsive actions? And was she herself prepared to be back under constant public scrutiny? She had told herself she could deal with it, because she would have to if she wanted to be with Alex. But now it was out there, witnessed by thousands and undoubtedly making global news, it suddenly felt very real.

TWENTY-EIGHT

Alex lay with her head on Ty's chest, mentally preparing for the day ahead.

She sighed. "We need to get up and spend some time with my daughter after she's made the effort to travel with us. There aren't many things worth leaving this bed for, but that's one of the many sacrifices of parenthood." She looked up at Ty. "I know the large part you played in Mhairi and Jamie's upbringing, but was there ever a time you wanted your own family?"

"I wasn't reliable enough when I was young. And I never met anyone I would have wanted to have kids when I finally grew up."

Alex ventured further, hoping for more insight. "Mhairi mentioned that you had someone once. A politician? She said you were together a while."

Ty's expression tightened. "Do you and Mhairi talk about me often?"

Damn. That's not a good start. She squeezed Ty's arm. "It was when we argued. She was trying to get me to understand you better. Mhairi is very protective of you, Tyra. I don't think you need to worry about her loyalty."

Ty shrugged. "Her name was Marianne Maxwell, and she was a politician in the Scottish Parliament. I was canvassing for the party before the first general election, and she won her seat with a large majority. We somehow became friends."

Alex watched her face cloud over with revisited emotion. "You don't have to talk about it if you'd prefer not to."

"No, it's fine. I haven't really thought about those times for years. It seems like a lifetime ago."

"How long are we talking about?"

"Just over fifteen years."

Alex smiled. "I was twenty-two and juggling newfound success with a young baby. A lifetime ago for me too."

"I was thirty or thereabouts. I forget our age difference, probably because you're a fully formed grown-up and I'm an elderly teenager."

Alex pushed her playfully. "Shut up and get on with the story, old lady. So Mhairi said she was a lot older than you?"

"Ha. She wasn't that old, but she must have seemed imposing to the twins. She was in her mid-forties and had a solid legal career before she decided to go into politics after the devolution vote." She hesitated, then sighed. "She was also in a twenty-year marriage to an advocate who was about to become a judge."

Alex raised her eyebrow. Ty getting mixed up with a married woman was the last thing she would have expected.

Ty shrugged. "The attraction between us was too intense to ignore. I suppose I was flattered a woman like her would be interested in me, but I also wasn't a homewrecker. She played the 'my marriage is a sham' card, which it probably was, but she hadn't been in any rush to end it, either. It was exhausting always having to be the one to say no, or to put some space between us. Eventually I told her we needed to spend less time together. She didn't want to hear it, so I pretty much avoided her for months. I ignored her calls and stayed away from the places she might look for me.

"Finally, she turned up at my flat. She told me she had left Desmond and got her own place, and that she wanted to be with me." She paused, taking a drink of water from the bottle by the bed. "I was swept away by the passion of it. She spent most of the week in her flat in Edinburgh, and a few days back in her constituency in Glasgow. We were together most nights, but it was never public knowledge, because she didn't think her career would be improved by it. Which is funny, because now it's almost unheard of for prominent Scottish politicians not to be lesbians." She laughed at her own joke and looked at Alex for approval to continue.

Alex nodded expectantly. "Don't stop now, I need to know what happens."

Ty laughed sharply. "Obviously, it didn't end well." She paused to plump the pillows before continuing. "Because we spent so much time together, it was inevitable she got to know the kids. I used to take them to Edinburgh for the weekend and they loved it. She made up this cover story that I was teaching her to play the guitar. I don't know how convincing it was, but we were together three years without any major rumors surfacing. She never did learn to play the guitar."

Alex smiled, wondering how anyone could ever let Ty

go. But then, hadn't she spent her whole career making decisions to avoid being outed?

Ty bit her lip. "And then the party gave her a chance to stand for election in the UK parliament. I didn't think she'd want that, I thought she was content with the career she had. But I was wrong, and she jumped at the opportunity."

She gave Alex a bitter smile. "She told me she would be under much more scrutiny and couldn't jeopardize her career with a lesbian scandal. I argued it was the twenty-first century and there were plenty of out gay politicians, but she'd made up her mind. She shed a few tears and said it was hard, but emotionally she was already four hundred miles away." Ty cleared her throat. "The kids were upset, especially Jamie. He had really enjoyed spending time with her. That added to my misery, and I started drinking a lot at night, mostly on my own." She looked at Alex as though trying to decide whether to continue.

Alex smiled encouragingly. There wasn't anything about Tyra she didn't want to know.

"One evening when they hadn't seen me for a few days Jim allowed Mhairi to walk around the corner to my flat. I didn't answer so she used the spare key and found me face down in a pile of vomit. There's nothing more sobering than waking up to a ten-year-old cleaning your face and crying." Tyra put her face in her hands for a moment.

Alex could see the shame of that moment was something Ty still lived with.

"I steered clear of the booze for a long time after that, until I was sure I was in a good enough place. Mhairi followed me around like a puppy, to make sure I wasn't lonely. That was nearly twelve years ago and until now I haven't had another relationship that lasted more than a couple of nights. How pathetic is that? One bad relationship and I give up." Her expression was sad as she looked Alex in the eye once again.

Alex was filled with a need to protect her, even from things that had happened in the past. She hugged her close. "I hate her for breaking your heart. But I also pity her for missing the opportunity to spend her life with you."

Ty laughed. "I may have thought it was true love back then, but with the joy of hindsight I can see she was a manipulative, overbearing bitch. I'd have been miserable with her." She pulled Alex in close, resting her chin on the top of her head. "You've made me realize what a relationship should feel like." Ty loosened her hold and slid out of the bed. "Right, that's today's ancient history lesson done, let's go and entertain a teenager."

Alex watched her head to the bathroom. Did Ty worry about again being with someone who had a history of putting her career before happiness? It brought home how much of a chance Ty was taking with her. She had a responsibility to ensure Ty never felt abandoned again.

TWENTY-NINE

As she left the stage after DandyLions' LA set, Ty smiled at Dory applauding ecstatically. She was taking her fan duties very seriously. Ty had watched earlier as Clara and Billy arrived with the boys, clearly keen to be reunited with their daughter. Dory had greeted them warmly enough, but quickly excused herself to follow Ryan to a prime viewing spot for the set.

Jamie stopped to ruffle her hair. "How did we sound, Dory?"

As she opened her mouth to reply, Jamie looked up to see Danielle Coburn standing nearby. He let out a whoop of excitement and launched himself toward her. They met in a raunchy kiss that made most onlookers turn away.

Ty saw the look of devastation on Dory's face. She slung her arm around her slumped shoulders and guided her to the dressing room. "Help me get ready and I'll show you my secret place for watching the show." Dory perked up a bit as she dug into the freely available snacks while Ty got showered and dressed. She shoveled some peanuts down and managed to get herself and Dory to the side of the stage just as Alex was about to go on.

Alex looked around, smiling when she saw them approach. Ty pulled her in tight. "Knock 'em dead." Her ritual encouragement was now backed up with a deep kiss. As she stepped back to let Alex go onstage, she was surprised to see Dory lean in to give her a warm hug.

"Good luck, Mom."

Ty had never seen Alex smile so widely as she ran onstage.

Ty quickly led Dory over to her favorite equipment case, showing her how to get a leg up via a speaker, until they had both pulled themselves up to the vantage point. "This is so cool." Dory craned her neck. "I can nearly see the whole stage."

"As long as you can't see the audience. If you can see them, they can see you." Ty grabbed her sleeve. "It's not too safe up here so try and stay put. It's a long way down!"

Dory leaned out again, looking down disdainfully to where her younger brothers were standing at the side of the stage. "We've got a much better view than they do."

Ty grabbed her shirt tighter. "Seriously, Dory. You've got too many protective mothers who will kick my arse if you break your neck."

Dory looked at her speculatively. "Do you think that's a good thing?"

"What? Of course it's a good thing. You can never have too many people who care about you. You've got two amazing women and a great dad looking out for you. Not to mention your grandmother, who terrifies me."

Dory nodded slowly and they watched the show in comfortable silence, Ty occasionally commenting on Alex's performance. Dory was watching so intently, Ty wondered if she had ever taken the time to watch Alex perform.

At one point she looked up at Ty, wide eyed. "She's amazing. I didn't...I didn't realize."

"Perhaps you could tell her that, after the show?" Ty suggested gently.

"No way! I'm not going soft." Dory looked guilty. "Maybe I could tell her she's good."

"Better than nothing, I suppose." Ty sighed. "Perhaps one day you can tell me where all this anger came from."

They fell silent again as Alex performed her most recent hit, the last song of the main performance. Ty knew she had to be onstage soon. "I need to get down. Are you coming? I don't really want to leave you all the way up here on your own."

"I guess." Dory shifted towards the edge. "The boys will be jealous when they know I've been up here."

Ty jumped down, ignoring the always present pain in her knee and reached up to give Dory a helping hand. Alerted by the noise, her family turned to them in surprise.

"We wondered where you went." Billy laughed as they turned back to watch the end of the show. The rest of the band left the stage while Alex got the crowd wound up, asking how much they wanted to see DandyLions back on the stage.

The crew had moved a pared-down drum kit to the front of the stage for Tyra. She held out her hand to Dory, who produced a set of drumsticks. "Good work, kiddo, you can be my assistant anytime."

Dory beamed.

With the crowd in a suitable state of excitement, Ty followed her cue to return to the stage, waving to Dory as she went.

After the show everyone crowded into Alex's dressing room to say their farewells to Dory and her family. "I'm hoping to come straight back to LA after the tour." Jamie had his arm around Dani's shoulders, and he looked to her for confirmation. She smiled and nodded. "So maybe you could show me some good surfing spots when I'm here, Dory?"

Dory's face lit up. But it couldn't compare with Alex's smile when Dory approached her without any encouragement and threw her arms around her. "Thanks, Mom, you were amazing. Can we do this again soon?"

"Did you see Alex's face?" Jamie was stuffing his mouth full of breakfast at a small café an amenable member of Alex's security team had driven them to. Alex was on a very long conference call with Linda and her PR manager, and they'd decided to take the opportunity to spend some family time together, just the three of them. Ty had lost track of how long it had been since they did it last.

They were discussing the success of Dory's visit and how much better her relationship with Alex had become.

"Did you put her up to saying that?" Ty looked at him suspiciously as she scooped up a forkful of egg from his plate.

He deftly knocked her fork, spilling most of the contents back onto his own plate. "You should've ordered the jumbo breakfast if you wanted more egg. And no, I swear that was all her. She said she'd never really bothered to listen to her mum before and couldn't believe how good she was live. She's a nice kid. A bit angry maybe." He looked up from his plate. "Oh, and I might have made her feel bad. She was moaning about having two mums to give her a hard time and I told her our mum died on the day we were born."

"Ah you didn't need to tell her that, Jamie." Mhairi shook her head. "She's young and doesn't realize how easy she's got things in life. And it probably doesn't seem that simple from her perspective."

He shrugged. "She looked a wee bit upset, but it's true. She's bloody lucky."

Ty smiled fondly. For all his desire to be famous, Jamie's feet were firmly on the ground, and she hoped that would never change.

They had talked about their future again, after Alex's record label had contacted Lachlan, offering the band a contract. After Ty, Mikki, and Mhairi had all confirmed they didn't want to continue with the band, Lachie had gone back to gauge the interest in signing Jamie as a solo artist. He'd found himself out of his depth in the negotiations, but Alex had advised him, and Ty knew she had made a couple of calls of her own. Jamie was still waiting to hear the outcome, but Ty suspected his life was about to change dramatically.

Mhairi was still giving her brother a hard time. "It's not like we grew up in an orphanage, Jamie. We've had Dad and Kirsty. And Ty's been so many things rolled into one, mother, big sister, bandmate and best friend. You wouldn't be sitting here looking at a deal with one of the big five labels without her, so I think we were pretty lucky ourselves."

Ty smiled to hide her sadness as she listened to them bickering, knowing they'd all be moving on soon, and things would never be the same again. She was pulled out of her reflection when she realized Mhairi was looking at her with an eyebrow raised.

She shook her head. "Sorry, what?"

"A couple of hours with your nearest and dearest and you can't even keep up with the conversation. Are we no' big enough stars to keep your attention anymore?" Jamie had finally finished his mountain of food and was sitting back watching her. His teasing tone didn't reflect the affection in his eyes. "Mhairi was asking if you're doin' okay. With all the attention and requests for appearances and that? It's kind of like all your worst nightmares come true. Apart from the finally finding the love of your life part of course." He smiled widely.

"Ah, shut up, will you, Jamie?" She knew she was falling big time for Alex, but there were plenty of things left unresolved about their future. The last thing she needed was reminding about how much it would hurt if they didn't manage to make it work. "I'm handling it so far, but I guess it's early days yet. We're protected on tour, so we can choose what we do and who we speak to. I don't know what it's going to be like trying to get back to normality afterwards."

"There's no normality after this, cuz. We're all celebrities now." Jamie just couldn't hide his glee, even when Mhairi fixed him with a cold stare.

"Can you not just have a bit of sensitivity, Jay. It's all exciting for you now but remember Tyra's been there and doesn't have such great memories. Just rein it in a bit."

Jamie's smile faded. "I'm sorry, Ty. I didn't mean you should have to take all the abuse and stuff. It just feels like a whole new life opening up." He rubbed his chin. "And to be honest, doing it without you two takes a bit of the shine off. What if I fuck it up? You won't change your mind and stay with me, will you?"

Mhairi rolled her eyes. "Great job of turning the sympathy back to you, Jay. You'll be fine and you know it. And no, I don't want to tag along on your quest for celebrity. What I want is to study, and compose, and play my bloody cello. You know I used to practice more in a week than I've done on this whole tour. My cello just sits there on the back of the bus, the case gathering more dust by the day. You chase your dream and leave me to pursue my own."

Ty was pleased to see her quieter cousin stand up for her own needs, but she knew it wasn't as straightforward as that. "And what about Ryan? You seem to be getting along awful well."

Mhairi turned to look at her, unable to hide her smile at Ryan's name. "He's so lovely, Ty. I've never met a person who's so in tune with what's going on in my head. He gets me."

"So is there a plan post-tour?" She was aware of the hypocrisy of the question. She and Alex had so much more choice and control over how they developed their relationship and yet they hadn't managed to discuss it properly. But she expected these kids to have a fully formed plan?

"I just don't know, Ty. Ryan's job is everything to him. He can't really do it on a different continent to Alex, can he? We've agreed to enjoy our time together now and talk about it more when we've got some free time."

"Meeting someone who's right for you is a big thing, Mhairi. Don't let it slip away just because you don't know how to talk about it."

The conversation was heading in a direction she didn't want to go, so before Mhairi had a chance to turn that observation back on her, she jumped up. "Right, you two, we've got a rehearsal to get to."

There would be time to talk about the longer term when she'd got through the terror of the next few weeks of public appearances and interviews. Despite the composed exterior she knew Alex had her own share of nerves about the reaction her very public announcement might produce. She needed Ty to be calm and reliable, not asking needy questions about their future. She put her doubts aside and made sure to give her cousins her full attention on the journey back.

THIRTY

As Ty had predicted the rest of the California dates flew by in a flurry of media appearances and interviews. Their first appearance was on the Owen Harvey Show. Owen was an old friend of Alex's and called her in advance to ask how she wanted to handle the interview. He promised to direct his questions at Alex and allow Ty to decide how much she wanted to contribute.

"Are you going to be okay?" Alex looked understandably concerned as they waited in the green room and Ty did breathing exercises to calm herself.

"I can't think of anything I want to do less. But we're in this together and I said I'd be there if you wanted me. So here we are." She took a long slow breath.

"I'll be right next to you, and you don't have to say anything you don't want to." Alex took her hand and didn't let go until they were sitting facing their host.

After a general discussion about the tour, Alex answered Owen's questions about their new relationship with her usual personable flair. She was in her element and Ty admired the way she could talk to viewers as though she was sharing all sorts of intimate information without actually giving much detail at all. Alex deflected the question about her coming out, making a statement about people needing to feel safe to be themselves and how everyone had a part to play in making that happen. Ty didn't contribute much, but Ryan's later analysis was that the audience, and the wider world of social media, had loved her dry humor.

"Ah, that's great, then. Can't wait for our next appearance." But she had to admit when pressed by Alex, it hadn't been as bad as she'd expected, and with each subsequent interview, her nerves subsided a little more.

Their final US date in Tacoma went well, and the following morning Ty was woken earlier than she expected by a beaming Alex brandishing a steaming mug of coffee.

She sat up rubbing her eyes. "What? Are we meant to be somewhere? I thought we were having a late start today?"

Alex handed over the mug. "Drink up. We're off to Seattle for the day. Mike's arranged for one of the security guys to drive us. We'll have the whole day to ourselves and catch up with everyone later."

Ty was immediately wide awake. "That's amazing. I've always wanted to go there. Can we go to the Space Needle?" She resisted bouncing on the bed and wondered if she appeared childish, but Alex looked pleased to see her so enthusiastic.

"I remembered you telling me. Don't worry, I've got the whole day planned, no sight will remain unseen." She sat on the bed and rested her hand on Ty's knee. "To be honest, I've got an ulterior motive. I just want to spend some time with you alone. Well, as alone as we can be in public. The last week has been so full on, I feel as though all we've done is perform, talk to the media, and sleep."

Ty pulled her close, and Alex rested her head on her shoulder.

"We've only got a few more nights, then there's just the Christmas shows and after that you can have a real rest. I'm gonna look after you and spoil you rotten."

Alex looked up at her, smiling happily. "You deserve a rest too. I can't wait to spend Christmas with you all alone." She jumped up. "But today we need to get moving. Out of bed, MacLean."

The traffic had been heavy when they arrived in the city, due to an anti-gun demonstration. Mike, Alex's head of security, had been a little nervous about the visit, but Alex had reassured him they would stay well away from where the demonstration was taking place. Now they were wandering around the Seattle Centre and Ty was on a high after their trip up the Space Needle.

"It was amazing. I could see the Rockies!"

When did I stop being that enthusiastic about everything? It felt so good to laugh with Ty and experience everything through her eyes. It was like the world had opened up again.

André, their driver and escort for the day, had been very good at giving them space while remaining nearby. It felt as though they truly were alone to enjoy the city. She turned and took Ty's hand. "Hey, there's a really great art museum here. I haven't been for years. Can we take a quick detour?"

Ty stopped abruptly, pulling Alex to a standstill. "You promised me lobster. Not art."

Alex laughed at her mock indignation and pulled her along. "We've got time for both." She waved André over to join them. "André, we'd really like to visit the art museum on our way to the restaurant. Would you be able to go pick up the car now and meet us there, please?"

André looked horrified. "But I'm supposed to stay with you at all times, Alex. Mike would kill me."

"Really, André, we'll be fine for twenty minutes. I've gone completely unrecognized all day. It'll save us all having to walk back after the meal." She smiled at him convincingly.

He scratched his head and frowned. "If you insist, but please head straight for the museum and call me if you have any problems." He jogged off up the road, looking over his shoulder repeatedly.

"You shouldn't have made him do that." Ty scowled. "He'll be in real trouble if Mike finds out."

"Well, he's not going to find out, is he?" She threaded her arm through Ty's. "And sometimes it's nice to have you all to myself."

"He's not exactly intrusive. None of your team are. I'd hate to have a job where I'm expected to be invisible until the shit hits the fan and suddenly it's all on me. It must be so stressful."

Alex tried unsuccessfully to keep the irritation out of her voice. "Unlike my job, which is just living the dream, playing my guitar and visiting interesting places?"

Ty rolled her eyes. "It's not all about you, y'know. I'm just saying I don't envy those guys."

They turned into a narrower street. They heard shouting in the distance, and Alex assumed it was from the demonstration. As they were halfway along the street, what sounded like a gunshot rang out, much closer. She looked at

Ty in alarm as the shouting grew louder. Ty was looking around, presumably searching for a building they could go into and wait for the car. But this street was mainly fire doors and delivery access to the rear of large buildings. The shouting was getting closer, and from around a corner a mass of people emerged, running in panic.

Ty pulled her forward, towards a doorway up ahead, as the wave of people rushed at them. They almost made it before they were hit by a wall of arms and legs. She felt Ty's hands on her shoulders as she was propelled forcefully into the doorway. She tripped on the step and sprawled in the entrance, her head jarring against the wall painfully. Alex lay there for a few moments, eyes closed, until the noise of the panicking crowd roused her, and she sat up slowly. Where was Ty? Had she been crushed by the crowd? She wanted to go look for her, but her head was spinning. She reached up and felt a lump forming on her temple.

She looked at the people still streaming past. Most of them looked terrified and they weren't paying much attention to their surroundings. She decided it was safest to wait until the crowd dispersed to look for Ty. She knew she could take care of herself and wouldn't thank Alex for putting herself at risk. As the mass of people started to thin out and her head cleared a little, she realized her cap and shades had fallen off. She reached for them, knowing she'd feel safer in her habitual disguise.

"Hey, Doug."

She looked up to see a slim man with thinning hair peering down at her, his beady eyes narrowed, and his thin lips curled in a snarl.

"Is this who I think it is? Isn't it that singer you used to have a thing for? Wasn't she playing near here last night?"

The beginnings of icy fear spread through Alex's body.

She tried to replace her shades but found them broken in half. She threw them down and slid backwards until her back was against the metal door.

A larger figure appeared alongside the first and gazed down at Alex, the expression on his unshaven face changing from curiosity to a leer.

"Dyke bitch! I really liked you. You're a fucking letdown!"

She saw the boot as it swung towards her face. She tried to duck away, but he made contact with her shoulder and the impact slammed her head into the wall beside her. The pain was excruciating, and Alex instinctively tried to protect herself. She scrambled desperately to get to her feet, grasping the side of the doorway to help herself up. A heel smashed into her hand, and she fell back in agony, the pain sweeping over her like a wave. She stayed down, cradling her hand and blinking to try and clear her hazy vision. She could see the silhouette of the man still standing above her.

"Try playing your guitar now, you prick-teasing cunt."

The other voice was more distant. "Fuck. Doug, man, she's seen our faces."

She looked up in horror as the boot swung back for another strike. Then, suddenly, the figure was gone. She heard Ty's distinctive voice raised in anger and could vaguely make out two figures struggling. She realized it was Tyra holding the large guy by his jacket. She pulled her arm back to swing at him, but the smaller man ran up and shoved her. She lost her grip, and they took off down the street.

Alex was aware of sirens but was unsure if they had been more distant and were suddenly nearby, or if they had just started up. She felt Ty drop down next to her and reach out to cradle her face. She flinched and tasted blood.

"Oh, fuck, Alex, I'm so sorry."

It sounded as though Ty was crying.

Alex knew she was safe now that Ty was here. She closed her eyes. The pain was so bad she just wanted to sleep. When she woke maybe she would feel better. As she started to slump, she felt strong hands bracing her under the arms.

"Not yet, Alex, we need to get you somewhere safe. Can you stand?"

She felt Ty's support on her loosen while she tried to get her phone out of her pocket. She tried to help, but her knees buckled when she attempted to support her own weight. Ty's arm came back around her waist. "I'll call André. He can't be far away. He'll get us to a hospital."

As if on cue she heard the screeching of car tires and then footsteps. She looked up to see André sprinting down the street, his face ashen. The street was suddenly full of patrol cars and officers running towards them. Alex was lowered gently into the back of a patrol car, after officers convinced Ty it was the quickest way to get her to an emergency room. Ty held her the entire journey, and Alex slumped against her with the side of her face that hurt the least. She didn't have the energy to speak, but she half listened as Ty gave detailed descriptions of her attackers to the officers, who relayed them by radio to their colleagues.

She drifted off to the sound of sirens and Ty whispering that everything would be okay.

THIRTY-ONE

Ty paced the room as an efficient nurse helped Alex remove her jacket and shirt carefully over her injured hand and get settled in bed. She wanted to help but the nurse had given her a look that told her to stay out of the way. It was only the need to be strong for Alex that was stopping her from curling into a ball. As she was helped into bed, Alex began to sob and shake uncontrollably.

Ty sidestepped the nurse and wrapped her arms around Alex. "You're safe now, sweetheart. I promise I'll look after you." *Like I did earlier?* She couldn't go there right now, not when Alex needed her. There'd be time for recriminations later.

When the nurse was happy with Alex's vital signs, she moved in to look at her injuries. After her face was cleaned up Ty could see Alex's cheekbone was bruised and swollen, but the blood that had appeared so copious earlier was from a small cut on the side of her face, where it had made contact with the wall. The nurse examined it closely. "That'll need a couple of stitches."

"She hit her head hard. She was confused and dazed." Ty remembered how groggy Alex had been when she first got to her.

The nurse took a closer look at the side of Alex's head. "You've got a hell of a lump there." She started an examination of Alex's head and neck while she asked questions about what had happened.

Alex didn't respond, so Ty replied. "The was some sort of mass panic and we got hit by a wave of people. Alex was on the ground and a guy kicked her and her head hit a wall. Then he stamped on her hand and shouted homophobic abuse at her." She heard the emotion in her own voice. Simply relating the events was enough to bring on a wave of panic.

The nurse's eyes widened. "Why would someone do that?" She shook her head as she took out a pen light and continued her examination. "You were really unlucky. The anti-gun rally met with a counter demonstration of right-wing groups at the city hall. They were getting up in each other's faces when someone fired a shot, and everyone panicked. We've had a few trampling injuries in tonight, but it could have been much worse."

The door opened and a dark-haired woman entered, looking decidedly fresh for what must be turning into a busy evening. "Ms. Knight, I'm Dr. Susan Tippler. I'm going to assess you now and decide what care you need. How are you feeling?"

"It's Alex. I'm feeling like shit. My head hurts like hell, and I can't move my hand."

Alex's voice was thick, but Ty was relieved to hear her speak.

The doctor inspected Alex's hand gently. "Please try

not to worry, Alex. We'll run plenty of tests and then give you some meds to reduce the swelling I'll come back later to discuss where we take it from there. Does that sound acceptable?"

"Yes, thank you, doctor."

"I'll see you shortly." She strode toward the door, but Ty intercepted her before she left.

"Thanks for your help, doctor. I'm sure the hospital is used to respecting the privacy of its patients, but Alex will need complete discretion about her whereabouts and her condition until her PR team is able to put out a statement."

The doctor smiled understandingly. "I understand that's all under control. Alex's team has already made contact with our media department so nothing to worry about there." She nodded her goodbye and left. At least Linda was good for something. But she couldn't help but worry about how Alex would deal with the fallout.

Ty and the nurse helped Alex out of the rest of her clothes and into a gown, just as an attendant arrived to take her to the X-ray department. Ty walked most of the way with them, but knowing she wouldn't be allowed into the room, reluctantly left to find some food, reassuring Alex she would be there when she returned to her room. Alex nodded vaguely.

As the attack had happened on their way to a late lunch, neither of them had eaten since breakfast. She forced herself to make the calls she knew were necessary, to Alex's mum and dad, and to Clara and Billy, though Dory was out. She repeated the details and reassurances each time, and then she called Ryan, who had been notified immediately by the security company and who had, in turn, called Linda. He promised to update the twins and bring them to the hospital later. She finally slumped into a chair in a deserted corner of the cafeteria.

The smell of the tuna sandwich in front of her was making her nauseous, and as she lifted her coffee mug her hands began to shake uncontrollably. Ty closed her eyes, reliving the moments of Alex's attack and her desperation in fighting the throng of people to get back to her. She had seen the boot make contact with Alex's shoulder, and the second blow to her hand. She had been near enough to hear the crunch. But not close enough to stop it from happening.

She clenched her fists to stop the trembling. The anger she felt when she'd reached the attackers had been all-consuming. If the police hadn't turned up when they did, she would have gladly taken them on with her bare hands.

Her stomach roiled and she struggled not to throw up over the table. Dragging herself to the nearby toilets, she went into a stall and retched until she was exhausted. Forcing herself to take slow, deep breaths she eventually managed to calm herself and rested her forehead against the mirror, enjoying the sensation of the smooth cold surface. *Get a grip. She's okay, and she needs you to be strong.*

The door opened. "Hey, there, are you okay?"

She forced herself to turn to look at the young woman in scrubs watching her with a concerned look. She managed a half smile. "Yeah, thanks. Just had a bit of a scare."

She ran the tap and started to splash water onto her face. She looked in the mirror to see the woman nod sympathetically and turn away. Ty wiped her face dry and peered more closely in the mirror. She looked like shit, but it wasn't like it mattered.

Stopping to retrieve her sandwich and coffee, she picked up a tea for Alex and arrived back to the room as she was being wheeled back in.

When they were alone Ty perched on the side of the bed. "Hey, how are you feeling? I brought you some tea." Alex's eyes remained closed, but Ty suspected she was awake. The nurse returned and roused Alex while she sutured and dressed the cut on her face, handing her more meds which Ty helped her swallow down with her tea.

When the nurse left, Ty stroked her hair out of her eyes and kissed the uninjured side of her face. Alex raised her eyes and looked at her.

"I called your folks," Ty said slowly. "They needed to know before it goes public." Alex didn't react so Ty kept on. "Your dad sends his love, and your mum wants to speak when you feel up to it."

Alex picked at the blanket. "Did you speak to Dory?"

"She was out. Clara is going to talk to her. I said to ring anytime if she wanted to speak to you. Clara and Billy send their love too. Linda is handling cancelling the last few shows and all the media stuff. She didn't think it warranted her traveling here unless you intended to stay in Seattle for long. I told her we would go home as soon as you're discharged." She hesitated. "Is that okay?"

Alex shrugged again.

Ty's phone buzzed in her pocket. She pulled it out. "Hey, Dory, don't panic. She's okay. A bit battered around the edges but she's safe now. Do you want to speak to her?"

She looked at Alex, who held out her good hand and took the phone, clearing her throat. "Hey, Dory. I'm fine, please don't worry... No, don't do that. The moment they let me out of here, I'll be going straight home... I don't know. Depends how bad my hand is... Yeah, my right... I know, honey, but it'll heal. I'm okay, honestly. Speak to Ty, and I'll talk to you again later, okay?"

Ty took the phone and did her best to reassure Dory,

promising to update her later. When she hung up Alex looked even more traumatized than before. Ty smiled as reassuringly as she could. "She'll be okay. She's a big girl."

Alex didn't respond and just stared ahead. The lack of interaction was starting to freak Ty out. "You should try and get some sleep."

"It hurts too much to sleep." Alex's voice was flat.

"Those pain meds should kick in soon, sweetheart. I wish I could do something to make you feel better." Ty rubbed her face. She was feeling so drained she didn't know how much longer she could keep this up.

To her relief, the doctor reappeared shortly with a file.

"Hi, Alex, we'll get you settled for the night shortly. I've got your X-rays here, and the good news is you sustained no fractures to your head or your shoulder, although there's no question they'll hurt for a while and there's some deep bruising. Your hand is another matter. You have a number of fractures to your metacarpals. Due to your profession, we think it would be best to pin them, to maximize the chances of regaining full mobility. It's a small procedure and definitely worth it, even though it will take some time to heal. I think you've got a mild concussion as well, so we want to observe you overnight to make sure you're okay there, too. We can do the procedure on your hand tomorrow morning and providing you recover well we can probably send you home the following day. How does that sound?"

"Whatever you think is best." Alex closed her eyes, dismissing everyone.

Ty followed the doctor out and said, "I'm sorry. She's taking it really hard. Not just the attack, but the cancelled tour and the effect on her family. She really needs to sleep tonight."

"We've given her something that should help, but with the concussion we're going to have to wake her up on and off throughout the night. There's a pull-out bed if you're staying. The nurse will show you." The doctor squeezed her arm reassuringly. "She's in good hands."

"I know, thank you." As the doctor walked away Ty felt her phone buzz. It was a message from Jamie to say he was in the waiting area with Mhairi. Ty stuck her head back in the room and seeing that Alex hadn't moved, she went to find her cousins.

Ryan was with them as they sat in a worried huddle in the waiting room. When they saw Ty they rushed over, drowning each other out with questions. Finally registering Ty's gray face Mhairi shushed the others and hugged her close. Ty felt tears sting her eyes as she grasped Mhairi back, not wanting to let go. Eventually she stepped back and sat down with them for a few minutes. When she had updated them, she promised both she and Alex would be fine.

Jamie didn't appear reassured. "You look like shit, Ty. Will you try to get some sleep?"

"You know you don't look great if this one notices." Mhairi elbowed him in the ribs as she handed over a bag of clothes and toiletries.

Ty accepted the bag gratefully. "Don't worry, I'll sleep like the dead the moment my head hits the pillow." She promised Ryan he could see Alex in the morning and herded them to the exit.

She got back to the room to find Alex fast asleep. Feeling guiltily relieved, she pulled out the camp bed as quietly as she could and settled down for the night.

The next thing she was aware of was an apologetic orderly knocking on the door to take Alex for surgery. Alex was still half asleep as Ty leaned over her. She brushed her hair back from her eyes. "I'll be here when you get back, sweetheart. Try not to worry. The doctor said it wasn't a big procedure."

Alex nodded and turned away, so Ty made do with a kiss to her forehead and stood back to watch them go. She pulled her jeans on and stumbled into the corridor in search of caffeine.

After a day of sitting in the chair watching Alex stare mutely at the wall, trying in vain to get her to talk, Ty was relieved when the doctor returned later in the day.

"We're happy with the resetting process, Alex. I'm confident that with a solid commitment to a physical therapy regimen you should be able to gain full use of your hand. We'll arrange for you to leave in the morning, and I'll refer you to a colleague in New York who will take over your care on your return."

"Thank you for everything. The care here has been amazing." Ty spoke up when Alex remained silent.

"Yes, thank you." Alex murmured absently, closing her eyes again.

The doctor indicated to Tyra to follow her outside. "I'm quite concerned about Alex's psychological welfare. Victims of violent attacks are often subdued for some time. I'm going to prescribe her some anti-anxiety medication."

Ty ran her hands through her hair. "Thank you. I'm worried too. She won't talk to me."

The doctor patted Ty's shoulder. "Just be there for her. Once she starts to physically heal, she should improve. It's very early days and she's in a lot of pain. Being at home should help, but you might consider getting some professional help to allow her to process what she's been through."

I hope that's true. Ty didn't feel optimistic as she headed back into the room.

THIRTY-TWO

Riding gingerly along the slush covered cycleway, Ty was doing her best to focus on the job at hand rather than the bigger situation. Six weeks of caring for Alex had taken its toll. The first few weeks had been about her physical recovery, and as her injuries healed Ty had hoped the old Alex would begin to resurface. But Alex had become obsessive about the media coverage around her attack, which had been extensive, if mostly sympathetic. She refused to leave the apartment for any reason, spending her days relentlessly scrolling through news feeds. A miserable downbeat Christmas had come and gone, and apart from regular appointments from the physical therapist, and a couple of short visits from Dory, it had been just the two of them in the apartment. Even Ryan had been banished, forcing him to run things as best he could with the occasional phone call for guidance. Linda hadn't given up calling, but Alex would drop her phone on the table and leave Linda to chatter on. Ty could hear her tinny voice lecturing on to a non-existent audience.

Alex had become more withdrawn and irritable as time went on, and it seemed to Ty all she ever did was make her angry. After another restless night in the guest room, she'd found Alex in a foul mood, trying to write new music. She had offered her help, and Alex had lost it with her, telling her to get out and give her some space. She'd grabbed her coat and her bike and headed out to clear her head.

Mhairi and Jamie had left New York soon after it became clear the tour wouldn't be rescheduled. Alex's label had offered Jamie a solo contract and he was currently hanging around in Hollywood enjoying Danielle's celebrity status before recording his first album in late spring. Mhairi was teaching music back home for the next few months to save some money before starting college, and Mikki had gone back to Sweden to get married and start a new band.

Everyone's moving on with their lives. She was getting restless. Her morning runs and bike rides took the edge off but sitting in the apartment all day was slowly driving her crazy. And New York was growing oppressive. She wanted to get out on the open road and ride for hours or go for a run and listen to birdsong. Here it was all noise and bustle and tall buildings blocking the precious winter sunlight.

Her recording studio back in Glasgow was just about managing without her, but she had a high-profile job in March producing an album for a well-known act, and the thought of getting back to the work she loved filled her with excitement.

But how she could she leave Alex in such a vulnerable state? She'd been hoping Alex would feel well enough to come home with her when the time came, but so far, she had refused to even discuss it. She'd put up a wall between them ever since the attack, and nothing Ty did seemed to breach it in any way. She'd also refused to talk to a therapist about whatever she was going through. As she rode the streets, she decided to try again to get Alex to leave the apartment, even if just for a short trip. That would be a start.

Alex looked out across a snowy Manhattan as she sat at her piano, flexing her fingers uncomfortably. Her hand had mostly healed but there was still a lot of stiffness that made her less agile than she was accustomed to.

She could play well enough to compose, and that was what she was trying to achieve as she sat staring out over the city. Tyra had hauled the digital baby grand out of her windowless rehearsal space and positioned it by the large floor-to-ceiling window in the living room, saying it wasn't good for her to be cooped up staring at the walls.

She had reluctantly agreed, knowing her desire to lock herself away was irrational, but she didn't feel the inclination to leave her apartment anytime soon.

She stretched her fingers again and played a few notes, stopping to scribble in a notebook. She begrudgingly admitted to herself she was making some progress, just not at her usual pace.

Hearing the elevator click, meaning Ty was on her way back up, she resumed playing, hoping to avoid yet another conversation about how she was doing.

A couple of minutes later she heard the door open, and Ty wheeled her chrome bike into the hallway. She had complained so much about how she missed her bike from home, that months ago Alex had sourced an identical one as a surprise for when they finished their tour. She had completely forgotten about it until they had arrived home from Seattle, and it had been waiting in the apartment. Despite the circumstances Ty had found it hard to conceal her pleasure.

At least it gave her something else to fuss over, thought Alex, watching her lovingly wipe it dry. She could store it in the extremely secure parking garage below, but she liked to have it where she could see it.

Ty finally stood up and walked into the room, her curly blond hair longer than usual. She looked tired but her blue eyes crinkled in a smile when she noticed Alex watching her. She was dressed in skinny black jeans and a thick skiing jacket, a look that normally made Alex's heart race. But these days she was either angry or numb, and nothing in between.

She came up behind Alex, placing her hands on her shoulders, and leaned in for a kiss. "Hey, beautiful, how are you doin'?"

Her Glasgow accent sounded stronger these days, for some reason. Alex instinctively pulled away from the contact and heard the quiet sigh behind her. She stopped playing and tried to engage. "The city looks beautiful."

Ty walked to the window and looked out at the view. "It doesn't feel so beautiful when you're trying to stay upright in all that slush." She moved away toward the kitchen. "I'll make us a coffee to go with the doughnuts you ordered."

Alex got up from the piano and threw herself on her favorite leather couch. Ty joined her a few minutes later, coffee and doughnuts in hand.

"Brought you a choice. I wasn't sure what mood you'd be in." She spread out a selection. "Salted caramel cheesecake, for your next top ten hit. Chocolate custard if you feel you've written something pretty good. And original glazed if it's most likely just an album filler." She sat back and grinned, waiting for Alex's response.

"I don't write fillers." Alex reached for the salted caramel.

Ty laughed loudly. "That's a shame 'cause you do love a glazed." She reached out to snag it and Alex slapped her hand away.

"That's why I'm going to eat it next. You can have the chocolate custard and be happy I haven't written three songs this morning."

Alex chewed her doughnut morosely. Her injuries had healed quickly, and the specialists had reassured that if she put the work in, she should get full mobility back in her hand. But she'd found it difficult to bounce back emotionally from her attack and she knew Ty was concerned about her mental health. But she couldn't seem to climb out of the hole she'd dropped into the day of the attack.

Ty had done everything she could have asked for. She was loving and patient, putting up with what Alex knew was self-pitying behavior. She only put her foot down when it came to Alex's physical therapy regime. The exercises Alex had to do religiously to regain full movement in her hand were painful and they made her angry. These were usually the times she lost it with Ty. She had told her on several occasions to get out, even to go back home, but Ty just retreated for a while until Alex called her back and changed the subject.

"I was wondering if you fancied getting out for some fresh air tomorrow. I bet Central Park looks cool in the snow." Ty looked hopeful.

Alex felt herself withdrawing at the thought of being

out in the open with crowds of people. "I don't think I'm up to that yet. But you go."

Ty groaned. "I don't want to go without you. You need to get out of the apartment, Alex. You've barely been outside in six weeks."

Alex got up and walked out without speaking. She closed the bedroom door firmly, knowing Ty would give her space and sleep in the guest room once again. She threw herself onto her bed and curled into a ball, sobbing silently.

Life had been amazing, and then the dream had been shattered in a single moment. She didn't want to push Ty away, but the need to take control of her life and remove anything that could disrupt it made her feel as though she had no choice. If she could get back to the way things used to be, life would feel right again. If, that is, she had the guts to do what she needed to, even if it broke what was left of her heart.

They were lounging on the couch while Ty flicked through her emails from the studio, muttering about things that hadn't been done.

Alex saw her opportunity and stood. "You need to go home, Tyra. You've got responsibilities and you need to go and face them instead of hanging around here." She turned away, unable to look at Ty's shocked expression. She stared out of the window, oblivious to the view.

"But I've got responsibilities here too, haven't I? Aren't we in this together?" Ty's tone remained mild, but there was underlying hurt in her voice.

She had to do this now while she had the strength. "We were, and I thought I could do the relationship thing, but it turns out I can't. I'm happier on my own. I just...I don't have anything to give you. Not anymore." In trying to keep her voice level she knew she was coming across as cold and remote, but it was all she could manage. Ty needed to believe she wasn't going to change her mind.

There was silence, so reluctantly she turned.

Ty was staring at her disbelievingly, tears running down her face. "You want to give up on us? You promised you wouldn't change your mind and I trusted you."

"I know, and I meant it with all my heart when I said it, Ty, but things change. I didn't know this was going to happen and now I just need some time alone. I'm sorry, but that's how it is. You need to go and live your own life."

Ty's tears were running freely now, and Alex found it difficult not to turn and run.

"I thought my life was here with you. I was prepared to give up everything and deal with living in a fucking goldfish bowl because I thought we belonged together."

"And now you don't have to give up anything." The desolation in her eyes was too much for Alex and she moved towards her room. "I was foolish to think coming out so suddenly was a good idea. I need to regain control of my life, and I have to do it alone, my way. I'm sorry this is how it has to end, believe me."

"Believe you?" Ty's voice cracked. "That's why I'm in this position, isn't it? This is it, Alex, there's no going back. If I walk away now, I never want to see you again. If you're not willing to fight for us..." Her voice faltered as she sobbed.

Alex couldn't believe she managed to keep her voice even, as she reached the door and turned, smiling sadly. "Goodbye, Tyra."

She closed the door to her bedroom and slid to the floor,

resting her head on her knees. She heard the sounds of Ty moving around for a short time, then the door slammed, and she knew she was alone. She mustered the energy from somewhere to drag herself up from the floor and throw herself onto the bed, where she lay staring at the wall for the rest of the morning. If this was what she wanted, why did it feel like she'd just lost a part of herself?

THIRTY-THREE

Tyra stepped off the plane into a driving rain that stung her already reddened eyes.

She had left New York in such a rush she hadn't called Mhairi to say she was on her way home. *That's not entirely true*, she corrected herself. She had five hours at the airport waiting for a flight when she could've rung her anytime. She just couldn't face telling Mhairi because it made it real. That wait, combined with a nine-hour flight had given her plenty of time to dwell on what had happened with Alex. She had finally stopped crying, but the empty feeling inside made her nauseous and her mood was so low she couldn't imagine ever smiling again.

She needed to get home and talk to Mhairi, who had been her rock for so long, and who understood her like no one else did, despite their age difference. She had left the apartment with barely more than the clothes she was wearing so she bypassed the crowd waiting at the luggage carousel and went out into the freezing rain to hail a cab for the short journey home.

"Where tae?" The driver asked. Ty stared for a

moment, surprised at how alien her native accent sounded, then she reeled off her address and they were on their way.

It suddenly occurred to her it was mid-morning on a weekday. Mhairi would most likely be at work and she had no keys to the house.

She sent a quick text. *Hey Mhairi, what are you up to today?*

To her relief the reply was almost instant. *You're up early! Not much going on here. I've got a day off but it's pissing it down. As usual. How's NYC?*

The taxi was pulling into their road, so she typed quickly. *Fancy a coffee?*

She paid the driver and stepped out just as the front door was flung open and Mhairi barreled down the steps and threw her arms around Ty.

As much as she had rehearsed keeping it together, as they stood there hugging in the rain Ty felt the tears run down her face and she sobbed against Mhairi's shoulder. Her cousin pulled back and looked at her for a moment before dragging her into the house. The fire was burning in the living room, and she was pushed into a chair and told to dry off.

Mhairi reappeared a few minutes later with two large mugs, kicking the door shut behind her as she sat in the chair opposite.

She leaned forward, elbows propped on her knees, blowing into her steaming mug. "Tell me what happened. Don't leave anything out."

Where to start? Ty stretched her legs and breathed in the scent of home. If she was going to live with a broken heart, at least it would be around people who really did love her. She poured out the whole story of the past six weeks, the reality, rather than the reassuring updates she had sent.

"Do you regret it?"

"What?" she asked dully. "Regret what?"

"Any of it. If you could change any of the stuff you did, would you?" Mhairi squeezed Ty's knee. "Not the attack, or Alex's reaction to it, or the way she announced your relationship to the world, you couldn't control any of that. But how you behaved, what you said. Acting on your feelings and taking a chance. Do you regret any of that?"

Ty stared down into her coffee pensively, then looked back up at Mhairi, her eyes stinging.

"No. Not a thing. I'd do it all over again if it meant I could be with her."

It felt good to acknowledge that. Yes, she was devastated it hadn't worked out for them. It was an almost physical pain she knew would take a long time to heal, but she was glad she hadn't been afraid to try. But one thing Alex had said was true. Now Ty didn't have to give up anything. She could get back to the quiet life she loved. It was a small consolation, but it was all she had.

Mhairi was enjoying her teaching and had been working hard to make up for all the practice she'd missed. She played her cello in the evenings and Ty could hear how much better she was now she was playing regularly. "Are you happy to be back playing the music you love?"

"Yeah, you know I love all music, but this is different. I get so much fulfilment from it. But I guess there's a part of me that misses the lifestyle on the road. My friends think I'm a freak for giving all of that up. They're always asking me questions about which celebrities I know."

"You could return to it later if you wanted. I'm sure Jamie would always have a place for you in his band."

Mhairi shook her head. "It was an amazing experience, but it wouldn't make me happy long term. Not like it will make Jamie happy." She pointed her bow at Ty. "And someone needs to be here to make sure you don't mope around."

Ty laughed softly. "I'm supposed to be the one taking care of you."

Mhairi shrugged and began to play again. "Family take care of each other. No matter what. You taught me that."

Ty settled back to listen to Mhairi play, her eyes closed as her thoughts wandered. She couldn't help but wonder who was taking care of Alex now. Was she getting out of the house at all? Was she remembering to do her exercises? The ache in Ty's heart hadn't receded yet, and she fought the desire to call. Alex had made her desires clear, and she'd respect them no matter how much it hurt.

"You know it's not really her fault, right?" Mhairi asked, still playing.

"Is that right?"

"She's scared, and she's letting that fear take over."

Ty shrugged. "But that's the thing. *She's* letting it take over. And that part is her fault. Pushing me away is her fault." She shook her head. "I knew better, but I believed her. Her type isn't meant for someone like me."

"Her type?" Mhairi asked, her eyebrow raised.

"Control freak. All about the image and the career. You know I've been there. I know." Even as she said it, she knew Alex had far more wonderful qualities that outweighed the bad, but she didn't want to think about those right now.

THIRTY-FOUR

The weeks passed quickly with Ty spending almost every waking hour in the studio. She had immersed herself fully in her work, leaving no time to think about anything else. It was working well so far and there was plenty to be getting on with.

Kenny had managed the day-to-day business well, but jobs that required her input had been piling up in her absence. She'd turned down anything that was time critical, but a number of artists had requested to work with her and were prepared to wait until she returned.

This was the work that was important to her. Performing in front of thousands and living the lifestyle that went with it had its perks. But it never felt as meaningful as when she found the hidden depths in a song that left a performer overwhelmed by what she had done with their work. And every happy paying customer meant more opportunities for talented but disadvantaged young people. She had trained a number of kids who had gone on to successful careers and it was the part of her job she was most proud of.

On a rare evening she was home before midnight, Mhairi looked at her closely. "You're not overdoing it, are you? You've got to allow yourself time to heal, Ty."

She was sipping a glass of wine, but Tyra was drinking tea. She hadn't touched alcohol since she came home and Mhairi would know this as a sign she was worried about losing control.

Ty put down her mug. "What am I supposed to do, Mhairi? Sit around moping? It's bad enough when I'm out for a run and I start thinking about her. You can't run and cry, I've discovered." Her voice broke and she covered her face with her hands. Why did it still hurt so badly?

Mhairi put her glass down and moved across to sit next to her. She drew her into her arms and waited for the sobs to subside.

"Oh, Ty, I'm sorry it's so hard. I didn't want to upset you but I'm worried if you put everything into your work and don't take time to grieve you'll make yourself ill."

Ty pulled back, taking the offered tissue to wipe her eyes.

"I don't know how else to handle it. And it's not like I'm making work up. I'm stacked. I have to get everything in order before the job with Liv, and that's in three weeks." She blew her nose.

"Are you gonna be okay dealing with Liv? She can be hard work."

Ty looked up into her cousin's concerned face. "I can handle Alivia Jensen. She's the least of my worries." She settled her head on Mhairi's shoulder and they sat in a comfortable silence until Ty started to doze and Mhairi packed them both off to bed.

But once she was in bed, she lay awake, staring at the ceiling. Was Alex hurting too? Or had their whole relationship been nothing more than a publicity stunt? She sighed and turned onto her side. She knew that wasn't true. She'd seen the emotion in Alex's eyes, felt it in her touch. But Alex's failure to use the attack to raise awareness of violence against LGBT people had disappointed her. There had been so much support online and LGBT+ organizations against violence had practically been knocking down Alex's door to get her to talk with them. Alex's refusal to speak out had made Ty consider stepping up, but she hadn't wanted to piss Alex off, so she'd stayed quiet. And that irritated her. It wasn't her style to stay silent.

In the end, maybe her initial instincts had been right. They were too different, ideologically, and personally, to make it work.

The big project Ty had always planned to come home for in March was to produce an album for an artist she had known for years. One of Ty's first jobs when she had set up her studio ten years ago had been to produce an album for a young singer who had just been signed by one of the majors. Her name was Alivia Jensen and they had got on from the moment they met. That first album had been a massive success, catapulting Liv to success and confirming Ty as a talented producer.

Liv had always wanted more from their relationship, but it had only once turned physical, when Liv was between boyfriends and Ty had finally succumbed to temptation. But mostly Ty had worked hard to resist, partly out of professionalism and also because their considerable age gap made her feel uncomfortable. Liv had most recently been in a relationship with a male guitarist from a top band, but it had ended, very publicly, a few months ago.

Ty had produced all of Liv's increasingly successful albums, so this job had been planned for some time. They rarely saw each other between recording sessions, but their relationship had always been intense when they were together. Ty had been a little too susceptible to her many charms and knew it was best to keep her at arm's length.

The week before they were scheduled to meet in the studio Liv called. "Hey, sexy, long time no hear. I'm up here early to spend some time with my folks. D'you want to get together for a catch-up? I know you, once you get me in that studio there'll be no time for idle chitchat."

Her tone was playful but there was truth to what she was saying. She didn't have the strongest work ethic, and Ty always had her job cut out for her just ensuring they kept to their schedule. It made sense to get the socializing out of the way, so she agreed to Liv's suggestion.

That evening as she was dressing, Mhairi stuck her head around the door. "Good to see you making an effort, but don't overdo it. I don't want to have to answer any emergency calls to come and rescue you."

Ty laughed lightly but swapped the fitted shirt she had laid out for a more casual option. "She's not that predatory. I don't think I'm in any danger."

"She was always after you. Even when me and Jamie were kids, she was resentful of us spending time with you. I was surprised you two never got together."

Ty looked away. "We did get together, briefly. The album before last, just before she met Dex."

Mhairi laughed loudly. "And now she's single and back for more. And with all the speculation in the media about you and Alex no longer being together she'll think she's in with a chance."

Ty rubbed her face. "Don't say that, Mhairi. I don't think I've got the energy to cope with any unwanted attention at the moment."

As she entered the restaurant Ty spotted Liv sitting in a corner booth, facing the door, her long legs stretched out in front of her. Her fine bone structure, a gift of her Danish ancestry, was so perfect her face was almost harsh, but as she saw Ty, she broke into a smile that softened her features and her pale blue eyes. Her ash blonde hair was perfectly straight and glossy. She was the opposite of Alex in every way, and Ty tried to ignore the pang of hurt that thought brought with it. Liv stood as Ty approached, dwarfing her by half a foot at least. They embraced warmly and as Ty leant in to kiss her cheek, Liv moved and kissed her firmly on the mouth. "It's so good to see you, Ty. We can't let it go this long again."

Liv declared herself to be starving so they ordered quickly and then Liv sat back and looked Ty up and down. "You're looking good, Tyra. I like the way you have your hair. So tell me what you've been up to these last two and a half years." She sniggered. "The bits that haven't made the celebrity news channels, anyway. I'm sorry things didn't work out for you and Alex." She didn't sound too sorry.

Ty shrugged. "And I heard you split with Dex. That's a shame. I liked him."

"It got boring. I grew out of him. We were together for *four* years." She yawned. "But tell me about the famous Alex Knight. What's she like? And what went wrong?

Coming out after all these years of speculation and then it was over in a couple of months, like she changed her mind. How did you fuck that up?" She laughed until she saw Ty's expression. "Oh, too soon?"

Ty chewed on her thumbnail. "I don't really want to talk about it, Liv. Can we change the subject?"

"Well, don't worry, I'm here now and I intend to take full advantage of having you all to myself." She flashed a killer smile, and as their drinks arrived Ty downed half of hers in one swallow.

The evening seemed to go at a snail's pace as Liv filled Ty in on every detail that had happened to her since they last met. Most of it was negative. Anything that had gone badly was someone else's fault and any triumphs were always ruined by a fellow performer's jealousy, or not being fully appreciated. She didn't have a good word to say for anyone, especially her band and crew. Ty's thoughts drifted to how kind and generous Alex was to the people who worked for her, and her deep sense of responsibility. What was she doing? There was no comparison between the two women. The only thing Liv had going for her was that she was here, sitting at the table, not hiding an ocean away.

One evening Jamie called Ty, moaning that the label was overruling his choice of songs. She did her best to sound patient. "You're a virtually unheard-of performer recording your first album, Jay. They're taking a big chance with you. You can't expect complete control."

"But I want to record a couple of your songs, the ones you wrote for the album we never made. It doesn't feel right otherwise." He wasn't quite whining, but it was close.

"What's your hotshot manager doing? I thought you had negotiated a good contract? Shouldn't he be helping you with all of this?" Ty calmed her own frustration. She had suggested to Jamie he come home and look for a record deal in the UK but one of the benefits of touring with Alex had been that she had taken Jamie under her wing and found him a supposedly efficient manager. Now he was thousands of miles away and outside of Ty's sphere of contacts. And where the fuck was Alex when he needed some help?

As if reading her thought Jamie cleared his throat. "Would you mind if I gave Alex a call? She said she was there if I needed her, and I could really do with some advice."

Ty let out a deep breath. "Of course I don't mind, Jamie. She's your friend and a valuable contact. You don't need to keep asking me if it's okay to speak to her. All right?"

"Cool." Jamie sounded relieved. "I'll give her a call tonight."

"Just do me a favor and don't talk to me about her for a while, okay?" She hung up and took a long breath. It was difficult enough trying to get over Alex without being reminded of the connections they still had. Mhairi did her best to keep Ty out of it, but she knew her feelings for Ryan were growing, despite the difficulties of a long-distance relationship. It was hard to ask Mhairi how Ryan was doing without finding out more about Alex, even though she wanted to know. She wondered if there would ever be a time when Alex was truly out of her life.

THIRTY-FIVE

The first two weeks of Liv's recording went smoothly enough. Liv floated in and out, putting in the minimal amount of work needed, but happy for everyone else to be working their arses off.

She'd changed, thought Ty. Fame and privilege had made her more self-centered. But once she stopped mentally comparing everything Liv did to how Alex would have handled it, she settled into the project and began to enjoy her work.

Liv invited herself to Ty's house for dinner towards the end of the second week. Ty didn't feel like she could refuse, although she would rather have spent the time in the studio than the kitchen. She recruited Mhairi as chaperone and made an effort, cooking up pan-fried sea bass.

Liv arrived early, armed with bottles of red and white. "Hi, sexy." She bounced in, kissing Ty enthusiastically on both cheeks as she handed over the wine. "Wasn't sure what you were cooking so I covered all the bases. Oh, hi Mhairi, I didn't know you were going to be here. What a lovely surprise. Last time we met you were still at school." Her voice had lost some of its enthusiasm.

Mhairi smiled widely. "I try never to miss dinner when Tyra's cooking. Why don't we go and sit down while she finishes in the kitchen?" She winked at Ty as she led the way.

They sat around the oak table in the dining room, Liv exclaiming her delight at the food. "I had no idea you were such an accomplished chef, Tyra. Or is this a newly acquired skill?"

"Ty's always been a good cook. My brother and I got to try out all her new dishes as kids." Mhairi said it sweetly, but it was a clear reminder that Liv was an outsider.

"I've always found it relaxing," said Ty. "And useful, obviously. I'm no' sure I'd want to do it for a job though."

"You're amazing, so many talents! I can barely make a boiled egg without burning the house down." She smiled seductively at Ty and leaned forward, providing a glimpse of cleavage.

The rest of the evening went pleasantly enough, although Liv showed no sign of leaving and Mhairi began looking at her watch and glaring at Ty.

"Had you not best be getting to bed now, Mhairi? It's getting late and you've work tomorrow." Ty hoped it would act as a nudge for Liv also.

Mhairi looked grateful and said her farewells. Liv, on the other hand, settled even more comfortably on the sofa, her long leg resting against Ty's, a full glass of wine in her hand. Ty sighed internally. "I'll need to be following Mhairi's example soon. I've got a full day tomorrow."

Liv, unlike Alex, was happy to leave all of the decisions to her producer and just do what was asked of her in the studio. She said it was because she had total trust in Ty to produce the best sound, but Ty suspected it was mainly because she was lazy. "Will you be staying up here the whole time or are you heading back to London?"

Although originally from Stirling, Liv had been London-based for all her career. She shrugged. "I don't have any firm plans. I've spent more than enough time with my folks. There's not much going on in this little city when you're accustomed to London."

"Well, don't look at me to entertain you. I'll be working fourteen-hour days for the foreseeable." She meant it as a semi-serious joke, but it fell flat.

"And that's why you need some quality downtime." Liv put her glass down, turned and put her hand on Ty's arm, looking into her eyes. "We could have fun together, Ty. I've missed your company, and now we're both single maybe it's time we made a go of it."

Ty's body was buzzing from Liv's proximity, and the wine. She had always found her incredibly attractive, and she couldn't control her physical reaction to her, however emotionally uninterested she was. "I don't think that's a good idea, Liv. I'm not in a good place at the moment." She stood up to get some distance.

Liv smiled up at her, unfazed. "Okay, Ty, if that's what you want, but you don't have the reputation you do for nothing. A few weeks with the superstar hasn't ruined you for everyone else, has it?" She stood and moved closer. "Just let me know if you change your mind."

Ty rested her head against the door and breathed a long sigh of relief. Liv had been difficult to get rid of. How did she ever end up in bed with her? She reminded herself that until a few months ago, a night with someone like Liv was exactly what she was always looking for. Until Alex had made her realize there was more to life. She didn't know when it would stop hurting so much, but she knew that one day, she would want to find someone to share her life with. Someone who wanted it as much as she did.

THIRTY-SIX

The days and weeks had passed slowly for Alex, but the crushing loss she felt after Ty left had galvanized her into action. If she was incapable of anything good in her private life at least she could do something about her career. Linda had taken advantage of her change of mood and was busy organizing a stream of chat show appearances and other PR opportunities.

Ryan was always close to hand, but Alex felt he was less warm towards her than usual. Or was it her imagination, fueled by guilt at how she had treated Ty? Did she deserve his warmth? She wanted to ask him how Ty was doing but she felt she had already caused enough problems for his relationship with Mhairi.

Fuck. How had it ended up like this? For a few short weeks she had been happier than she ever imagined she could be. She'd told Ty she'd be happier on her own, but she was more miserable than she'd ever been.

When Dory announced she was coming to stay for a week, Alex did her best to put her off, explaining she was busy writing and preparing for media appearances. Dory ignored the excuses. She hadn't hidden her shock at the news that her mother and Ty had split. She had lectured Alex on being less of a control freak and told her she would regret it if she let Ty slip away. Alex had been forced to explain that it was truly over and there would be no going back. Just saying the words had brought on the hurt all over again but as usual, she kept her game face on and didn't let it show.

Dory's imminent arrival also forced Alex to address the guest room. She hadn't been able to face going in there and couldn't bear the thought of a stranger messing with Ty's belongings, so everything had remained as it was the day Ty left. Now she opened the door and stood in the room, looking around. Ty must have left with the clothes she was wearing. Her favorite, most worn leather jacket was still slung over the back of the chair and Alex gathered it up, inhaling the familiar woody scent of Ty's perfume. Most of her other clothes were in a duffle bag in the bottom of the closet, not in the dresser. *I didn't even let her feel at home*, thought Alex sadly as she gathered the other belongings and packed them away carefully. She took the duffle to her room and placed it at the back of her closet. She wondered if she should have it boxed up and shipped back to Ty, along with her guitar and her bike. The bike still stood in the hallway, despite Ryan asking a number of times if he should move it to the garage. She made a mental note to ask him to have it moved and to request the cleaning service prepare the guest room for a new visitor. As for Ty's belongings...she'd hold onto them for a while longer, if only to have a little bit of Ty still with her.

Dory sat across from her in the restaurant, watching her appraisingly. Alex was uncomfortable under the scrutiny, as well as being out in the public eye. She knew she needed to get used to it with all the interviews she had coming up, but so far she had avoided crowds of people like the plague. She would have loved to stay home and order food in instead of coming to a bustling restaurant, but Dory had insisted.

"I've never seen your hair so short, Mom, are you trying to steal my look?"

Alex looked up sharply. She'd lost weight over the past few weeks. She had no appetite and after the delicious home cooked meals she had become accustomed to, she had little interest in food. When she looked in the mirror, she could see the change in her face. That, combined with the hair she had cut short because she didn't have the energy to do anything with it, gave her a more severe look than usual. "I know. I overdid it. It got so long while I was recuperating, I just wanted a fresh look." She paused. "Does it make me look old?"

Dory laughed lightly and reached across to squeeze her hand. "No, you don't look old. But you do look sad. I don't think that's because of the haircut though, is it?"

She shook her head, tears pricking her eyes. "Not here, Dory, please." She cleared her throat. "Why don't you tell me about your plans for the summer?"

Dory looked at her for a moment as though debating whether or not to pursue it, then launched into the catalogue of things she wanted to do over the next eight weeks. But later, at home, Dory continued her grilling. "So how are you feeling about things? You know all these media appearances are going to involve questions about your coming out, the attack and your split with Ty. You've had a lot going on, Mom. Are you sure you're ready for all of this?"

Alex ran her fingers through her short hair. "Honestly? I have no idea, Dory. I just know I need to move on and the only way I can do that is to get all of this over with. The public memory is short when they feel like there's nothing of interest going on, but the longer I stay quiet the longer people will remain interested."

"But in the restaurant, I asked you if you were sad and you almost started crying. How are you going to cope with insensitive questions on a TV show? I don't want to see you break down on national television."

Dory looked so concerned, Alex did her best to sound reassuring even though she felt far from confident she could hold it together. "You know me, I'm a professional. I've been doing this your whole life. Don't worry about me."

"But I do worry about you. How are you? Really, I mean, when no one's looking?" They were sitting side by side on the leather couch, Dory turned to look at her mother, demanding an honest answer.

Alex leaned back until her head was resting on the leather. She looked up at the ceiling to avoid her daughter's gaze. "I'm not too bad, Dory. Better than I was. Now that my hand is healed and I'm able to work, it's made a massive difference. Still need to keep up the exercises though." She flexed her fingers to demonstrate.

"And Ty? Are you sure you can't talk things through? You were so good to—"

"No, Dory, we weren't." Alex didn't want to hear how perfect she and Ty had been. "We were good until something went wrong and then I reverted to my need to be in complete control of everything. I treated Ty badly and shut her out. People like me are meant to be alone."

Dory frowned, looking taken aback. "Is that what you really think? Or is it easier to say that than to sort it out? I mean, if I said that to you, would you tell me I was right, to just give up?"

Dory left Alex to think on that while she went to get a drink. When she returned, she asked, "Do you want to end up like Grandma?"

Apparently she wasn't going to let it go. "What's so bad about being like your grandmother, Dory? She has a highly successful career and travels wherever she wants."

"She's alone, Mom, and she's been alone since you were fourteen."

"She's not alone, Dory, she's got Piers." Francesca had a fellow professor she pulled out for occasions where a plus one was required. Alex knew it was nothing more than a convenience for her mother, but she didn't like the point Dory was trying to make.

"D'you know she's kept Piers waiting for nearly *ten years*? She claims she's made it clear she doesn't want anything serious, but he's hanging on in there, convinced she might change her mind." She turned sideways on the couch. "I think it's cruel."

She did have a point. Her mother definitely had the power in that relationship and was happy calling all the shots. Was that how she herself had been with Ty? Unwilling to yield any control over what was happening between them. She had a sudden need to shut the conversation down.

"I appreciate your concern, Dorothy, but I am an adult and capable of making my own decisions about my life."

Dory laughed and jumped up. "Cool. If you're not worried about your future as a sad old spinster, neither am I.

Let's go out and find some live music. I bet you can get in anywhere in this city."

Alex sighed. She had no desire to go out, but anything was better than being interrogated for the rest of the evening. She called for her car and followed her daughter to prepare to hit the town. But as she got ready, the notion of ending up like her mother began to sink in, and the thought was distinctly uncomfortable.

THIRTY-SEVEN

Ty let herself into the house, closing the door behind her in relief. A solid month of work and she had finished the Liv Jensen album. She didn't have to face another day of Liv standing too close to her, trying to get her in bed, or waving bags of coke in her face. She'd got through it and was pleased with the result, but it had been hard work and she was taking a few days off.

She could hear the TV in the den and wondered what Mhairi was watching. She grabbed a couple of beers from the fridge and found an open bag of crisps on the worktop. Feeling guilty, she returned to the fridge and retrieved a bowl of guacamole Mhairi must have prepared earlier. *It's green. Green is healthy.* She gathered everything in her hands. She knew she needed to get back into shape after a month of little exercise and a diet consisting of whatever fast food her crew ordered during their long working days. Now it was spring she was planning to go up to the cottage in the Highlands and spend some time running and cycling. Maybe she'd even dig her kayak out of the shed if the weather was mild enough.

She pushed the door open with her hip, her hands full. "What we watchin' then?"

Mhairi visibly jumped, then scrambled for the remote. Ty saw what looked like a chat show before the screen went black.

"Shitting hell, Tyra, I nearly died. You could've let me know you were coming home early."

Ty slung herself over the back of the sofa, holding up the beers. "It's eight-thirty, hardly early. An' we finished the album today. I thought you might want to celebrate with me."

Mhairi leaned over and retrieved the bowl before Ty managed to decorate the upholstery. "That's fantastic news. And ahead of schedule. You can take a break now, can you?"

"A few days, yeah. I've got a job I need to be back for next week." Ty opened a can and passed one over, while she waved her own in the air. "To another successful job completed."

"I'd rather drink to you managing your workload a bit better and not working yourself to death."

Ty laughed and smacked her lips in satisfaction. "So, what were you so quick to hide when I came in? Have you got a secret soap opera addiction you've been hiding from me all these years?"

Mhairi glanced at the TV shiftily for a moment, before looking at Ty. "I'm sorry. I was going to watch Alex's interview from the Owen Harvey show last night. Ryan was really worried about her doing it and I've not had a chance to ask how it went." Her expression became even more downcast. "I'm sorry, I feel as though I'm betraying you by even keeping in touch with what's going on in Alex's life when it's so hard for you."

Ty put her beer down and raked her fingers through her curls. "I don't want you to feel you can't live your own life, Mhairi. You and Ryan have got something good together, don't let my failure at relationships ruin that as well." She stopped to think about how she was really feeling and decided what she said was true. "I work in the same industry as Alex, I can't avoid seeing anything about her forever. I've only managed it this far because she's been out of the public eye. The moment she announces a tour or releases an album her face'll be everywhere and I'm just gonna have to deal with it." She took a long swig of her beer. "Come on, let's watch it. How hard can it be?"

Mhairi's eyes narrowed. "Are you sure? It's only a few months since Alex was on that same show with you, talking about your relationship."

"Hey, okay! I know that, but thanks for the reminder." Ty got up and went to the cabinet in the corner, returning with two glasses and a bottle of her favorite whiskey. "Just put the bloody thing on, will you?"

Mhairi fast forwarded through the other guests until the moment when Owen stood up to introduce Alex. She paused the recording and looked over. Ty poured herself a drink, and ignored the unspoken question, so Mhairi pressed play and sat back in her chair.

Alex strode out onto the stage with her usual presence, smiling and waving at the enthusiastic audience, and greeting her host warmly. Ty looked into the face she hadn't seen since she walked out of the apartment in January. Alex had lost weight, making her features more angular than ever. Her hair was cut shorter than Ty had ever seen it, and the combined effect was an austere beauty that made Ty's heart ache to hold that face in her hands and taste those lips again. She feigned indifference and picked up the bowl of snacks. The loud crunching caused Mhairi to roll her eyes and turn up the volume as Alex started to speak.

Owen had opened with a question about her plans for the future after some time out of the public eye, and Alex was explaining her intention to start recording a new album in the autumn. *The album you asked me to produce.* The better part of her was pleased to see that Alex looked well. Apart from the weight loss she looked a lot happier than the last time Ty had seen her, when she had been seriously worried about her mental health.

Maybe she was right, and she truly was happier alone. That thought made Ty feel unbelievably sad. If there was one thing she'd learned from what had happened with Alex, it was that being with the right person was the best feeling in the world. *But she wasn't the right person if she didn't feel it too.*

She forced herself to focus on the interview, where Alex was now explaining that she would start her next world tour in Canada to make up for her missed dates due to the events of last year. This allowed Owen to shift the conversation to those events.

"It doesn't feel like it's been long since you were sitting on my couch in the middle of your most successful tour to date and talking about your new relationship with Tyra MacLean." He didn't ask a direct question, allowing Alex to decide where to take the conversation.

God, she's got him well trained. Ty couldn't help the mix of admiration and distaste at Alex's inability to do anything without having complete control over the outcome.

Alex smiled, but there was clearly sadness beneath it. "As you know, a lot has happened since then, Owen, including being attacked on the street in Seattle by a homophobic thug who's now serving ten years in prison."

Owen nodded sympathetically. "A vicious attack that horrified the world. And how are you recuperating?"

"The physical and psychological effects have taken a long time to recover from. I'm lucky to have regained full movement in my hand." She held up her right hand and flexed it. "But it's still not up to prolonged use, which is why I'm holding off on going into the studio until the autumn. And I'll wait until I'm one hundred percent before embarking on a tour. I'm sure I can make it up to my fans when I do go on the road." She smiled at the audience as they cheered and clapped and returned her attention to her host.

"That's good to hear. I'm sure the anticipation will make it all the better." Owen cleared his throat. "And your relationship with Tyra? It's public knowledge she returned to the UK some months ago and has been working with Alivia Jensen on her latest album. Will you be spending time together in the future?"

Alex shook her head and took a moment before answering. "I'm afraid not, Owen. Ty is the most wonderful person I have ever met, and I feel honored to have been with her, but it turns out I truly am a solo performer, on stage and off." Her smile at the camera didn't quite reach her shining eyes. "I wish her every happiness for the future."

Ty had seen enough. She jumped up and muttered something about getting an early night, scattering crisps everywhere as she strode out of the room, determined not to spill another tear over bloody Alexandra Knight.

THIRTY-EIGHT

The next month went by in a flurry of activity for Alex, as she made one appearance after another around the country.

The more she talked about the events of the last year, the easier it got. It was exactly what would have happened sooner had she talked to a therapist, she had to admit to herself. But ironically, the more she got back into the swing of her old life, the hollower she felt and the louder the nagging voice in her head became.

She was on her treadmill, trying to run off the growing feeling of dread as she considered her life. Perhaps it had always been this shallow, but because it was the norm, she hadn't had anything to compare it to. But after Ty...

She was making a conscious effort to eat well and regularly and to spend more time in the gym and as a result was gaining some lean weight, making her feel much healthier. She was slowly increasing the amount of time she could play, and she knew she would soon be back to her usual ability on both guitar and keyboard. She had written a number of good songs, more emotional and not quite as upbeat as her usual material, but she knew they would make a reasonable album.

Things with Dory were better than they had been for years, and she'd been relieved to find Dory had enjoyed their time together as much as she had, even when there was no chance of meeting Jamie. On the surface her life was back on track. *So why am I so unhappy?*

She ran harder to silence the voice, working out until she could no longer stand. But as she dragged herself to the shower, drenched in sweat, the doubts and regrets were just as strong.

Alex was flicking through some music news sites when Tyra's name caught her eye. It was all the more surprising that it was an article about Ty herself, not the band. Unusual when she worked so hard to keep a low profile.

Alex clicked onto the article. It started with a reference to Tyra's recent performing career with DandyLions, and that after a brief spell in New York with Alex she appeared to be back in her hometown and single. But the main story was that she had been filmed, performing, for the first time in years, some of her most famous songs. A video of the performance accompanied the story, and Alex paused for only a moment before playing it.

The recording was of reasonably high quality but clearly recorded secretly from under a table or somewhere with a restricted view. Ty was on a low stage in what appeared to be a small venue. Her hair was long enough to reach the collar of her leather jacket and that and the mix of dirty blond and silvery grey in her curls suggested a visit to a hair stylist was long overdue. She took a guitar from a woman holding it out to her from the side of the stage and said something inaudible which drew a loud laugh from the audience.

Alex was torn between the pain of seeing Ty after so long, and frustration at not being able to see her clearly enough. She ditched her cell for the laptop and continued the video. Just the sight of her made Alex's breathing more rapid and her stomach churn with emotion.

Ty sat on a stool on the stage, adjusting the microphone stand for a couple of minutes before chatting to the audience while she fine-tuned the borrowed guitar to her satisfaction.

"Y'knew you'd wear me down eventually, didn't you?" The crowd laughed and there were a few shouted comments. Alex was struggling to translate. She realized Ty had been making an effort to be understood when they were together. On her home ground she had no such qualms.

"Do me a favor, okay? No filming please. Tonight is just for you."

There was a buzz of agreement and Alex could see cellphones being placed on the tables at the front. Ty smiled at the crowd. "All right, what d'you want to hear?"

She heard people in the crowd shouting for various songs. "Vita" seemed to be a popular choice. Ty shook her head and smiled a reserved smile. "How about this?"

Alex recognized the song immediately. "A Chance to be Better" was a real singalong anthem from Ty's heyday. She realized she knew all the words as she joined in with the chorus, transfixed by watching the woman she knew so well, singing a song she had only seen her perform as a teenager.

The camera angle, although distant, clearly captured Ty's face, and the emotion displayed as she sang. She finished the song to loud applause and paused to listen to the shouted comments, smiling slightly. "Nah, too obvious. As you're such an appreciative audience, I thought I might play you something a bit more special."

She played the intro to "Sleepless Nights" and the crowd, small as it was, roared in approval.

"You want to hear it then? I can play something else if you'd prefer?" she teased, throwing her head back in laughter as she was drowned out by noise.

Alex felt nauseous, transported back to her roof the first week they were together, when she had coaxed Ty into singing her most beautiful song. Less than a year ago, but it felt like a lifetime from where she was now.

Ty was introducing the song, drawing out the anticipation of her small audience. "For anyone in the room who doesn't know this song, and it doesn't sound like that's many of you, this is from my third album. I hadn't played it for over twenty-five years until someone reminded me it wasn't as bad as I remembered. So here goes. It's called 'Sleepless Nights.'"

The room fell utterly silent as she began to play. The camera moved around a little as though its operator was trying to get comfortable in their surreptitious recording position, but mostly it stayed trained on Ty's face as she played, utterly engrossed in the song and singing the lyrics with a passion Alex had tried to forget.

Fuck! She physically dragged herself away from the laptop, throwing open the doors and gasping in ragged breaths of fresh air. "You. Fucking. Idiot." She punctuated each word by knocking her head against the glass door, hoping the physical pain would distract her from the feeling in her chest. It didn't and she slid to the floor, collapsing in a heap, holding her throbbing head in her hands. She couldn't deny her mistake any longer.

THIRTY-NINE

Tyra threw her phone across the table, Mhairi expertly catching it before it fell off the edge and hit the stone floor of the kitchen. She looked at the screen with interest.

"Is this you? When? Was it when you went to Frankie's the other night? You never said you were playing?"

Ty was rubbing her fingers across her forehead and staring at the table.

"I didn't go there to play. I went for a drink. I used to love it there, no one bothered me. But the band was a wee bit shit, and everyone was all 'Go on, just one song.' I knew most of the women in there, so I thought it'd be safe. But some fucker recorded the whole thing."

Mhairi played the video and "A Chance to be Better" played. She looked up after a couple of minutes. "You sound great. Stop stressing."

"It's the other song I did. It was 'Sleepless Nights.'"

Mhairi's eyes widened. "No shit. You've never even sung that for us. What made you choose that one?"

"I dunno. It was in my head. It seemed fine for that tiny

crowd but now it's out there." She gestured futilely towards the world beyond the window.

Mhairi handed Ty her phone back and squeezed her shoulder. "Don't sweat it, Ty. Your real fans will love it, but most people have probably never even heard of the song."

Ty sat and played the recording back a couple more times. She had written the song just before her life had gone off the rails, when she had still thought love could be simple and beautiful. But it had always been bound up in the misery of what came afterwards, until Alex had convinced her to play it again on that rooftop. And suddenly the thought of perfect love hadn't seemed so completely unrealistic. What had she been thinking, playing it in public, now?

Jamie had finished recording his album and had plans to come home for a few weeks over the summer. Ty had only spoken to him briefly, and she knew he had managed to get one of her songs on the album, but she hadn't heard any of the tracks yet. She was excited to see him and wondered how his time in LA would have changed him. She hadn't been away from him or Mhairi for that long in their entire lives.

When she got back from the studio one evening, she found Mhairi in the kitchen eating toast and reading over some sheet music. "Hey, what plans have you got for when Jamie's home? Do we need a road trip?"

Mhairi looked up briefly and went back to her music. "Dunno how much free time he'll have, Ty. He's doing two festivals and one of them's near London. He's gonna be traveling up and down the motorway half the time he's here.

And he'll have his entourage to show around." She bit into her toast with a crunch.

"Entourage? Do you mean Dani? I think it's lovely she's coming over to meet your dad. I'm even more impressed they're still together." She studied Mhairi, confused by her offhand manner. "You're not jealous, are you?"

Mhairi looked up, still chewing slowly. "Why don't you have a chat with Jamie? Sooner rather than later, maybe?" She got up, gathered her music, and left. Ty heard her steps on the stairs and wondered what was bothering her.

She got out her phone. *Hey, Jamie, what's up with your sister? Ring me when you're free. Remember the time difference.* It had taken Jamie a while to stop calling at three in the morning for a catch-up.

"You're doing fucking *what*?"

Jamie was doing his best to sound reasonable and confident, but Ty didn't miss the panic in his voice.

"You told me to get on with it and you didn't want to know. I've done that, Ty. My album's gonna be a success and my couple of appearances back home will be a fantastic way to warm up for the autumn tour."

"I told you to ask Alex for advice, not record a fucking song with her. A song I bloody wrote. For fuck's sake, Jamie!"

"The label was really keen, and it gave me a chance to use one of your songs." His voice was more distant as though he was holding the phone at a distance from his ear. Which was probably a wise move.

The anger left as quickly as it had come, and Ty felt

hollow instead. "It's fine, Jamie, you're right. It's a good career move, and I'm sure it sounds great."

"Ah, that's great, then." He didn't sound convinced at the sudden change of heart. "So you're good with us all coming over?"

Ty was starting to feel lightheaded. "What? Who's all? Danielle's coming with you, isn't she?"

There was a long moment of hesitation. "Well, Alex has agreed to do a guest appearance during my festival sets and everyone thinks that'll be awesome. And Dory's looking forward to seeing you. And Ryan, although he doesn't really care about seeing anyone except Mhairi, the saddo."

There was a pause, but Ty just didn't have the energy to respond. She stared at the phone, wanting the call to end but not able to deal with it.

"So...is that all good then?"

"Yeah, Jamie, it's all good. See you soon." She dropped her phone and wrapped her arms around her legs. The thought of Alex being in the same country, let alone performing with Jamie, was all too much. Why couldn't she stay on her side of the world? Was it too much to ask? She was finally healing, even playing again, and getting back to some sort of normality. But now Alex would be here opening old wounds. She took a walk to the gym to work out her frustration.

Mhairi came in just as she was struggling with her final pull up. "I thought I'd find you here. How are you doing?"

Ty dropped to the ground and pulled her T-shirt up to wipe the copious amounts of sweat from her face. She looked closely at her cousin as she collapsed onto the bench. "You been to the hairdresser? It looks great."

"Why, thanks for noticing, I thought I'd turned invisible over the last week." Mhairi squeezed Ty's fingers, pulling her hand away instantly and wiping it on her jeans. "You can always talk to me, Ty. It doesn't matter what you're thinking. You don't need to keep it all in your head."

Ty shrugged. "I don't want to ruin anything for Jamie and his triumphant return, and I know it's not all about me, but I don't think I can do this, Mhairi. I can't be around her and act normally."

"I don't think anyone is expecting that of you, Ty. We'll have a couple of days with Jamie by himself and then when the others arrive you can leave him to it. Although..."

Ty raised her brows impatiently.

"Jamie says Dory has asked a few times if she'll get to see you. I don't think Alex has been party to the conversation, but Jamie doesn't really know what to say."

Ty began to do dips on the bench. She didn't know what to say either. The last thing she wanted was to see Alex's carbon copy daughter, but she had built a relationship with Dory in the time she'd spent with her last year. Back when Ty thought she and Alex had a future that Dory would be a part of. And she knew from experience how hard it could be on kids when relationships moved on. She couldn't just turn her back on Dory.

Mhairi sat and watched her until she couldn't bear it any longer. She pulled herself back onto the bench. "Just give me half an hour here. Find us something for dinner and I promise I'm all yours for the evening." She watched Mhairi leave then headed for the weights room.

"Good choice with the lasagna." Ty piled her fork for another mouthful, feeling she'd earned it with her intensive workout.

"I just put it in the oven." Mhairi smiled as she sat back. "I don't know what I'll do when we no longer live together, and my fridge isn't magically stocked with amazing dishes."

Ty chewed slowly. If Mhairi really thought she might have a future with Ryan, was she thinking about moving to New York? She wasn't sure how she would cope without Mhairi's steadying presence in her life, but she was an adult now and needed to find her own path in life, just as Jamie was doing. Ty decided to enjoy their time together now and worry about the future when it happened. "Let's clear these plates and go and play some music."

Ty had been writing in her spare moments at the studio and realized how much she missed Mhairi's input. In the few years they had been touring and recording together she'd always been there as a sounding board. Ty played through what she had been working on and they discussed and made changes. Mhairi played a few pieces she had been practicing for a performance she had coming up soon, until Ty noticed the time and stood up, resting her guitar in the corner.

"There's just one more thing I wanted to play for you." Mhairi's voice was soft. She started to play the string arrangement from Sleepless Nights. Ty had always known it was a beautiful piece of music. She had been so proud when she wrote it all those years ago. And hearing it now, played so exquisitely by Mhairi, with all the more recent emotions the song now stirred up, she felt her eyes start to burn. She turned to the door.

"Stay and sing it with me?"

"I can't, Mhairi. I just can't." She closed the door firmly behind her but could still hear the melody as she climbed the stairs. Whether it was Mhairi still playing or just in her head, she wasn't sure.

FORTY

Alex landed in Glasgow with a blinding headache and an impending sense of doom. Dory was chatting away as they cleared security and headed for their car. Dory had been to Europe before but never to the UK, and she was excited about visiting a new country, but also because she would see Jamie soon. Dory's crush had settled down. and after spending some time with Jamie and Dani in LA, it had become more of a case of hero worship. Alex had been delighted that Dory wanted to accompany her on the trip but had soon realized how demanding traveling with a teenager could be. She was hoping Jamie would entertain her long enough for Alex to execute her plan.

She had no idea if she was doing the right thing by coming to Tyra's hometown, but she knew she had to try to fix things. She had recorded the song with Jamie to try to help his career, and because she genuinely enjoyed performing with him. But when the label suggested a guest appearance in his festival sets would be a good move for both of them it seemed too good to be true. And Jamie wanted her there, so she must be doing the right thing. She hadn't managed to convince herself, and she had a nagging fear she would make things worse with Ty, instead of better.

"Mom, stop drifting off. It's like you're only half with us."

Ryan gave her a sympathetic look as they sat in the car on the way to the hotel.

"I'm here, Dory, what were you saying?"

"I was asking what that monument was called. This is an amazing city."

Alex ran her fingers through her hair, mentally slapping herself in the face. "It's not a city I know very well. I performed here on my last European tour, but I was in and out, and I didn't get to see much. Great crowd, though."

"Do you think Jamie will have time to show me the sights?"

"We've got a whole week before we have to travel south. He invited us over early for that reason so I'm sure he'll be ready to play the tour guide."

Ryan leaned forward. "Mhairi's looking forward to seeing you as well, Dory. She can show us both around." He was almost as excited as Dory but was better at hiding it. Alex wondered how he and Mhairi would make things work if they decided that was what they wanted. He had spoken to Mhairi nearly every day they had been apart, and Alex knew they needed to have the conversation she had been dreading. But she had needed him more than ever these past few months, and the time had never seemed right. She decided to have a serious talk with him about his options before they returned to the US. *You don't get to choose who you fall in love with.* She sagged into the seat of the car, wondering for the thousandth time if she should have stayed at home.

The hotel suite, large as it was, felt overcrowded as

everyone gathered to say hello. Jamie and Danielle had arrived with Jamie's father and stepmother in tow, Mhairi and Ryan were inseparable, and Dory was bouncing off the walls. She wished they'd all go home and leave her in peace. Half the population of the city had descended on her hotel room, but the one person she wanted to see was nowhere in sight. What did she expect? That Ty would come running to give her a second chance? She'd thrown Ty out of her apartment after she'd put her own life on hold to look after her. Alex couldn't blame her for staying well away.

After the introductions she withdrew from the socializing and stood staring out of her bedroom window at the grey city below, her arms wrapped tightly around herself. She heard a noise and turned to see Mhairi approaching, smiling kindly as always.

"You okay? You're looking kind of drained. I'll get everyone moving and we'll leave you in peace."

"I had to come, Mhairi. I need to see her. I need to be with her." The words came out as though she had no control over them.

Mhairi failed to hide her surprise. "Is that the reason you came? I think you might be disappointed, Alex. She's *very* determined not to see you. She's been trying so hard to move on and she's finding this really difficult."

"Fuck!" Alex turned back to the window. "I don't want to cause her any more pain, but I need to see her." She forced herself to face Mhairi. "Please? I tried to call her, but she's blocked my number."

Mhairi shrugged. "I'll tell her what you said, but she's out of town and doesn't plan to be back for a while. You may need to accept that she's not prepared to hear you out." She bit her lip. "You really hurt her, Alex, and she's just starting to heal. You might do more harm than good."

She turned and left the room, and Alex heard her encouraging everyone to leave the visitors to get some rest after the long flight. What was she doing here? The doubts flooded back in. She didn't want to cause Ty anguish, and if Mhairi, who was closest to her, thought it was a bad idea maybe she really had blown her chances. Should she just accept defeat and go home? She couldn't bear the thought of leaving things as they had in New York, when she couldn't think straight and said such terrible things. She had to try and put things right.

Jamie had been helpful on the Dory entertainment front and Alex had managed a couple of restful days with enforced early nights and was now beginning to feel more energized. There had been no more information forthcoming from Mhairi, and Jamie, when asked, had vaguely said he thought Ty was away somewhere. Mhairi had handed Dory an envelope which she took away to read in private. Later, she came back out and handed Alex a sheet of paper along with a postcard of a long beach of yellow sand. She opened it slowly.

Hey, Dory,

Hope you're enjoying Glasgow. I'm really sorry I can't be there to see you. Something came up and I had to leave town.

This photo is of Machrihanish, the beach I told you about. Ask Jamie to take you. When he's back in LA, I'll come over and visit, I promise.

Enjoy the rest of your stay and sorry again we couldn't catch up.
All my love,
Tyra

Alex reread the neatly printed words until they started to blur. Dory gently retrieved it from her grip and slid it back into the envelope. "I'm sorry, Mom." She went back to her room leaving Alex to her thoughts.

She had known there was little chance of Tyra being around, but the disappointment of seeing it confirmed in writing was painful. And yet, for all the hurt Ty was feeling she had gone out of her way to leave a handwritten note for Dory. A caring gesture that made the pain in Alex's chest feel a little bit worse.

FORTY-ONE

Two days later Alex waved Dory off on her surfing trip with Jamie and Dani and slid behind the wheel of the sporty coupe she had rented. It had taken a lot of effort to get the address of Ty's cottage. Jamie had gently refused to give it to her. "If she wanted you to know where she was, she'd have told you. If she wants to be on her own it's best to leave her, Alex."

Mhairi had been equally stubborn. Alex had tried every tactic she could think of until she'd finally given up. Ty had told her enough detail she was fairly confident she could find the cottage by herself. But the evening before, Mhairi had taken her aside and punched an address into her mapping app.

"If you fucking hurt her again Alex, I swear I will come and find you."

Alex flinched at the unfamiliar fierceness of Mhairi's tone. "I promise you, Mhairi, all I want to do is spend the rest of my life making her happy."

"Well, you'll have to find her first. She's not even at the cottage. She's gone on a trip along the coast in her kayak.

There's no phone signal in that area so I can't even warn her you're coming." Her voice softened a little. "Please be gentle with her, she's been through a lot."

Five hours of driving along winding roads gave Alex plenty of time to play out her speech in her head. It was also enough time to overthink everything, and by the time she pulled on to the gravel forecourt of the rambling Victorian seafront hotel Ryan had booked, she was half tempted to turn around and give up. But she knew she had to try or spend the rest of her life regretting it. After checking in she took a stroll down to the quaint little harbor, bustling with life as small boats docked and departed. She could see why Ty spent so much time here. It was truly beautiful.

Her plan was to ask around if anyone knew when Tyra was due back. Mhairi was sure she would have left her estimated return with someone in the village, in case she got into trouble. She knocked on the harbor office door and stuck her head inside. A young man with light-reddish hair was poring over a map on his desk. He looked up.

"Good afternoon. I was wondering if you know the whereabouts of Tyra MacLean?"

The young man smiled in a friendly fashion and maneuvered around his tiny office to reach the door.

He thrust out a hand. "Hi there. I'm Andy."

"Alex." She shook his hand and he moved past her to go outside, where he led her up some steps onto the harbor wall.

"Tyra doesn't come to the harbor unless she's borrowing a bigger boat." He pointed across the bay. "You see that little blue jetty right over there? That's her wee place. If you ask at the pub up the road, they usually keep an eye out for her when she's out alone. Just follow the coast road till you get to the pub. You can't miss it, the Swinging Sporran."

Alex thanked him and walked back to the hotel to pick up her car. She checked the directions Mhairi had provided, and a ten-minute drive took her around the coast until she pulled up at a blue five-bar gate. She double checked the address; it was definitely Ty's place. She slipped through the gate into a garden of wildflowers that sloped down towards the water. A path had been mown through them and she followed it to a small white cottage with pale blue doors. She knocked loudly and shouted but the house was locked up and empty.

Leaving the car in the gateway she walked back towards the pub she had passed half a mile up the road. There were quite a number of cars in the parking lot, and she was suddenly aware she was without security for the first time since the attack. But she knew this was something she had to do alone and even Mike had thought the danger in such a remote location was minimal. She pulled her cap further down on her head, leaving her shades in place as she entered.

The bar was one long room with a long window opening out onto the view of the bay. There was a deck running the full length of the building too, and the benches outside were busy with people taking advantage of the unusually good weather. Alex approached the bar where a few older men sat, who turned to watch her approach.

"Afternoon." The short woman behind the bar greeted her with a smile. "Go and find a table outside and we'll come out to take your order."

"Uh, I'm not here to eat, thank you. I was wondering if

you knew when Tyra MacLean is due home. I understand she's been away for a few days."

Her accent made her feel even more conspicuous as she spoke, and she saw a couple of men at the bar looking on with more interest. One of them nudged his neighbor but they stayed silent. If they knew Tyra, the chances were they would know who she was too.

"She's due back this evening. Seven at the latest, she said. But there's a storm coming so she might try and get back a wee bit earlier." The woman regarded her closely. "If you wait here, you can watch out for her. She'll be paddling across the bay right in front of you there." She waved in the direction of the window.

Alex hadn't eaten since before she started her long journey and suddenly realized she was famished. "Yes, that sounds like a great idea, thank you. And I'll order something to eat after all, please." She quickly selected a salad from the menu and ordered a Coke, which she carried outside to a free bench in a quieter corner of the garden. She sat back and closed her eyes, enjoying the sun on her face and trying not to think about why she was here.

"You should make the most of it. We don't have too many days like this." The woman put down a plate and some cutlery on the table in front of her. "Enjoy your meal."

When she had finished, there was still no sign of a kayak in the bay, so Alex took her things back inside and placed them on the bar before paying. From the look on her server's face, she wasn't used to such generous tipping.

"Thank you. Hope to see you again before you leave. And good luck catching up with Tyra. She'll be back anytime now."

Alex strolled back down the lane until she reached Ty's cottage. She had a closer look around the outside and was surprised to find that along the water-facing side of the house ran a full-length glass sunroom. She peered inside to see two overstuffed old chairs facing the window. A battered looking half-strung acoustic guitar sat on one of them, while a nearby table was piled with books and magazines and sheets of paper scrawled with what Alex assumed were lyrics. She had a vision of Tyra sitting there, looking out at the stunning view, and writing her beautiful words. Was there a future where she sat alongside Ty, working together on their music? She hoped with all her heart there could be.

The exterior of the house was well-maintained, and the garden, while clearly designed to encourage wildlife, wasn't untidy. Ty must have someone looking after the property for the long periods she was away. She followed the garden down towards the water, where she found the jetty. Close up it was a ramshackle affair that had seen better days, but it had been painted recently in the same calming blue as the doors of the cottage.

Alex sat down on the edge of the jetty and stared into the water. It was crystal clear. No wonder Ty loved it. It was idyllic and serene, and most certainly a different world from New York. She understood why Ty had felt hemmed in by the big city. Leaning back against the post she closed her eyes. The only sounds she could hear were birdsong, the lapping of the water, and the rhythmic creaking of the wood.

Ty was sweating as she paddled back around the bay. She had spent a couple of nights wild camping on a beautiful beach of white sand that could only be reached by water.

Pitching up on the sand dunes and fishing for her meals was her idea of paradise. The only thing she missed on her wild camping trips was a chance to have a shower and she now felt caked in a mixture of sweat and sea salt.

The unusually hot sun had been welcome while she walked on the beach and swam. But her twenty-mile paddle back around the coast was beginning to feel a bit much, even with the wind that had started to pick up, luckily in her favor. She'd packed plenty of water, knowing there was no fresh water at her camping spot, but she was down to her last few mouthfuls now, and would be glad to get home and rehydrate fully with a couple of nice cold pints she'd most definitely earned.

She stopped again to wipe the sweat out of her eyes and looked towards her jetty in anticipation of getting ashore. There was someone sitting there. Why did tourists think it was okay to treat her garden like it was a public park? She calmed her irritation. It didn't happen often and who could blame them when it was such a beautiful spot? Getting closer, her heart sped up when she saw the dark hair. She reproached herself, wondering when she would stop mistaking every dark-haired woman for Alex. The woman was stretched out on the jetty, seemingly asleep. She really did look like Alex.

When she was still five minutes from land, the woman woke with a start and scrambled to her feet, shielding her eyes to look out at the water. *Shit. No fucking way.* She felt nauseous. What was Alex doing here? She knew she was in the country. That was part of the reason Ty was hiding away up here. She didn't know what to do, but unless she wanted to turn around and paddle back around the bay, her options were limited.

As she pulled up to the jetty Alex was standing, cap

and glasses in hand, watching her, uncertainty at her reception clear in her expression. She had on a pair of denim shorts and Ty couldn't help but take in the view. Glad she had on her sunglasses, she dragged her focus back to Alex's face and kept her own expression blank. Alex shuffled her feet, still watching. She jumped out and started to pull her boat up the slope she had added to the jetty. Her knees were stiff from being cramped in the boat, and the kayak was heavy with her camping gear, but she waved Alex off dismissively as she leapt forward to help.

Finally, the boat was on dry land and she abandoned it, heading for the tap at the top of the jetty. She filled her hands with fresh water, tipping it over her head and face to give her time to think. *Keep it calm. And keep it simple.* She turned, pushing her wet hair out of her eyes. "What do you want, Alex?"

Alex looked wretched. There were circles under her eyes, and while she looked less gaunt than when Ty had seen her on TV, she was still too thin. She wrapped her arms around herself, looking around as though she wished they were somewhere more intimate than standing on a jetty in the blazing sun.

Partly out of sympathy, but mostly because she was exhausted, Ty motioned toward a picnic bench in the shade. She filled one of her large bottles with cold water and went to sit opposite. But she wasn't about to make it easy.

Alex finally spoke, looking into her eyes with sad sincerity. "I'm sorry I came here uninvited. I know this is your special place." She rubbed her face. "But I had to apologize to you. For how I treated you."

Ty started to speak, to say it didn't matter anymore, she was over it, but Alex held her hand up and spoke in a voice crackly with emotion. "Please let me say what I came here for. It won't take long."

Ty nodded. She couldn't make it any worse.

"I'm not blaming the attack. I'm responsible for how I behaved afterwards, but I was trying to regain control of my life, control I felt I'd lost by coming out and making myself a target for bastards like that. And I misguidedly believed it would be easier to regain control without you in my life. I made a terrible mistake, Tyra, and I hurt you horribly. I know that. But I know now that there's no point being in control of my life if you're not in it."

Ty started to speak again and forced herself to shut up. Painful as it was to hear what Alex had to say, she knew it wouldn't be over until she had heard her out.

"I love you, Tyra. I've loved you for a long time, but I was too afraid to admit it." Alex reached across the table and took Ty's hand.

She hadn't expected to hear those words from Alex, and she had to use every inch of resolve in her body to firmly remove her hand from the warm touch.

Alex flinched at the rejection. "Please just think about giving me another chance. I promise you will never regret it."

Ty was trying to keep her face unreadable, but she couldn't hide the frown when Alex used the word promise. She'd made promises before. But she had no desire to hurt Alex. In fact, the thought of hurting her made her feel sick to her stomach. She just wanted to get out of there as quickly and painlessly as possible.

She took a deep breath. "Alex, I appreciate you coming here to say this. I think we both have a lot of regrets. But I've really struggled over the last few months, and I'm not putting myself back in that situation for anyone. I'm sorry, I think you should just go back home and forget about us. There are issues we can't get past, so there's no point trying, only for me to get hurt again." She was amazed she had kept her shit together, especially when she saw Alex's face crumple at her words. "Please." She spoke more softly.

Alex nodded and slowly got up from the bench. "I understand." Tears slid down her cheeks. "Maybe one day you'll change your mind. Good-bye, Tyra. I truly am sorry, and I do love you."

FORTY-TWO

Ty waited until she heard the car leave the lane, then she got up and walked down to her kayak, tipping out all the camping equipment and dragging the empty boat uphill towards her shed. Leaving it outside, she threw herself back down on the bench and ran her hands through her hair. The emptiness that welled up inside almost floored her. *Oh, fuck. She said she loved me, and I told her to bugger off.* She'd been in love with Alex for so long, and while it was true there was still plenty of shit to sort out, if she let Alex walk away like this, there'd be no going back.

She jumped up and ran back to the cottage, fumbling under a rock for the door key. Once inside she raced to the table, covered in newspapers and sheet music, and rummaged through it until she located her phone. "Mhairi, I need you to—"

"Ty, you're back." Mhairi sounded relieved. "I need to tell you something."

Ty gritted her teeth in frustration and tried her best not to shout. "I fucking know, Mhairi, she just left. Listen to me. Ask Ryan where Alex is staying. Now."

She heard murmuring. "The Highland Hotel on the seafront. Is everything okay?" Mhairi sounded concerned.

"Hopefully. Gotta go." She hung up and ran down to the shed. She made some mental calculations. The hotel was a ten-minute drive away so Alex would have arrived back by now. If she packed and checked out straight away Ty probably had twenty minutes at most to get there before she left.

She swung the shed doors aside and looked at her options. Her motorbike was tucked away at the back, where she'd stored it when she arrived, assuming she wouldn't need it during her stay. She would need to use her mountain bike. On a good run she could make the hilly five miles in twenty minutes, but she'd already spent the day paddling and it was so warm. But she needed to try.

She threw on her helmet, pulled her bike free of the other items in the shed and dragged it up to the road, hoping the traffic would be minimal. Luck was with her, and her tired legs moved as fast as they could to get to the hotel. She pulled into the drive, skidded on the gravel and almost fell off. There were no cars visible on the forecourt. Gasping for breath she dropped her bike where it was and charged up the steps with her last bit of energy, throwing herself through the wooden doors of the hotel. Inside the elegant reception she was suddenly very aware of her own heavy breathing. She doubled over, desperate to get enough air into her lungs.

"Tyra, what's wrong?" Iain, the general manager of the hotel and one of her evening drinking buddies at the pub, was alone at reception and she staggered over to lean on the desk as she pulled off her helmet.

"Has something happened?"

She tried to croak a response.

"D'you need a drink of water?"

She nodded and he turned to the water cooler while she drew in deep breaths, trying to calm her breathing.

As he turned back his attention was drawn by something, and Ty turned. Alex had appeared at the top of the staircase, bag slung over her shoulder. She was adjusting her sunglasses as she looked down into the hallway. She stopped dead as she saw Ty, and then continued down the stairs slowly.

Ty grabbed the glass of water from Iain's hand and downed it, wiping her hand across her grimy face and through her disheveled hair. Alex reached the bottom of the stairs and pulled her shades off. Her eyes were damp and red rimmed. Ty's heart clenched.

"Shall I just go and put your bike somewhere safe, Tyra?" The front door closed audibly.

She owed Iain a pint. Now alone with Alex she felt lightheaded, whether from exertion, dehydration, emotion or a combination of all three, she couldn't tell. Alex continued to stare at her, an unreadable expression on her face.

"Okay." It came out as a gasp and wasn't quite what she'd planned to say, but it was the best she could do.

Alex looked confused. "What?"

Ty inhaled deeply, her breathing finally slowing. "Okay, I'll give us another chance."

Alex's expression didn't change immediately, and she wondered if she had missed her moment. She raised her eyebrow. "If that's still on the cards?"

She saw Alex's face slowly light up as they moved towards each other, and she was filled with the need to make her smile forever. "You're right. This is too good to be scared of. I love you with every inch of my being. And I trust you to love me. God, Alex, don't make me regret it, but I need you beside me, always."

Alex took her face in her hands, searching her eyes as if for any last doubts.

Then they kissed, and Ty knew they would find a way to make it work.

FORTY-THREE

The sky had darkened to an ominous gray and fat spots of rain were starting to hit the windshield. Alex tried to keep her eyes on the unfamiliar lane in the failing light but couldn't help looking across at Tyra to make sure she hadn't imagined the last half hour. Ty grinned her cocky grin and she felt her own wide smile reflect her happiness. She'd left the cottage truly believing she had destroyed any chance of fixing things with Ty. The desolation she had felt only made it clearer to her now how much she wanted—no, needed—Ty in her life. She didn't want to be alone anymore, but she knew they had a lot to talk about. When they'd finally pulled apart in the hotel lobby, Ty had suggested they go back to her cottage and talk about their future and what they needed to do to be together.

Ty sat with her hand resting on Alex's leg. The touch was light, but Alex felt it like a white-hot heat through the denim. Beneath the happiness and relief, she could feel a knot in her stomach. They had a lot of things to talk through and what if they couldn't find a way forward? She tried to put aside her worries. They would find a way.

As she pulled up to the blue gate, Ty jumped out in the rain and opened it, directing her to a space behind the house. She pulled up in front of a large shed, with Ty's canoe lying in the open double doors. She could see a jumble of outdoor equipment, and tucked away at the back, a gleaming motorcycle. She jumped out of the car, pulling her bag from the compact back seat as quickly as she could, keen to get out of the rain. Ty ran past her, pulled the doors together quickly and fastened them. She turned back and grabbed Alex's bag, leading her by the hand to the front door. "Don't expect too much, it's just a wee holiday cottage for one."

The rain was heavy now, and they hurried through the door, shaking off water as they went.

"Don't you ever lock anything up around here?"

Ty pushed the door closed with her foot and pulled Alex in close. "I left in a bit of a hurry." Her breath warmed the wet skin on Alex's neck. "I know we need to talk but I just want to take you to bed."

Alex felt the heat build inside her, but she forced herself to hold Ty at arm's length. "It's a very tempting offer but you're soaking wet, and it doesn't feel too warm in here. Why don't you go and get a shower? I'll get this place warmed up." She looked around for the first time. "Is there heating or do I need to light that fireplace?"

The room they were in was the width of the cottage. Tyra went to a door on the far side, opening it onto the sunroom she had seen earlier. The change in temperature was noticeable immediately. "These old stone cottages never get warm even on a day like today. The garden room's a different matter. I usually leave the door open, but it wasn't this warm when I left a couple of days ago." She turned back, kicking off her sneakers. "I really do need a shower. Make yourself at home." She leaned in for a quick kiss as she passed on her way to the only other door in the room. She left it open, and Alex could soon hear the sound of running water.

She took in her surroundings fully. The cottage was a combination of old features, such as the stone fireplace that dominated the middle of the large room, as well as newer ones like the open plan kitchen area to her right, small and compact, but fully equipped. She filled the kettle and looked through the cupboards, finding them well stocked with a range of foods. She found some tea, figuring she didn't need to add more caffeine to today's emotional rollercoaster, and went for a look around while the water boiled.

She stuck her head through the doorway Ty had left by, to find a cozy bedroom, with just enough room for a large bed. A further open door led into what looked like a walk-in closet, and beyond that she could hear the running water, and Ty's low voice. She smiled to herself, remembering Ty's love of singing in the shower, and decided it was sensible to steer clear of the bedroom for now.

She made her way back to the kitchen and as she made tea, she realized she was hungry. Ty had been active all day so she must be famished. She found some almost-fresh bread and sliced and buttered it, topping it off with some slices of cheese she found in the refrigerator. She took the plate of sandwiches and the tea out into the sunroom, which was still warm, despite the rain hammering on the roof. She set them down on a small table and moved the guitar from the spare chair, pulling it up alongside the other. She sat down just as Ty emerged, towel drying her hair and dressed in faded sweatpants and a DandyLions hoody, the same as the one she had given Dory, what felt like a hundred years ago.

"Sorry about the state of the place. I don't really have visitors, so it's got a bit cluttered." She looked around. "Mhairi comes for the weekend sometimes and it's much better after that. But she's been busy." She shrugged and dropped into the empty chair, catching sight of the food.

"Ty, I think this is the most idyllic place I've ever been." Alex waved at the view, slowly re-emerging from the retreating rain clouds. "A few books lying around don't matter to me."

Ty smiled happily.

"Now eat up. I'm guessing it's been a while since you ate?"

"I'm starvin'. I hadn't really thought about it until now." They made quick work of the food and sipped their tea in silence for a few minutes. Knowing the conversation needed to be had, Alex shifted her chair around so she could look directly at Ty. "I can't give up my career and I know you would never ask that of me, but I will do whatever I have to do to make room for you in my life, Ty. You just have to tell me what you need."

Tyra looked at her over the rim of her mug. "I need to feel like our relationship is an important part of your life. Not just something you can try, and then throw away if it becomes inconvenient."

Alex cursed herself for the behavior that had made Ty feel this way. She pulled her chair closer, gently took the mug from Ty's hands and placed it on the table. She held both warm hands in her own and held her gaze. "I am *so* sorry for the way I behaved but I promise you it taught me just how much I need you in my life. And I have no intention of letting you go again, for as long as you want me."

Ty's smile was wide. "That makes me very happy because it's exactly how I feel about you." The smile faded a little. "Is there anything I could do better? I felt like I really pissed you off last winter."

Alex squeezed her fingers. "No, that was all me. I need you to keep being you." She took a long breath while she considered. "But my workload can be overwhelming, and you might get sucked into that. If you find you're losing your own direction you need to say something, and we'll find a way around it, I promise."

Ty nodded. Alex looked down at their joined hands and hoped Ty could put aside some of her stubbornness. "There is something else. I would be honored if you would produce my next album. But...I don't think it will work for me to record it in the UK. I've started to build a real relationship with Dory, and I wouldn't want to be that far away for so long. I know you said you don't work anywhere else, but will you at least consider another studio? We can choose one that meets your standards."

She looked up and Ty was smiling, but not her usual cocky grin. "I'm sorry if I'm a bit stuck in my ways. I need to learn to compromise too. I would love to work with you again, maybe we can find something that suits us both." She leaned across and they kissed, slow and sensual.

Alex almost forgot what else she needed to say. She pulled back, forcing herself to focus on one last thing. "Have you heard of the Stars Are Out charity?"

Ty nodded. "Of course. They do amazing work raising money for LGBT+ youth causes. I wrote a charity single for them a few years ago. Why?"

Alex smiled. "Of course you did. Well, not long after you... left, they approached me to become an ambassador. At the time the last thing I wanted was more visibility, so I told them I'd think about it." She shifted in her chair as Ty frowned. "But before I left home, I asked how I could get involved and now they've invited me to co-host their next big charity event. I really want to do this, Ty, but it's way out of my comfort zone. I need you to help me to be brave. I'm very lucky to have a voice and I want to use it. I want to do everything I can to help make a world where people feel not only safe to be themselves but celebrated." She sighed. "Sorry, that sounded like a speech, but I need you to know how important this is to me."

Ty was smiling warmly, her eyes shining. "That may be the sexiest thing you've ever said." She stood quickly, pulling Alex toward the bedroom. "Let me show you to your luxury accommodation."

They undressed each other slowly, stopping often to kiss newly bared skin. Their lovemaking in the past had often been urgent, born out of lust or a need to connect. This was something new, as if they both knew without a doubt where they belonged. Alex had waited so long for this moment she didn't need to rush it.

Ty pushed her gently back onto the soft linen and lowered herself so the full length of her body covered Alex. She felt as though she was on fire and the blaze was centered between her legs. She pulled Ty's head down and kissed her hard, and her hips bucked involuntarily as Ty's warm tongue slid its way into her mouth. Ty pulled back, smiling, her arms holding her weight. Alex slid her hands up the hard muscle, and then down Ty's body to where the curves were softer, coming to rest on her hard nipples. She gave then both a firm nip and the smile disappeared as Ty groaned and lowered herself to nibble at the sensitive skin of

Alex's neck. She shifted her weight to one elbow and Alex felt her hand run down her body, fingers skimming over her chest, her abs and lower still, until a single finger reached where she wanted it most. She pushed her hips towards the pressure and Ty lifted her head, smiling once more.

"Please, Ty, I need you to touch me." Her voice was hoarse with need, but as she felt Ty's fingers slide through her folds she didn't care. "Oh yes." She thrust again and Ty looked into her eyes as she slid inside. Alex thought she was going to die from the sensation of being filled. She moved against her, desperate for more, and Ty understood and slipped another finger in. Alex gasped, her eyes fixed on Ty's, recognizing the love and desire reflected back at her. She forced herself to slow her movements and shifted her hands to Ty's hips, lifting them until Ty was straddling her thigh. She pushed herself against the wetness, evidence Tyra needed this as much as she did. Ty responded and they moved together, eyes still locked as the rhythm increased. Alex knew she couldn't hold out much longer.

"Come for me, Alex."

The words were too much, and her cry rang in her ears as she tightened around Ty's fingers, and her whole body stiffened, the pressure of her thigh sending Ty over the edge as well, as she let out a gasp. "Oh fuck, Alex, I love you." She finally collapsed, and Alex held her close. She couldn't seem to get enough of their intimacy. She ran her fingers through her hair and gently kissed Tyra's closed eyes. She wasn't letting her go ever again.

Ty awoke to the sound of her own stomach growling. She turned to see the bed beside her was empty and the smell of cooking filled the house, probably what had woken her. The last twenty-four hours had been full-on, physically as well as emotionally, and she hadn't eaten anywhere near enough. She sat up, plumped the pillows behind her, and wondered if she should go and see if Alex needed help. Before she could move, the door swung open, and Alex appeared with a tray piled with plates and mugs.

"Wow, how did you manage to find a chef all the way out here?"

Alex placed the tray in the middle of the bed and Ty held it steady while she settled. "Don't be rude. I did survive as a student for a number of years before caterers saved me from the more mundane tasks."

Ty looked down at the bacon sandwiches piled up on the plate. "Full marks. They look entirely edible." She gave Alex a kiss on the cheek and tucked in without another word and Alex's enthusiasm suggested she was equally ravenous.

When they had finished, she gathered the plates and rolled out of bed, throwing on a T-shirt and boxers. "There's something I wanted to tell you, but I got a wee bit distracted last night. Join me in the garden room at your leisure." She left with a cheeky smile, dumped the plates in the kitchen and retrieved her guitar from its case.

"I'm jumping in the shower. Won't be long." Alex's voice was distant.

Ty opened the doors to the garden room. It was another sunny morning, but as she opened the outer bi-fold doors she could feel a fresher wind in the air. Just the sort of breeze she would have appreciated the day before on her long trek home. She thought about all that had gone on in those intervening hours since she paddled into the bay and smiled happily.

She settled herself on a cushion and leaned her head back against the door frame for a moment, soaking in the view of the bay and the mountains behind. Then she picked up her guitar. It hadn't been played since before she went on her camping trip, so she tuned it quickly and started to strum, singing along softly. She was finishing one of her oldest hits when Alex walked through the door, wrapped in a towel and nothing else. Ty stopped playing and her eyes followed the length of Alex's bare legs until they disappeared under the short towel. She looked higher to see Alex smirking at her.

"Sorry, I didn't mean to distract you. Do I need to get dressed if I want to hear you play?" Her short hair was wet, and a droplet of water slid down the side of her face.

Ty nodded dumbly, absently wondering if she was actually drooling.

Alex turned on her heel, whipping the towel off as she left the room, giving Ty a full view if what she had been picturing. Ty sighed and tried to remember how to play the guitar. She wondered if she would ever grow accustomed to Alex's beauty. She hoped not.

Alex reappeared a few minutes later, her hair messy from a towel drying, and wearing Ty's old hoodie and sweatpants, which came to mid-calf. She was still stunning. She pulled a chair across from Ty and sat, watching her play. "So, what is it you want to tell me?"

Ty continued to play quietly. "I'm thinking of doing some gigs. Solo, I mean. Mostly my old stuff and a few new songs I've written." She watched Alex for a reaction.

Alex's face lit up with a wide smile. "Oh, Ty, I'm so pleased. There's a whole world of new fans out there waiting to hear how amazing you are."

Ty felt her cheeks go warm. "I don't know about that,

but I was filmed playing at my local club and some idiot put it online. It got shared a lot and I've had loads of interest online since. But I enjoyed it. Just a small, intimate venue." She hesitated. "I was playing—"

"I know what you were playing, Ty, I watched it. Over and over."

Alex's eyes were so full of love. Ty wondered how a song she had written so many years ago could so perfectly capture how she would feel when she finally found the love of her life. She played the opening chords, a smile spreading across her face.

EPILOGUE

Three months later

Tyra looked around the unfamiliar workspace and kept her gaze neutral. Alex had brought her to the most prestigious recording studio in New York City and she was impressed. She had always known, aside from being geographically inconvenient, her own studio lacked both the space and the cutting-edge equipment required for an album of Alex's standard. But she'd been enjoying the novelty of Alex negotiating, so she wasn't making it too easy.

She kept her expression blank as she turned back to Alex, who was perched on the edge of a nearby desk, chewing her lip. "It'll do, I suppose."

Alex's shoulders slumped a little. "C'mon, honey, it's the best studio in the city, and you'll have free rein to bring in anyone you want to work on the album."

Ty couldn't keep up the pretense any longer. She felt her face split into a wide grin as she stepped between Alex's knees and pulled her into a tight embrace. "I love it, it's perfect. And I'm so excited to be making this record with you."

Alex's face lit up as she leaned in and they kissed, not pulling apart until they heard a throat clearing loudly in the next room. Alex chuckled. "Sounds like someone's keen to get to our dinner date."

She jumped down, slipping her arm through Ty's. They emerged from the studio to find Ryan pacing, typing hastily on his phone.

He looked up. "Are we all done here?" He had limited success with his attempt to sound casual.

Alex squeezed Ty's arm. "I think we'd like to have a better look around, Ryan. Would you see if the reservation could be moved back a couple of hours?"

"Uh, yeah, sure." Ryan nodded dutifully, forcing a smile as he looked for the number.

"Stop tormenting him, Alex." Ty was laughing as he looked up in bewilderment. "Alex knows how keen you are to see Mhairi. She's just windin' you up. We're ready to get going."

Ryan threw Alex a filthy look before leading the way out to the car, audibly muttering about unbearable bosses.

Alex laughed. "You'll miss me when you run away to England," she shouted at his retreating back.

"It's Scotland, as you well know. And you'll wish you hadn't teased him so much when he's gone." Ty followed behind, still often surprised by this new relaxed version of Alex.

Ty looked out at the tall buildings surrounding them as they drove to their lunch appointment. The city felt very different now she was happy here. And she knew it wasn't for too long. Alex had promised sun, sea and deserted beaches as soon as they finished their work on the album.

And they'd spent a good part of the summer at the cottage. Alex couldn't seem to get enough of it, and so far they had managed to keep the location secret. Alex had become a regular at the pub, where she couldn't believe that the locals knew who she was but treated her just like anyone else. Ty often had to drag her away from late night rambling conversations with a group of local fishermen. Being able to relax and be herself had helped Alex's mood no end and Ty was so pleased to see her happy. She roused herself from her thoughts to see Alex grinning across at her and her heart raced, knowing she was responsible for that smile.

Dory had been delighted to see them back together, and she and Alex had spent a month driving around the UK in a motorhome half the size of a tour bus. Alex had been keen to give Ty some space while she did a tour of some well-established but intimate folk club venues in Scotland and the north of England.

Ty's return to solo performing had received plenty of critical acclaim and she enjoyed it enough to know she wanted to do more of it, so she'd made an effort to step back from the running of the studio. The success of Liv Jensen's album had made her more in demand that ever, but she'd stopped taking all the work she was offered and picked out a few of her most important clients to work with over the next year. Kenny had finally agreed to a promotion, and they were focusing on renting the studio out to visiting producers. There would be plenty of work for their army of apprentices and trainees to learn their trade.

The restaurant was crowded when they arrived, but Alex's party was seated with the efficiency Ty now accepted as normal.

Mhairi was already there, having arrived straight from the airport for an extended stay, paid for by Alex's recording budget when Ty had declared she needed her multi-instrumental talent. She threw herself into Ryan's arms, both of them giving the impression they had been separated for longer than a month.

Ty caught Alex's eye and smiled. It had been difficult for her to tell Ryan to go and live his own life, and their search for a replacement PA was still ongoing. But Ryan had promised not to leave until they found someone. He was moving to Glasgow while Mhairi continued her studies. She had applied for a music school in New York, but the transfer would take time, and they didn't want to be apart any longer.

When Mhairi finally released Ryan, she slid onto the seat next to Ty and wrapped her in a warm hug. Ty relaxed into it until Mhairi pushed her away to observe her at arm's length. "You look fantastic. And so happy. Love suits you."

Ty felt the warmth in her cheeks. "I've only been gone a few weeks."

"But I didn't see much of you when you were home, did I? Between driving around the country to gigs and hiding away at the cottage. And then you took off for your big charity event. You make a good 'celesbian' by the way."

Ty scowled. "Shut up, will you." She was coping with the exposure, and Alex's newly discovered role as an LGBT+ ambassador, but she didn't want a reminder, here, among the people she most felt at home with, that her life had just got a whole lot more public. She couldn't be prouder of Alex, though. She'd totally embraced the opportunity to speak up for the queer community, especially those who struggled to have a voice of their own.

"I'm just saying it's good to see you taking all the changes in your stride. You took some chances and it's working out for you. That makes me very happy."

Ty pulled her back in for another long hug, using it to hide the tears that were threatening to spill.

The moment was broken when Jamie rocked up to the table, sporting a new full sleeve of ink. Ty roared with amusement, regaling everyone with stories about the hard times Jamie had repeatedly given her over the years about her tattoos. As he tried to defend himself Mhairi started teasing him about his accent. She turned to Ty. "What's he sayin'?" She put on her strongest Glasgow accent.

"I'm no' sure. I think he's one of those Americans now."

Jamie shook his head in defeat, knowing anything else he said would make things worse. He and Danielle were still together, and although he remained his usual over-the-top self, he'd done a lot of growing up. His career had taken off, and Ty was so proud of him.

As they sat around the table laughing, Ty sat back and took a moment to appreciate it all.

She and Alex had planned their work schedules for the next six months, giving them both time for their own work, but ensuring they were never apart for too long. It wasn't perfect but she was optimistic it would work, as long as they kept talking and spoke up about how they were feeling.

As if sensing her reflective mood, Alex reached across and covered her hand with her own. As the waiter arrived with a magnum of champagne Ty knew there was plenty to celebrate.

The end.

ACKNOWLEDGMENTS

This book has taken me A Long Time to write.

Thank you...

To Victoria and Nicci at Global Wordsmiths for all the advice and editing and putting up with me having no idea what I was doing.

Jamie and the Hunter S Thompson Appreciation Society for being there at the beginning and inspiring me to actually write. Even if only on Tuesday lunchtimes.

Gustaffo for 'that conversation', the type you can only really have over a beer. For anyone who hasn't got a Peruvian cyberpunk comic book artist muse, I would highly recommend getting one.

The friends who were press-ganged into reading it at various stages of completion, and who gave me the best support and feedback anyone could wish for; Alison, Jo, Niki, Helen, Valden and Gill.

And Louise, for having more patience than anyone should really need. You are my inspiration.

Printed in Great Britain
by Amazon